PROTECTION
FOR HIRE

D0366329

Also by Camy Tang

The Sushi Series

Sushi for One?

Only Uni

Single Sashimi

PROTECTION FOR HIRE

Protection for Hire Series

- Book One -

CAMY TANG

ZONDERVAN.com/
AUTHORTRACKER
follow your favorite authors

ZONDERVAN

Protection for Hire
Copyright © 2011 by Camy Tang

This title is also available as a Zondervan ebook. Visit www.zondervan.com/ebooks.

This title is also available in a Zondervan audio edition. Visit www.zondervan.fm.

Requests for information should be addressed to:

Zondervan, *Grand Rapids, Michigan* 49530

Library of Congress Cataloging-in-Publication Data

Tang, Camy.
        Protection for hire : a novel / Camy Tang.
            p.   cm. — (Protection for hire series)
        Summary: "First she served as a mob enforcer. Then she found Christ in prison.
Now, Tessa Lancaster is protecting an heiress whose spouse seeks to kill her. In this
action-packed read, Tessa and a handsome Southern lawyer discover the reality of
being made new in Christ" — Provided by publisher.
            ISBN 978-0-310-32033-3 (pbk.)
            1. Bodyguards — Fiction. 2. Ex-convicts — Fiction. 3. Heiresses — Fiction. I. Title.
PS3620.A6845P76 2011
813'.6 — dc22   2011024797

Any Internet addresses (websites, blogs, etc.) and telephone numbers in this book are
offered as a resource. They are not intended in any way to be or imply an endorsement
by Zondervan, nor does Zondervan vouch for the content of these sites and numbers
for the life of this book.

All rights reserved. No part of this publication may be reproduced, stored in a retrieval
system, or transmitted in any form or by any means — electronic, mechanical, photo-
copy, recording, or any other — except for brief quotations in printed reviews, without
the prior permission of the publisher.

Published in association with the Books & Such Literary Agency, 52 Mission Circle,
Suite 122, PMB 170, Santa Rosa, CA 95409-5370, www.booksandsuch.com.

Cover design: Jeff Gifford
Cover photography: IStockphoto®
Interior design: Katherine Lloyd, The DESK

Printed in the United States of America

11 12 13 14 15 16 17 18 /DCI/ 21 20 19 18 17 16 15 14 13 12 11 10 9 8 7 6 5 4 3 2 1

PROLOGUE

Tessa Lancaster's rather freakish paranoia was what almost got her in trouble.

Her automatic reaction as she exited her uncle's club was to scan the dark streets. Seven cars, two on this side of the street and five on the other. Hard to tell if anyone sat inside them, but she didn't catch shadowy movement. A homeless man huddled in a doorway of a shop a few doors down, the same man she remembered seeing when she entered the club.

Her cousin, Ichiro, saw her movements and laughed. "Like somebody's going to jump you right outside Uncle Teruo's club? Nobody's that stupid."

"They may not know who owns the club. It doesn't exactly have 'Japanese mafia' in neon letters over the door."

"Everyone knows it belongs to Uncle Teruo." Itchy's arrogance was about as extreme as Tessa's paranoia.

A stiff breeze from the San Francisco Bay cut through her black leather jacket, and she curled her body tight as they headed toward his car, parked a block down the street.

They walked past the homeless man. Even though she remembered seeing him an hour ago, she still cast a furtive glance at him through lowered eyelashes. His clothes were worn and dirty, and his body was coated with mud, but in streaks — as if he'd slathered it on himself. His hair was dirty, but maybe not quite as oily as it would be for someone who hadn't washed in weeks. And as she drew closer, she realized he also didn't smell ripe enough.

Her muscles bunched just as the homeless man jumped at them.

She reacted faster than Itchy, so she couldn't be sure who the man meant to attack first. She stepped directly in his path and captured his arm in an armbar.

However, instead of the counter-move she expected from an assassin, he yelped like a dog. "Ow! I'm sorry, it was just a joke!"

"What do you mean, a joke?" She didn't immediately release him.

"My dormmates ... a stupid bet ... how much I could get panhandling as a homeless person in one night ..."

A college prank? Tessa thrust him away with disgust.

"He was only going to ask you for money?" Itchy smirked as they walked away, leaving the man moaning and clutching his tender arm. "Your paranoia is getting psychotic, cuz. You could have killed him."

Maybe he was right. She'd been working for Uncle Teruo for seven years, since she was sixteen, and seven years was a long time to be always on the alert, to be expecting attacks from her uncle's enemies and her own.

Uncle Teruo had never given her orders to kill anyone, but she knew it was only a matter of time. She could take down a 250-pound man and knock him out with a rear-naked choke in less than thirty seconds, but she wasn't sure if she'd be able to take a killshot or snap a man's neck.

She rubbed her forehead. She realized that she was tired of all this. And she could see that her lifestyle and the danger in it was going to make her seriously crazy.

She had Itchy's car keys since she hadn't drunk anything tonight. She fumbled for the remote in her pocket when movement from a shadowy building made her spine stiffen. Itchy saw it a few seconds after she did and pulled his gun. She did the same with hers.

A scuffed sound came from the alley between a nail salon and Chinese restaurant, both of them dark with their windows glinting in the dim street lights like glowing orange eyes. Itchy raised the gun.

"Tessa," came a reedy voice.

She recognized it, although she almost didn't because her cousin Fred usually had a snarling, sneering tone when he said her name. She holstered her gun. "Itchy, it's Fred."

Itchy hastily stowed his gun, not wanting to get in trouble by accidentally shooting the son of the Japanese mafia boss.

Tessa approached the alley carefully, because even though she knew it was Fred, she didn't like the darkness shrouding him or the strange thinness of his voice. "Fred?" She paused, allowing her eyesight to become accustomed to the darkness before moving any closer.

"I'm here." He sounded tired. "You have to help me."

She listened, and caught the sound of movement in the distance. Footsteps. Maybe boots. Men's voices. Then she heard something she had never heard before—Fred sobbing. Alarm shot through her and she walked quickly toward him. "Fred, what's wrong?" The acrid smell of garbage burned her nostrils as she passed a dumpster.

He seemed to materialize in front of her, his face a pale moon, but she could see dark splotches across his chin and cheeks, like black paint had splashed at him. This close to him, she could detect a sharp metallic scent that filtered its way past the smell of garbage.

"She's dead," Fred moaned, his eyes becoming crumpled lines in his face. "I killed her."

"Who's dead?" This wouldn't be the first dead body she'd had to dispose of, although most of the time, it was for her uncle, Fred's father, not for Fred himself.

"Laura."

It took a second for her to realize why the name was familiar. Fred's girlfriend. That's right, Laura Starling lived in a loft apartment in this area.

"What happened?" Itchy asked.

"We got into a fight. And I got so mad. And the next thing I know, she's dead and there's this in my hand." Fred held up his right hand, holding a bloody steak knife. He glanced behind them. "Where's your car? We have to get away."

"It's fine," Tessa told him. "You'll be fine. We'll get rid of the knife —"

"The police are after me."

"What?" Itchy cast frantic glances around them.

"A neighbor called them when we were fighting. I ran."

"Did they see you?" Itchy asked.

Tessa already knew they had. The booted footsteps were sounding closer, probably coming from the narrow street that ran behind these buildings. They were pursuing Fred.

They only had a few minutes.

They could take Fred in the car and go, but Fred's fingerprints were all over Laura's apartment, and the police would come to question him right away. How likely was it that he hadn't been seen running away by a neighbor? Maybe the police would lie and tell him someone saw him, just to get him to confess. Regardless, Fred would crack like a crystal glass. He just wasn't strong.

Not like Tessa. The only way to save Fred was to deflect suspicion away from him.

Did she really want to save Fred? No. But she loved her uncle, and she'd do it for him, because he loved his only son.

"Give me the knife." She spotted a gallon container of bleach against the wall of the restaurant and nabbed it. It had maybe a half cup left, but that was enough.

She slid off her jacket and pulled off her black long-sleeved shirt, shivering in her sports bra. Tessa used the shirt to wipe the knife down, then cleaned it again with bleach. Luckily, the steak knife was one of those fancy modern knives that had been forged from one piece rather than having a tang and handle. She hoped she could compromise the blood so any of Fred's blood wouldn't show up on a DNA swab.

She tossed the bloody shirt to Itchy along with his car keys. "Take Fred and go. Put him in the backseat and make him lie down so no one can see him — knock him out if you have to."

"Hey," Fred protested weakly.

Tessa slid her jacket back on and gave Itchy her gun. "Tell Uncle Teruo. Make sure he has your car cleaned so there's no blood, and give him the bloody shirt to burn." She didn't trust Itchy to do a thorough enough job of it.

"What are you ..." Itchy's eyes were incredulous as he stared at her. "What are you going to do?"

"What I have to." She tossed the knife in the dumpster. It would have her fingerprints on it and it would take them a few minutes to find it. The footsteps were coming closer. "Go, hurry!"

Itchy dragged Fred with him. Luckily he was smart enough to drive sedately away rather than burning rubber and attracting attention.

Within a few minutes, she heard the footsteps at the other end of the alley. "Stop!" someone called to her.

She broke into a run.

A cruiser pulled up in front of the alley, lights whirling. She hesitated, then tried to run around the car.

Someone rammed into her from behind, slamming her into the asphalt, scraping her cheek and smearing motor oil on her face.

As they cuffed her, the full realization of what she was doing finally hit her.

She was going to prison for a murder she didn't commit.

Chapter 1

The young woman was as out of place here as a Ferrari in a used car lot.

The first thing Tessa Lancaster noticed about the mother watching the kids in the game of Simon Says were her expensive shoes, gold and pearl colored heels with a dark gold rose over the peek-a-boo toe, which sank into the grass of the tiny backyard.

The second thing Tessa noticed about her was the gigantic black eye swelling the entire left side of her face.

She must be new at the San Francisco domestic violence shelter, because when she noticed Tessa looking at her, she smiled instead of turning away with a nervous glance.

With shoes like that, she didn't quite look like she belonged. Then again, the shelter was for any abused woman needing a place to stay, and who said rich women didn't get knocked around the same as prostitutes or waitresses?

Tessa raised her voice above the boisterous throng of children. "Simon Says . . . jump on one foot while patting your head and rubbing your tummy and turning in a circle!" Tessa bounced around in front of them, her hair flying out of its ponytail and hitting her in the face, while the kids giggled and screamed and twirled in circles. They loved her. They didn't care who she'd been or what she'd done. They only cared that she would play with them for her entire volunteer shift at the shelter.

"Snack time!" Evangeline, one of the shelter volunteers and one of Tessa's only friends, called to the children from the doorway behind Tessa which led back into the main building. Like a gigantic blob, the kids raced into the shelter from the building's tiny backyard, still screaming, and some still whirling around from the Simon Says game.

One tow-headed boy ran toward the woman with the expensive shoes, clasping her around her knees and laughing up at her. She smiled as she reached down to pick him up, but he squirmed to be let go. He scurried after the other kids.

"He hasn't laughed in so long," she said wistfully as Tessa walked up to her. Her accent was like maple syrup. Southern. She could have been Scarlett O'Hara in the flesh—flashing eyes, graceful hands, svelte figure.

Tessa squelched a sigh of envy. "What's his name?"

"Daniel."

The sight of the woman's black, yellow, and purple mark in the distinct shape of a fist made a dark, growling blaze burn in Tessa's gut. She tried to keep her voice light. "He's made friends quickly. One of the little girls was already flirting with him."

"He's just like his fa ..." Her smile faded as her voice caught on the word.

The boy's father? "Is he the one who gave you that shiner?" The words burst out of Tessa's mouth before she could think to temper them.

Oh, no. She looked away from the woman's shocked face and breathed in deep through her nose, trying to calm her temper.

The one thing she'd battled the most since giving her life to Jesus three years ago, and it still rose like a gladiator in her soul. "I'm sorry, that wasn't very sensitive of me."

A beat of silence. Then Tessa asked, "So, where are you from?"

"I grew up in Louisiana, but I've been in San Francisco for five years. Daniel was born here."

"Oh. What do you, uh, do?"

The woman gave Tessa a small smile. "I can shop like nobody's business."

Tessa laughed. It seemed like that's what she wanted her to do. But someone affluent like this ... "How'd you find the shelter?" Wings Shelter wasn't exactly in the Presidio area of San Francisco.

Tears gathered like jewels on her long, dark lashes. "I was at the San Carlos Motel, but we had to leave."

She didn't have to say it, but Tessa knew her story, the same story as many other women here. She'd probably left her home and checked into a hotel under a false name, but the man who abused her found them there.

"A man on the street saw us. He led us to the shelter."

Wow, how likely was that? God really had led this woman here. An otherworldly stirring in Tessa's heart made her suddenly feel both small and huge at the same time.

"Tessa!" Evangeline called to her from the shelter doorway. "I know your shift is over, but Mina wants to see you."

Ooh, good news? She couldn't think of any other reason the shelter's employment coordinator would want to talk to her. "It was nice chatting with you."

"I better make sure Daniel doesn't get into trouble." The woman smiled at Tessa and then headed into the shelter.

She didn't even know the woman's name. But it didn't matter—the other women here would eventually tell her who Tessa was—or specifically, who her uncle was—and then the woman would delicately avoid Tessa the next time she saw her.

The thought made her feel like a thin glass ornament. She should be used to it—now that she'd been out of prison for three months, women still feared her just as they had seven years ago when she'd been an enforcer for her mob boss uncle and her dangerous reputation on the streets had been slightly exaggerated.

Now they feared her because they weren't quite sure what she was doing here at Wings.

Tessa took the stairs of the old Victorian house two at a time, each step punctuated by a creak. The second floor landing opened up into a long narrow hallway, and she remembered to skid to a stop and knock on the office door before entering.

Tessa had to wiggle between two of the three desks crammed in the small office—once a bedroom—to plop herself in front of Mina's desk. "You wanted to see me?"

Mina's light brown eyes clued her in—not the joyful, we-found-you-a-job look, but a sad, these-employers-are-idiots look.

"Oh." Tessa sagged a bit in the narrow folding chair. "What happened?"

"Well, I've been the one taking calls from employers because you put the shelter down as a reference."

Tessa wasn't supposed to know that. She straightened at the information. Why would Mina break the rules by telling her?

"There's a, um ... theme to the questions they ask."

"Theme?"

"They almost all want to know if you're *the* Tessa Lancaster. The niece of Teruo Ota. The head of the San Francisco yakuza."

"Seriously?" Tessa closed her eyes, leaned forward, and bonked her forehead on Mina's desk a few times. She just couldn't get away from her past with the yakuza, the Japanese mafia. Would she ever be able to?

She suddenly sat up again. "They're not journalists, are they?"

"No, although I had a few of those. I always check the caller name and company with the list you give us each week of where you've applied for jobs. If the person isn't on the list, I tell them to go away."

Whew. The last thing she needed was some rabid dog reporter with grandiose dreams of using Tessa to somehow take down the entire San Francisco Japanese mafia. Or worse, some gossip mag wanting the scoop on why one of the yakuza's unofficial strong-arms was now volunteering at a battered women's shelter and applying for a janitor position at Target.

Tessa bit her lip. "You, uh ... tell them the truth?"

Mina's eyebrows raised. "Of course I do. Well ..." Her eyes slipped away from Tessa's gaze. "I'll admit after the third one of the day, I'm always tempted to tell them you're Amish."

Tessa giggled, then sighed. "I wouldn't want you to lie. If there's one thing I've learned, it's that I have to take the consequences."

"It's just unfair, because you really have changed, but they don't believe it."

"No, it's more like they don't want to get involved." Tessa had known it for a few weeks now, but hadn't wanted to admit it to herself. She seemed to have acquired a highly developed ostrich mentality lately. "They don't know why I'm applying for these minimum wage jobs, if I have an ulterior motive or if I've had a falling out with my uncle. They're not stupid—they're not going to hire someone who might cause problems for them, and they're not going to hire me if it's going to make my uncle mad."

Mina pitched her voice low and leaned in to ask, "What exactly did you do for your uncle? You didn't ... kill anyone, did you?"

"No, never. Aunty Kayoko saw to that."

"Who?"

"My Aunt Kayoko. Uncle Teruo's wife." More of a mother to her than her own mother. An ache blossomed under her breast-bone, and she rubbed at it. "She protected me. She dissuaded Uncle from giving me any job that crossed some invisible line she had in her head. She was closer to me than my own mother, in some ways."

"Was?"

"She died last year." And Tessa had cried in her cell all day the day of her funeral, wanting to go but not allowed to. If Tessa had been released a year early, she'd have been able to say goodbye.

Mina cleared her throat. "So, you roughed people up?"

"I did whatever my uncle asked me to do." Tessa looked down at her hands. "It's probably best I not talk about it."

"Oh, of course. I was just thinking ..." Mina flipped through a stack of file folders on her desk, then grabbed one and skimmed through the pages. "You can ... basically take care of yourself, right?"

"Uh ... yeah. I studied Muay Thai from when I was in grade school, and I also studied Brazilian jiu-jitsu, tae kwan do, and a little Capoeira." And basic no-holds-barred street fighting too, with a reputation among her cousins and her uncle's *kobuns* for having a streak of creative ruthlessness.

Mina's eyes widened at the list, but they also shone with excitement. "So how about a bouncer?"

Tessa wasn't sure what to think about that. "You really think someone would hire me as a bouncer?"

Mina made a face at Tessa's job applications folder. "They obviously won't hire you as a janitor, a burger flipper, a cashier, or a stock boy. Why not a bouncer?"

Why not? "I guess ... although I don't know if I'd be comfortable working for a particularly shady nightclub. I've known the girls who work there, and sometimes it's only a step above slavery."

"It might be a step toward doing bodyguard work." Mina was on a roll. "You'd be perfect for that. Your own private company, you can pick and choose what clients you'll take, and you can more than take care of yourself."

Wow. That would be really cool. "Yeah. Okay, got any leads on bouncer jobs?"

"Uh ... no."

"Oh, right. Battered woman not at the top of the bouncer qualifications list. I'll look online." Tessa rose and held out her hand to Mina. "Thanks for the idea."

"I'm sorry about those other jobs. I thought for sure that Fat Burger would hire you, but ..."

Yeah, but was she really surprised? Aside from the fact she was an ex-convict, being an ex-yakuza didn't place her high on anybody's hiring priorities.

She walked down the stairs much slower than she'd gone up, and she headed to the quaint living room on the first floor, situated near the back of the house. A fire might be lit in the antique fireplace, and she loved the crackling sound and the smell. As she entered the room, she spotted the Southern woman's glossy dark head next to a couple other women at the shelter. They all glanced at her with identical Oh-my-gosh-there-she-is-stop-talking-about-her expressions.

Tessa looked away, just in case they could see the sting in her heart reflected in her eyes. She didn't want to be feared anymore. She wanted to have friends who didn't know how to shoot an automatic weapon or boost a car. She wanted somewhere she belonged ... but where would that be? She was drifting in between the world of the yakuza and the world of normal, and she wasn't in either one. She didn't want to belong to the yakuza world, but she was starting to think she'd never belong to the normal world either.

A stampede of footsteps. Tessa expected to see a rampaging gang of suspiciously quiet kindergartners come to attack their favorite playmate. Instead, the woman's perky head popped up in front of her.

"Tessa? Hi, I didn't introduce myself earlier, I'm Elizabeth St. Amant."

Tessa took the smooth, manicured hand. "Uh, hi." She glanced at the women Elizabeth had been talking to, and they had alarmed looks in their eyes.

"Oh, don't mind those cats," Elizabeth said. "They thought they were warning me off of you, but as soon as they talked about your unsavory past, I just knew you were perfect."

"Excuse me?"

"Even though they don't believe you've changed, why, as soon as I saw you with those children, I knew that you'd done a 180 like a flapjack on a griddle."

Flapjacks? Elizabeth had a way of talkingreallyfastanddraaaawlingatthesaaaametiiiiime that made it hard for Tessa to follow her. "What exactly did they tell you?" Tessa asked carefully.

Elizabeth actually started ticking them off on her fingers.

"Let's see. First, you used to do some nasty things for your uncle, who's some sort of head for the yuck ... yak ..."

"Yakuza. Japanese mafia."

"Second, you've been in prison for murder."

"Manslaughter," Tessa automatically corrected. Not that it made that much difference, since she hadn't done it in the first place.

"Third, the only reason you're volunteering at this shelter is because Evangeline, who used to be your cellmate, stayed here a few months ago because of an abusive boyfriend, but then she started volunteering here, and she vouched for you when you wanted to volunteer here too."

The problem was that some of the women here didn't trust Tessa because she wasn't really one of them. Tessa had never been abused, had never been a mother. In fact, because of her background, she had never been afraid for her own life.

"Fourth, you've been going to the church here at Wings. And after hearing that, and seeing you with my Daniel, I knew you must be trying to turn your life around. You're exactly the kind of person I need."

"What do you need?" The woman didn't seem too loco, so Tessa wouldn't mind helping her. She guessed.

"My husband is trying to kill me," Elizabeth announced, "so I want to hire you as my bodyguard."

Chapter 2

Heaven must smell like homemade ramen noodle soup.

Tessa stood in the doorway of the Japanese restaurant and breathed deep, closing her eyes and picking out Jerry's signature spices in his ramen broth. She was drooling and she didn't care.

Well, it had been seven looooooooooooong years. Considering she'd eaten Jerry's ramen once a week up until then, she ought to be excused an excessive Pavlovian reaction. Since she'd gotten out of prison, she'd moved into Mom's house and began looking for a job, so she hadn't had time to come here to get her fix.

"Can I help you?"

The young, perky voice interrupted her olfactory cloud of ecstasy and made Tessa open her eyes.

The restaurant hostess, a young woman with long, glossy black hair, stood in front of the wooden hostess podium just inside the restaurant's glass doors. She had a plastic smile and her eyes were just a little wary of the crazy lady smelling the restaurant. Tessa realized she knew her—Karissa Hoshiwara, one of Jerry's granddaughters. Of course she wouldn't remember Tessa, she'd only been a high school freshman when it all happened.

"I'm a friend of Jerry's. Is it okay if I go in back to see him?" The politeness sounded stiff on Tessa's tongue, but after so many years, she didn't really have the right to barge into Jerry's over-heated kingdom unannounced.

"Oh." Karissa's smile lost its edge, as if being her grandfather's friend explained all sorts of you-ought-to-be-in-therapy behavior. "Sure, go ahead."

As Tessa turned to head back to the kitchen, Karissa suddenly asked, "Do I know you?"

Tessa turned to meet curious eyes. Innocent. *My eyes were never that innocent.*

No, she had to remember that she was a new creation in Christ! With copious exclamation points! She had to act like it! "Yeah, actually, your mom is friends with my mom."

"Oh." Karissa's brow wrinkled faintly, marring the perfect skin of a young twenty-something. "What's your name?"

"Tessa Lancaster." She couldn't help the tension in the back of her neck, waiting for the reaction.

Karissa's dark eyes blinked. Then widened. And then she smiled. "Oh! You're *that* Tessa."

She'd provoked a lot of reactions in her life, but never one like this. "Excuse me?"

"I saw your picture from that old newspaper clipping."

So did everyone. Still didn't explain the one-step-below-rock-star glow in the girl's eyes. Tessa wasn't sure what to say, so she smiled weakly. She probably looked like a sick pig.

"Evangeline showed me the clipping," Karissa added.

"Evangeline?" The name made Tessa's smile widen. "How do you know her?"

"I, uh … I met her at Wings." Karissa's cheeks were faintly pink.

"You went to Wings?" Karissa didn't look old enough to be married, let alone at a domestic violence shelter.

"I used to live with my boyfriend," Karissa confessed. "He started getting rough with me, and we lived nearby the shelter, so I went there one night. Evangeline was volunteering that night. The shelter asked me about my family, and when Evangeline found out my Grandpa Jerry worked for the Otas' restaurant, she told me about you."

"She was my cellmate for three years," Tessa said.

"Oh. I liked her. But I haven't seen her in a few months."

"You moved out of your boyfriend's apartment, right?" Tessa hated that she sounded like a mother but she'd seen too many horrible stories at Wings.

Karissa nodded. "I'm living with a girlfriend in an apartment near San Francisco J-town."

"You drive from San Francisco to San Jose every day to work?"

"Oh, no. I'm only here today to help Grandpa Jerry out. He's short-staffed today."

"That's nice of you, to give up your Saturday to help him out."

Her eyes flickered away. "I didn't have anything else planned."

Tessa recognized that look, and the meaning behind Karissa's words. Many of the women at Wings had lost touch with their friends during their abusive relationships, but in trying to regain their normal lives, they battled loneliness and the struggle of making new friends. She wondered if Karissa was the same way.

"Lots of the women staying at Wings could use someone to chat with," Tessa said. "Uh ... if you came to church at Wings with me and Evangeline one Sunday, you could meet them, maybe ... be a friendly face." And maybe Karissa wouldn't be as lonely herself. Evangeline had helped Tessa find the church at Wings soon after being released, but this was the first chance she'd had to invite someone else.

Karissa looked uncertain.

"You don't have to," Tessa said. "But in case you wanted to. You could see Evangeline again."

"I ... I think I'd like that." She looked like she even meant it.

"Call me and I'll pick you up. This is my mom's home phone number," she added with a pained sigh. No job, no cell phone. Mom's cell phone was on one of Tessa's aunts' plans and Tessa didn't want to utilize yakuza cell phone minutes.

A harsh voice gave a short bark of laughter. "Still living with your mom, Tessa?"

Rita, one of the waitresses, approached them with two steaming bowls of ramen. Rita had always been jealous because Tessa's close relationship with her uncle caused her to receive a kind of respect not typically given to women in the world of the yakuza. In contrast, Rita, the sister of one of the older yakuza members, had only received this waitressing job at Jerry's restaurant. "It's been what, four or five months? Still haven't moved out yet?" Rita managed to say the innocuous line with a sneer in her voice.

Tessa reached out to oh-so-accidentally knock those bowls into Rita's ...

No. Tessa drew her hand back, blinking to clear her head. She had to control her temper better. She wasn't that person anymore.

"Get back to work, Karissa," Rita hissed, with a significant glance over Tessa's shoulder. A couple had entered the restaurant while Karissa chatted with Tessa, they now stood waiting patiently just inside the glass doors. Tessa hadn't even noticed.

Karissa gave her a small smile and turned to greet the newcomers. Rita wove through the tables to deliver her ramen bowls.

As Tessa headed through the main dining area toward the kitchen at the back, passing patrons in teakwood chairs, her heart started tap dancing. She'd met a new friend. Invited her to church. And in a few minutes, Jerry would crush her in a ginger-scented embrace, then sit her down with a bowl of ramen the size of a wok, stuffed with vegetables and his homemade noodles.

"Coming through!" Rita's voice sounded almost at her shoulder.

Tessa jerked in surprise, and her elbow connected with something hard. Then the sound of a shattering clay bowl sliced through the buzz of restaurant patrons, and she felt a lash of pain against her ankles.

"Yow!" She grabbed her stinging leg and tried not to hop on her other one as she spied steaming liquid streaming through the grout in the floor tiles. Knowing her luck, she'd twist her knee and do a double back flip landing square on her behind. She side-stepped the river of noodles.

"Now look what you've done," Rita hissed.

"I'm sorry."

"You did that on purpose."

Tessa's temper snapped. "What is your problem? I have better things to do than waste calories making your life miserable."

Tessa's raised voice sounded abnormally loud in the small restaurant.

Rita's face paled. It was the same fearful look Tessa had seen when fellow prisoners found out who she was and what she had done for her uncle. Rita's reaction made Tessa realize her reputation as a bully hadn't changed, even though she wasn't working for her uncle anymore.

And that thought made her anger die away. Because she *had*

changed. She wasn't a bully anymore. And she needed to act like it.

"Let me help you clean up," she said.

The normal restaurant noises rose again, although some patrons gave her sidelong looks. Tessa found a mop in the broom closet near the restrooms at the back of the dining area and started cleaning up the spilled ramen broth. Rita bent to pick up the clay bowl pieces, head down, but casting occasional glances her way—filled with fear.

It hurt.

"Got a new job so soon, Tessa?"

The taunting voice shot adrenaline down Tessa's spine and she snapped to attention. She whirled around to face her cousin Fred, Uncle Teruo's son, striding through the restaurant like he owned it.

She had expected Fred to at least be obligated to come see her or talk to her in the three months she'd been out, yet this was the first he'd shown his face to her, and it looked like it was entirely by accident.

Fred had always hated her for being stronger, faster, and smarter than him. Then one night she discovered him panicked because he'd murdered his girlfriend. Because she knew her uncle would want her to, she'd taken the bloody knife and shouldered the blame for Fred's crime.

Now her cousin owed her, but rather than gratitude, it made his hatred slice even deeper than before. That hatred glared out of his eyes as he stalked toward her.

Fred had always unfairly lashed out at her with his nasty temper, but Tessa had never let him get away with it. She wasn't about to let him get away with it now.

She'd never been so grateful for her Caucasian father's tall genes as she straightened and stared down at Fred's beady eyes. He stopped a few feet from her, probably because he'd have to crick his neck to glare at her and that would just be embarrassing for him.

"Dealing with garbage suits you." Fred's lip curled.

"Don't worry. I'm not after your day job." Tessa smiled.

Her comment went over his head. "I don't clean up messes."

"No, I clean yours up for you."

His neck reddened.

To think she'd gone to prison for this moldy tomato.

No, she hadn't gone to prison for him. She'd gone to prison for his father.

She flashed him a smile. "Fred, do you have a point to make, for once in your life, or are you just here contaminating the air?"

She caught a few gasps from the quiet restaurant that had stopped to witness their tense conversation. She realized that because of what she'd done for him, she could freely insult this rat dropping whereas others could not.

"You can't speak to me that way," he spat at her.

"I just did, you squashed slug." And Fred knew that if he touched her, she'd use his head to clean up the spilled ramen instead of the mop in her hand.

He sputtered. Fred didn't have many brain cells devoted to quick comebacks. "You ex-convict."

"What's wrong, Freddy-weddy? If you're going to insult the ex-convict, you better be prepared to take what you dish out."

"Tessa, leave him alone."

A commanding voice filled the restaurant even though he hadn't raised his voice above its normal growl.

Rita and the other waiter scurried away, and patrons suddenly turned back to their meals, although the volume was barely half what it had been before. Subtly, the air became denser, as if blanketed by an invisible fog.

Not a fog. The presence of the man walking into his restaurant—one of several he owned—was more charged than a mere fog.

"Uncle Teruo." Tessa stood her ground as he approached her, aware of Fred scuttling out of his father's way like a cockroach. She dropped her eyes and bowed at the waist in a sign of respect.

He paused, acknowledging her greeting, then suddenly his large square palms were cupping her face, rough against her skin but tender in their touch, raising her gaze to meet his. His eyes, half-shadowed by eyelids puffy with age and responsibility, gleamed with the familiar tenderness that was like water to her parched soul. He shook her face gently, playfully, then drew her to him in a brief embrace. "How are you, Tessa?"

"I'm fine, Uncle," she spoke into his suit jacket, breathing the familiar scent of his favorite brand of cigar. He had hugged her like this the day she'd been released, and the smell brought back that feeling of being free, of being home. Her fingers curled briefly on his back, then he straightened and stepped away.

"Have you eaten yet?" he asked her.

Now those were the words she wanted to hear. "Nope." There was that drool again, right on cue.

He turned her by the shoulders and pushed her ahead of him toward the kitchen, where Jerry was still blissfully unaware of the almost-fight between the niece and son of the San Francisco yakuza boss.

••••

Tessa had thought Uncle Teruo's arrival was something along the lines of a rescue from a fate worse than death, but now she wasn't so sure. She felt a bit like she'd jumped from a wok into hibachi coals.

She'd gotten her hug from Jerry—today, more garlic-scented than ginger-scented—and her massive bowl of ramen, which was thankfully very garlic-scented.

Eating in Jerry's office with Uncle Teruo sitting across the desk from her ... not such a happy place.

Normally she loved talking with Uncle Teruo. Except not when he asked things like, "How are you feeling?"

Read: Up for anything more strenuous? Like something that involves beating the stuffing out of somebody?

"I'm doing fantastic now that I have this." She indicated her bowl, peering through the steam at the floating bean sprouts. She wanted to say grace, but somehow saying grace in front of her sociopathic cellmates had been easier than saying grace in front of her Buddhist, gangster uncle.

"You're still staying with your mom?"

Read: So I know where to find you if I want you to do something for me, especially anything involving breaking fingers.

Tessa nodded at the corner of a gigantic cube of tofu peeking out of her soup. "Until I can get a job and move out." She closed her eyes and bowed her head. Maybe Uncle would get the hint ...

That would be a *no*.

"What kind of job are you looking for?"

Read: I'm delighted you're willing to return to the workplace, because I have the perfect job for you.

Inspiration struck for how to neatly avoid the question. "Uncle, hang on a second. I need to say grace." She jerked her head down. *DearLordThankyouforthisfoodAmen.*

"Grace? What grace? Who's grace?" His bushy salt-and-pepper eyebrows lowered over his eyes.

Read: You don't tell your uncle to "hang on."

"I needed to pray before I could eat." Tessa picked up her chopstick and the boat-shaped spoon. She took a magical sip of broth, ignoring the stinging heat, rolling the salty, savory goodness on her tongue before letting it slide down her throat, warming as it went down. She didn't need crack—she had Jerry's ramen.

"Are you done eating? I need to discuss things with you."

Tessa froze with the noodles on her chopstick only inches from her mouth. She sighed and let them plop back into the soup. So much for the hoped-for casual chat, non-related to the work she'd done for him before getting arrested.

Uncle reached over and took her hand. "I want to say again, thank you for what you did."

It took her a second to realize he was referring to Fred, to inserting herself under suspicion for his son's crime seven years ago. Despite his humble words, the cool, dry skin of his palm lay heavy over her knuckles. "You're welcome, Uncle," she replied.

He released her and leaned back in Jerry's chair. "I can give you a job."

From anyone else, it would have been a generous, innocent offering. From Uncle Teruo, it carried the weight of a royal statement and deep undercurrents. "Uncle, I already explained this to you."

He waved his hand dismissively. "You're just worried. You're too smart to get caught again."

As opposed to Fred, who was stupid enough to have been wandering around with the bloody knife in his hand when Tessa found him that night. Fred would have folded under police questioning and led to trouble for Uncle if he'd actually been arrested.

"And I would not ask any more favors from you," Uncle continued.

If she'd been eating, she would have snorted ramen noodles. That was a loaded promise. Uncle might not actually voice any requests for Tessa to take the heat for someone's crime again, but the situation and Japanese sense of duty would compel her to offer to do it or be held in disfavor by the old-fashioned *oyabun*.

She wasn't sure how to put this delicately, so she plunged full-steam ahead. "Uncle, I told you in my letters from prison and when I first saw you after I got out. I am a Christian now, and I'm trying to learn to love people, not break their kneecaps."

His frown looked suspiciously like a pout. "I never asked you to break kneecaps."

She rolled her eyes. "Unnnncleeeee ..." Her exasperation drew the word out into six syllables. "You know what I mean."

He lifted a forefinger as a thought came to him. "Your cousin Ichiro became a 'Christian,' too, but he still works for me."

Tessa rolled her eyes. "Itchy's girlfriend grew up Episcopalian and has no idea what he does, so he went to church with her so he could get into her pants."

He glowered at her. "Are you saying you're going to church so you can ..." His mouth worked silently while red stained his cheeks. "... with some boy?"

Tessa choked. "What? No." This was not going the way she'd hoped. "I go to church because I've become a different person." She'd been tempted to say better person, but the way her luck was going, Uncle would think she was insulting him and order a hit on her. Or just send Fred to poison her air space.

An indulgent smile hovered around his stern mouth. "This

is new for you. Don't be so hasty to make a complete life change until you know this is who you want to be."

Three years as a Christian wasn't long enough? Then again, she'd had only a few months as a Christian outside the prison walls, so maybe he was justified in thinking it might be a temporary thing.

Except it wasn't. She knew it wasn't, with a knowledge deep in her gut, a knowledge deeper than the secret places of her heart. A knowledge that gave her both peace and strength to say, "Uncle, I'm not going to change my mind."

"Be reasonable. What kind of job can you get?"

She mutinously glared at her cooled bowl of ramen. "I got my college degree in prison." Psychology. It had fascinated her because she'd spent so much of her life reading the emotions and thoughts of the people she talked to on behalf of her uncle. She wasn't exactly proud of what she could do—knowing when people were lying, what they were feeling, being able to manipulate their emotions—but she wanted to use that skill for helping people rather than making or collecting money for the yakuza.

Uncle Teruo's face gentled. "You know that I believe you can do well at anything you set your mind toward, but with only a Bachelor's in Psychology, there aren't many jobs available. Plus …" He sighed. "I'm sure you've realized by now that there aren't many people who would hire an ex-convict, especially for any type of psychology job."

She had known that even when studying for her degree. She just hadn't really wanted to admit it to herself because her studies had been so fascinating and she hadn't wanted to switch to a different degree program.

"Don't be stubborn," he said. "You haven't had any job offers, have you?"

Telling her to stop being stubborn did what it usually did — made her completely pigheaded. "I have had offers. I just chose not to take them."

"Oh? What?"

"A woman offered me a job as a bodyguard."

"Paying how much?"

"Er ... we didn't discuss it."

"Why not?"

"Well ... her assets are still being held by her husband, whom she ran away from because he was using her as a punching bag."

"So she couldn't pay you?" he said slowly. Uncle's face had that expression that wondered where his niece's brains had suddenly dribbled to.

"She said she'd pay me as soon as she got her money back. She called some family friend who was going to get her a really good lawyer."

"I see." He stared at her for a moment, eyebrows raised, mouth a thin line. "And you turned down this incredibly lucrative business deal because ...?"

She stared down at her soup bowl. "She has a three-year-old son. And I wasn't sure about the kind of trouble I'd attract, considering what I used to do."

"Your ruthlessness is what makes you an Ota," he said proudly. "But it does collect some enemies."

Only her uncle would praise her for her ability to cause physical pain.

Tessa had been sorely tempted to take Elizabeth up on her offer, especially after talking with Mina about her own body-guard business, but she realized that it wasn't fair to Elizabeth to saddle her with an even more dangerous person than her fist-flying husband. Tessa would rather try to find a legitimate job first and prove to the world that she was no longer working for her uncle. Once Tessa was off people's radar, then she could protect her clients without bringing even more danger to them.

The old Tessa wouldn't have cared who she put in harm's way, but the new Tessa hopefully thought about other people more than she used to.

"And this is the only job offer you have?" Uncle Teruo asked. He settled back in his chair, the very picture of an uncle indulging his niece's pipe dreams.

"I'm interviewing at OWA tomorrow," she said.

"Didn't you already apply to OWA?"

"Yes." Twenty-two times. "So?"

"This is for another salesperson position?"

"Uh, no. Janitor."

His brow darkened. "My niece is not a janitor."

She was when even McDonald's wouldn't hire her. Maybe they thought she'd kill someone by flipping a burger in their eye. "It's a foot in the door," she said. "From there, I can get promoted. Outdoors and Wilderness Adventures is my favorite store." Just the name made her want to smile.

He sighed heavily and opened his mouth to protest, but she said softly, "I really want this job, Uncle." *I really want to go legitimate.*

He surprised her by reaching across to grasp her chin between his square fingers. "I miss having you around," he said.

Tessa stilled. Uncle Teruo and his wife, Aunt Kayoko, had always given her more affection than Tessa's own selfish mother and irritable sister. With Aunt Kayoko gone, Teruo was her family. She may not want to do illegal things anymore, but she couldn't deny his hold on her heart. She knew that as long as she had him, she'd never feel alone.

"Uncle." She swallowed. She hated denying him. "Please understand."

"I do." He sighed heavily. "I do. And I owe you a debt I can never repay."

"You don't owe me anything."

"I owe you lunch." He gestured to the soggy noodles in front of her. "Eat. I don't want to be accused of starving my niece."

He stood with stately grace. On his way to the office door, he paused as if suddenly remembering something. "You said you're still staying with your mother?"

"Yes." The tightness of her voice gave her away.

Uncle Teruo found that vastly amusing. He chuckled as he turned the door handle, he chuckled as he exited the office, and he was still chuckling as he turned in the doorway to lean into the office to tell her, "Six more months."

"What?"

"You'll come back to me begging for a job so that you can move out, because I know my sister. You won't be able to live with Ayumi for longer than six more painful months. Have fun!" He shut the door with a soft click.

Chapter 3

Tessa should never have brought her mother to OWA, Outdoor and Wilderness Adventures retail store.

"And what in the world is that monstrous thing?" Mom pointed to the indoor climbing wall, where a tall, lean man was inching his way up. Tessa could tell he was a novice at rock-climbing, but his movements had the grace of an athlete. An OWA store employee was belaying him—controlling the rope to catch him if he should fall—but the employee seemed a bit distracted by the Kim Kardashian look-alike flirting with him.

"That's a climbing wall, Mom." Tessa steered her away from the giant structure near the front door of the OWA store and toward the main floor.

"Don't they know they could get sued? Honestly, Tessa, you say you like this store? It's full of dangerous things." Mom held up a headlamp.

Tessa eyed the Mammut 2-in-1 headlamp/lantern combo. "Um, okay, yeah, you could use that to *blind a raccoon*."

Mom dropped the item back down onto the shelf. "Well, how am I supposed to know what it is? It looked obscene."

With a bored expression, Alicia returned from sorting through the workout clothes. "How much time before your interview?"

"Twenty minutes."

"Do you always arrive this freakishly early before your interview?"

"Only the ones I want." Which, these days, was all of them.

"Well, since you brought us here to help, let's do a last-minute check." She surveyed Tessa's crisp white button-down shirt and slim gray skirt with a critical eye. "You have creases on your shirt, your hair is hopeless as always, and you have a panty line."

There was something wrong about being accompanied to a job interview by her mother and her sister. Not that they could walk into the back office with Tessa to make sure she wasn't putting the hiring manager in a choke hold or something equally guaranteed not to get her hired.

But this was Tessa's favorite store, and she wasn't above withstanding her family's usual criticism on her hair and clothes if it might get her a job here.

"The crease is from the car seatbelt. I did my hair this morning but it's just naturally straight and hairspray won't keep it up for long. And I can't change my underwear," Tessa said.

"Well, fine, if you don't mind men looking at your rear end." Mom shook her head and cast her eyes toward the ceiling.

"Let's hope the hiring manager will be looking at my face, not my backside."

"Try to slouch without looking like you're slouching," Mom said. "It'll make you look shorter."

"Men don't like hiring women they have to look up to," Alicia said.

"You shouldn't have drunk so much milk when you were

younger," Mom said. "It probably boosted the height genes you already had from your father."

Tessa didn't blame her for the disdain in her voice for the man who'd ditched them when she was ten, but she made it seem like it was Tessa's fault for possessing said genes. "If I slouch, it'll seem like I'm hiding something."

"I don't know why I bother helping you get a regular job," Alicia said. "This whole religious thing will wear off in a few months and you'll be back working for Uncle Teruo."

"I became a Christian three years ago while surrounded by convicts. I'm pretty sure this religious thing isn't going away anytime soon." A part of her regretted her snippy tone as soon as she said it. If she'd really changed, shouldn't she be able to relate better to her sister rather than degenerate into their old bickering? She'd been able to bypass the drugs, drinking, and hanging out with her yakuza cousins since she got out of prison, but it was so hard to change old behaviors when it came to her sister and mother, mostly because they'd never understood her or approved of her even before she worked for the yakuza. When they were children, feminine and self-centered Alicia had only been embarrassed by her tomboy younger sister, and Mom had favored her older daughter, leaving Tessa feeling left out and lonely. Was it any wonder she'd hung out with her male yakuza cousins, who liked her feistiness and boldness?

"Well then, hurry up and move out so I can finally sell my house and move into Mom's. I would think you'd have done it by now," Alicia said in an accusatory tone.

Tessa couldn't understand why Alicia was still just as hostile toward her as when Tessa had worked for the yakuza, which Alicia had disapproved of. Even though Tessa had been working so hard to change, it was as if she wasn't good enough, no matter what she did. That frustration was making her respond with the same sarcasm as the old Tessa, even though she did her best to control her temper.

"When I first got out of jail, you were still blissfully ignorant about Duane's extracurricular activities and there was no reason for me to move out. Maybe I'll just stay at Mom's house," she threatened.

Alicia's skin, fairer than Tessa's, showed all the motley splotches of her irritation. But to Tessa's surprise, her mother almost smiled. Maybe Mom actually wanted her to stay. Why, she couldn't fathom. Loneliness? Boredom?

No, probably the live-in, unpaid maid.

She squelched a belated niggle of guilt that she was the reason Alicia and her daughter, Paisley, couldn't move out of her soon-to-be-ex-husband's house, but it wasn't Tessa's fault no one would hire her. And just like stay-at-home-mom Alicia, Tessa couldn't rent an apartment without a job.

Mom reached into Tessa's shirt and started tugging at the cups of her bra.

"Mom, we're in public," Tessa hissed as she tried to squirm out of the way of her hands.

"Too bad you were so opposed to padding these."

"Mom, I hope the hiring manager doesn't look at my chest."

Mom ignored her and reached into her purse. "I know what will help—duct tape."

"What?" Tessa couldn't believe Mom carried a roll with her. Then again, this was Mom.

Mom pulled out a short length. "Works wonders to lift the bosom."

"Mom! No way." Tessa quick-stepped backward out of range of her mother, who held the piece of duct tape in front of her.

"Oh, don't be such a baby. I used this all the time when I was in the Miss Cherry Blossom pageants. We'll go into the bathroom really quick and—"

Tessa stumbled and she registered the shift in padding under her feet. Uh-oh, she had walked into the area under the climbing wall. She'd better get out of here, quick. She was surprised the OWA staff worker belaying the climber hadn't yelled at her to—

"Edddiiiiieeee!"

The shouted name came from directly above her, but before she could even react, a sack of potatoes crashed onto her shoulders.

Actually, it fell a bit slowly, but it still fell on her.

"Oops," a male voice said from several feet away. The OWA employee.

"Tessa!" her mother shouted, sounding either concerned or embarrassed. Or both.

She lay sprawled on the floor at eye level with a pair of sneakers running toward her, probably those of the OWA employee/belayer.

How strange, the sack of potatoes smelled incredibly sexy—male musk, sage soap, and a thread of cologne that screamed *money.*

"Are you okay? I'm so sorry." The muffled voice had a slight drawl that tingled down her spine.

The OWA employee attached to the Nikes in front of her nose pulled the potatoes off of her, and she sat up and turned to look.

She couldn't believe she'd thought he was a sack of potatoes.

He was lean, but wide, and chiseled shoulders burst out of the tank top he wore. From the way his long legs were folded up under him, he would be even taller than she was.

But why in the world were his blue-green eyes looking at

her as if she were a ghost? And not the see-through, squinty, I'm-not-quite-sure-I-see-something-there type of ghost look, but the Oh-my-gosh-it's-the-dead-nun-who-hurled-herself-off-the-balcony-after-her-illicit-lover-plunged-to-his-death type of look.

"Tessa Lancaster?" The hesitant young voice tore Tessa's attention from golden-brown curls, high cheekbones, and a Roman nose to a twenty-something woman in the coveted uniform of an OWA staff worker. The girl's face registered confusion and wariness.

"That's me." Tessa tried to spring to her feet with the eagerness of a future OWA employee, but nearly kissed the ground again when her knee buckled.

"Uh ... we're ready for your interview."

Perfect timing.

••••

He'd seen a ghost.

As the tall, slim figure walked away from him, Charles Britton blinked rapidly to make sure it was really Tessa Lancaster. Was she out of prison already? It had been so long. He almost hadn't recognized her—rather than the sleek all-black she'd worn to the courtroom, today she was dressed in a white button-down shirt and dark gray pencil skirt, and her hair, which he'd previously seen falling halfway down her back, had been twisted up into a professional-looking French knot, from which straight brown strands were already escaping.

Probably due to him nearly flattening her into the ground.

"Eddie!" he roared, turning toward his brother. "You were supposed to be holding that rope-thing."

"The climbing rope," Eddie corrected him absently, his gaze riveted to Tessa's disappearing figure. "She was cute."

"I'm sure she'd like the phone number of the guy who *dropped his brother on her head.*"

That finally got Eddie's attention away from Tessa. "Sorry about that. I was talking to this girl ..." He glanced around. "Hmm. She's gone. She was cute too. Although not as cute as your landing pad."

"So if you'd been holding my climbing rope when I was out on a real rock face, I'd have left my brains over the mountainside?"

Eddie grinned. "Only if there was a cute climber like her to distract me from my belaying duties."

"Tessa Lancaster is not cute. She causes a man more trouble than two girlfriends."

"Hey, you know her?"

Charles should have kept his fat mouth shut. "I saw her in court once."

"She was your client?"

"No." But a shot of alarm made his blood fizzle. Now that he worked for Pleiter & Woodhouse, would Tessa's mob boss uncle hire Charles's law firm to defend mafia clients? No, Teruo Ota had his own fleet of well-greased lawyers, and even if he did hire Charles's firm, Charles wasn't partner—yet—so it'd be unlikely that he'd be asked to take on a case involving such a high-profile client. And especially not Teruo Ota's jailbird niece.

Charles started unhooking himself from the climbing apparatus. "Help me get this stuff off."

Eddie started helping him. "So how do you know her? And can you introduce me?"

"No, I can't. She doesn't know who I am."

Eddie's hands stilled as he unhooked yet another strap. "She doesn't? So how do you know who she is?"

"Because she's the niece of the Japanese mafia boss in San Francisco."

"Whoa." Eddie's eyes became like Mama's antique blue china saucers.

"I know she's cute, but now you see why I said she was trouble?"

Eddie paused, giving him a searching look. "You think she's cute."

"So do you."

"You never think girls are cute."

Charles glared at his brother. "I assure you, I like girls."

Eddie rolled his eyes. "That's not what I meant. You would never *allow* yourself to notice a woman connected to a criminal family." He gave an evil grin. "Until now."

"Just get me out of this harness," Charles said. "I can't believe you dropped me."

"Technically, you fell. And I, with my lightning reflexes, put friction on the rope to slow you down for the last few feet."

"Why didn't you slow me down the *first* few feet? Your only job was to prevent me from hitting the ground."

"What can I say? I'm a babe magnet." Eddie struck a pose.

"I saw only one girl, and she ran away from you."

"Don't forget Tessa. And she walked away only because you landed on her and not me."

In that brief moment Charles had looked into her face, she'd seemed different from when he last saw her. Then, she'd been hard, with a dark, dangerous air to her. Today, she'd seemed ... lighter.

No, it was probably the fact she'd been stunned by having all 200 pounds of him try to pulverize her into dust, tempered only by the rope going taut at the last second to soften the blow.

"Does this mean you're not going climbing with me next month at Mount Shasta?" Eddie asked.

"Are you trying to kill me so you can get all the inheritance money?"

"There won't be any. Mama will make sure to blaze through the last penny on her deathbed."

Actually, Charles had just done her accounting last night, and unless Mama bought a couple private islands, she was in good shape for a couple lifetimes. "Did Mama call you?"

"Yeah. Uh . . . did she tell you anything about coming to live with us?"

"What?"

"It's apparently a sudden decision."

"I thought she had just moved in with Aunt Coco. That Aunty Coco was looking forward to having her stay with them for a few months." After Mama and Daddy divorced several years ago, Mama had been very well off with her settlement and the trust fund set up by Mama's father, General Durand. She found that if she didn't have to pay for the taxes and upkeep of her house, she would be able to live nearly exactly as she had before Daddy cheated on her and left her. Also, as she got into cooking, it was more fun for her to cook for others. So she sold her plantation home and began living with relatives for several months at a time.

Eddie coughed. "I think the reason it's such a sudden decision is *because* of Aunt Coco."

"Oh. Is it because of Mama's cooking?"

"I got my own earful. You'll get yours when Mama calls you."

Charles sighed. "Aunt Coco likes to stretch a dollar into six. I told Mama that I thought Aunt Coco invited Mama to stay with her because she thought she'd be getting a free chef."

"Well, I *didn't* tell Mama, but I think the relatives purposely didn't tell Aunt Coco about Mama's cooking," Eddie said.

And Mama's love of excess pepper, unusual combos like beef and guava, and her new favorite spice, turmeric. All mixed together.

"She was a great cook when we were growing up," Charles said. "I just don't like these new exotic recipes she's been trying the past few years. But I can't exactly say no when she cooks for me."

"You could sue the Food Network for existing."

"It would be fine if she watched Paula Deen. The problems happen when she watches Iron Chef — once she tried to recreate some octopus pudding dessert she saw on the show."

"Blech." Eddie made a face, then slapped Charles on the back. "And Mama's staying with you again. Good luck."

"If she serves sushi gumbo, I'm forcing you to come over for dinner."

"Hmm, now if *Tessa* made me sushi gumbo ..."

"You're a moron," Charles said.

However, inwardly he couldn't blame his brother. He'd been mesmerized during that short moment he'd met her eyes — dark brown with flecks of green, framed by long dark lashes. And her mouth had been soft and full and pink.

He gave himself a firm mental shake. She was yakuza, for goodness' sake, and he knew exactly what she'd done because he'd been a law clerk at her trial. And he was thinking she was cute?

Actually, he'd thought back then that she was cute too — until he'd researched all the unsolved assaults and murders her cousin Ichiro had been involved in, and since she'd been part of his gang, he knew she had been involved in most of those as well, even if it wasn't proven.

So when she'd pled out for manslaughter rather than murder, he'd advised the judge to extend her sentence beyond the maximum, and the judge had done it, giving her seven years instead of five.

Ironic that now, as a defense lawyer, he had defended a few corporate criminals.

Why was Tessa Lancaster applying for a job at OWA when she could just go back to working for her uncle? Had something happened between them?

Charles had no doubt that eventually she would go back to hanging out with her cousin Ichiro again. He had escaped conviction a couple times already. Tessa probably would too, unless she messed up again like she did with Laura Starling's murder.

Regardless, he'd probably never see her again.

Chapter 4

The living room couch was like a torture rack from the Spanish Inquisition. And probably just as old.

When they'd been younger, Tessa and Alicia had loved sleeping on the living room couch. Twenty years ago, the springs had already been sagging and swaying, and it had been a dark-blue corduroy cloud. Plus, sleeping in the living room had been reserved for sleepover parties and Christmas Eve, both happy-pink-fizzy-skies events.

But the arrival last night of Alicia with a pale and shaking Paisley had relegated Tessa to the couch so Paisley could be bundled up in her aunt's bed. So, not such a happy-pink-fizzy-sky event.

What had caused Alicia to leave her house in the middle of the night to bunk at Mom's house? After putting Paisley to bed in Tessa's room, Alicia had holed up in Mom's bedroom until Tessa finally went to sleep on the couch, concerned but too tired to stay up.

She spared a fleeting thought for the dangers of her niece in her bedroom. When Tessa had still been living with her mom in her teens, she'd accumulated a highly illegal weapons collection that had been hidden in various places in her room. Because of her toys, she had also fortified the room so that G.I. Joe couldn't get in.

She'd taken her weapons with her when she moved to her condo in her early twenties, and then after she got out of prison, they were all (tearfully) sold because of her parole. But Tessa didn't quite trust herself to have remembered all the hiding places in her bedroom. Alicia would eat her alive if her daughter found a forgotten *wushu* chain whip or something.

She twisted to try to ease the ache in her back and would have rolled off the couch if she hadn't thrust her hand out to plant into the olive-green shag carpet. She pushed her body back over the edge of the faded blue corduroy cushions.

She sat up and swung her legs down, intending to stand up, except: (a) the couch which had seemed so large when she was eight was in reality only eleven inches from the floor, and it was like trying to stand up after sitting in a kindergarten chair, and (b) since she'd grown a few feet since she last slept here, her feet had dangled over the edge uncovered all night and were now numb with cold.

She managed to hobble to the bathroom, then to the kitchen. Faint noise from her room—Paisley was up. What time was it? She glanced at the clock—seven-ish. She opened the fridge, grabbing a carton of yogurt. She opened it and yelped.

Mom had apparently been trying to conduct a science experiment. The entire inside was coated with greenish dark gray fuzz. She thought a section of it might have reached out to her with a spiny tendril before she slammed the lid back on.

She opened the cabinet door under the sink, but the garbage can sitting there was already full, so she pulled it out. May as well empty it.

"Morning, Aunt Tessa," Paisley said from the doorway of the kitchen. She yawned and scratched at her wild blonde-streaked brown curls. "What's for breakfast?"

Not yogurt, that was for sure. "Did you want me to make you some eggs and toast?"

"Naw, I can just get cereal." Paisley opened the fridge.

And promptly burst into tears.

Alicia chose that exact moment to walk into the kitchen. She took one look at her crying daughter and turned to Tessa, who looked innocent of all wrongdoing while peeking into the garbage bin like a trash lady.

"What did you do?" Alicia demanded.

Tessa actually took one-billionth of a second to consider a calm, mature answer. But of course her temper sprinted past and won the race. "I friended her on Facebook. What do you think I did? Nothing."

"That is not nothing." Alicia thrust a hand toward her daughter, whose face was buried in her hands with tears running between her fingers.

"I was only trying to save her from more emotional trauma in the form of thousand-year-old yogurt." Tessa gestured to the carton of yogurt sitting on top of the full garbage can.

"It's not her fault, Mom," Paisley said in between hiccoughs. She reached into the fridge and gingerly handed her mom a can of whipped cream.

Alicia made a disgusted noise. "I could kill your father."

Now Tessa was completely confused. "Over whipped cream?"

Paisley covered her mouth with her hand and squeezed her eyes shut.

"Look what you've done!" Alicia yelled at Tessa.

"Considering the wealth of information you gave me last

night, you're lucky I didn't offer it to her with her morning pancakes. I have no idea what's going on."

Alicia pressed her lips together and didn't answer. Neither did she apologize for unfairly accusing Tessa of wrongdoing or even explaining what exactly Tessa had done wrong.

"So are you going to tell me why we're instituting a Redi-Whip ban?" Tessa asked.

"You want to wait for my daughter to leave the room first, O Sensitive One?"

"Oh, I'll tell her." Paisley sniffed and swiped at her eyes, which were still red, but the rest of her was quickly returning to normal. While Tessa had often been tempted to hang her niece off a tall building for her smart mouth, for once she was glad for the resilience of youth.

"I was at Adele's house doing homework—"

"Did you get it done?" Alicia said.

"Mooooooom, I'm telling a story here. And yes. Can you stop being a mom for a second?"

"Well, you can't fire your mom, so deal with it," Alicia said.

Ah, the huggy-huggy kissy-kissy bond of a mother and teenage daughter.

"I came home," Paisley said. "I knew Mom was with you guys at OWA so I just let myself in. Oh, how did your interview go, Aunt Tessa?"

"Badly. Continue."

"I went into the kitchen for something to eat because Adele's family only eats vegetarian and while some of it's good, yesterday her mom served this weird brownish-blackish baba-something that tasted like the underside of a rock."

"Baba ghanoush," Alicia said. "It's eggplant ..."

Paisley sent her an exasperated look.

"Okay, okay, tell your story."

"So I walk into the kitchen, and what do I see?" Dramatic pause.

Was Tessa supposed to say something? "Uh ... what?"

"My father, naked."

"Ew!" Even if Tessa had liked Duane, the thought of a daughter seeing her daddy in the buff was too horrible to contemplate.

"With his girlfriend, naked."

"What?"

In an aside to Tessa, Alicia said, "They weren't doing anything ... you know."

"What do you mean?" Paisley protested. "Of course they were doing something. They were covered in whipped cream."

"That's a tragic waste of whipped cream," Tessa said.

"See, Mom? I'm not the only one who thinks that."

"You're not helping," Alicia told Tessa.

"So I screamed," Paisley said. "And his girlfriend screamed. And Dad screamed too."

Tessa could believe Duane screamed, all right. The pansy had called Tessa the night Alicia found him in his office with his girlfriend, crying and begging Tessa for protection from his Michael-Myers-crazy wife. "His stripper girlfriend should be used to performing."

"Oh, it wasn't the stripper," Paisley said airily. "He dumped her the week Mom found them together. Dad's had three girlfriends since. This one's a flight attendant."

The man needed to be neutered. "Why was he at your house?" Tessa asked.

Alicia took up the story. "After I put Paisley to bed, I called him to tell him I had to tranquilize his only child. He explained that he lost his condo."

"How'd he lose it? The man makes six figures."

"Because he also bought a Ferrari, a houseboat, a vacation home in Cancun, and a diamond tiara for the whipped-cream girl."

"Which she was wearing," Paisley added.

"I thought he couldn't buy anything. Isn't that how divorce works in California?"

"Not for the money he makes after the official separation."

"He doesn't make *that* much. Did he buy all that on credit?"

"And reneged on the condo. He's homeless. Since the house is still in his name, he decided to move in."

So that meant ...

"Good morning," Mom said as she entered the kitchen, then stopped at the sight of the three of them in intense conversation. "What's going on?"

"I was explaining about Duane," Alicia said.

Mom's mouth twisted at mention of his name, then she changed the subject. "Everyone sleep okay?"

"Yes," Alicia said.

"I guess." Paisley shrugged.

"Like Def Leppard was playing a concert next door," Tessa said.

The three of them looked at Tessa. "Tell us how you really feel," Alicia said.

"I'm not sleeping on the couch again. Paisley can sleep there."

"I don't want to sleep on a couch—"

"How dare you make your niece sleep on a couch—"

"I'm sure we can fit everyone somehow," Mom said.

"I'm six inches taller and almost twice Paisley's age," Tessa said.

"You could just move out," Alicia said angrily.

Mom cleared her throat.

"And live where, on what salary?" Tessa asked.

"You could get a job," Alicia sneered.

Mom coughed.

"I send out fifty to sixty resumes a week," Tessa snapped. "And I was here first."

"Oh, so you'll send your sister and niece out into the streets?"

"You could get a job," Tessa replied silkily.

Alicia's mouth puckered shut and she looked away. "I've been too busy raising Paisley to get a job."

"A-hem!" Mom nearly coughed up a loogie to get their attention. "We have plenty of space. We'll clean out the spare room and put that storage stuff in the sunroom."

Tessa was a little surprised at Mom's sudden willingness to clean out Dad's old office. Right after Dad left, her mother had been hysterical-psycho insistent that they leave Dad's old office the way it was. A few years later, her bitterness had foamed over and she'd gone through the room, intending to throw away everything inside, but something about being in the room for the first time in years calmed her down, and instead she'd simply boxed everything up and used it as a storage room. She became angry-psycho agitated whenever her daughters asked to clear out the room, so they stopped mentioning it and pretended it didn't exist.

"I, uh, think it's still got the daybed in there," Tessa said.

"In the sunroom, that stuff will be fine over the winter, but come spring, the sun will damage it," Alicia protested.

She could just say, "I want my sister to enjoy the torture of sleeping for months on a three-foot-long saggy couch rather than work to clean up an old, unused room."

"We'll install those dark shades on the windows," Mom said. "It can even be a spare bedroom if we can get rid of enough stuff."

"And how are we going to afford it?" asked the jobless sister who was too lazy, scared, and unmotivated to find a job for the first time since her daughter was born.

"We'll be cleaning out the room—garage sale!" Mom's face lit up. Garage sales were like Macy's stores to her—hours of unceasing, endless wonder and amazement.

This friendly, reasonable version of her mother was completely unfamiliar and maybe a little unpredictable. But Tessa said, "I'm cool with it." Anything to keep her room. She'd already gotten rid of all the knives and swords from her personal collection, but she never knew if she had forgotten a stiletto hidden somewhere from her teen years, and if Paisley found it, Alicia would go Michael-Myers-crazy again.

"I'm not," Alicia said. "Can't you just find a place to stay with some of your yakuza friends? I don't understand why you sold your condo. For a supposedly smart woman, sometimes you act completely crazy—"

Tessa didn't really expect her selfish sister to suddenly become unselfish and easygoing, but this constant attacking put her back up. "Alicia," Tessa interrupted in a low, succinct voice, "I am going to tell you this *one more time.*"

Alicia paused in the middle of her tirade with surprise in her eyes and pink in her cheeks.

"The reason I won't go back to my yakuza friends is the same reason I sold my yakuza-money-purchased condo, and the same reason I won't work for Uncle Teruo again. I'm done with that life. I'm trying to be normal, which is what *you* kept harping at me to be all those years before I went to prison."

The flush in Alicia's cheeks deepened.

"As soon as I find a job, I will move out," Tessa said.

Mom pouted, but didn't say anything in response.

"When I do, you can rule this castle the way you want. Until then, you're going to just have to deal with it."

Alicia's eyes narrowed. "Well, work harder to find a job fast."

Tessa was quite proud of herself when she refrained from retorting, "What about fifty to sixty resumes a week is not working hard?" Then again, she did bite her tongue hard enough to draw blood.

"You should take that bodyguard job," Paisley said. Tessa had forgotten she was here.

"The unpaid one?" Mom asked.

"Elizabeth did promise to pay me when she got her money back."

"Yes, yes, just take it, take it," Alicia said impatiently. "She'll probably pay you before you actually find permanent work."

Were the only jobs available to her jobs like the one yesterday? (The interviewer for the janitor position had asked her to take her top off. Tessa had walked out.)

Not if she was careful. And she thought she'd actually be a really good bodyguard. Hadn't she worked to disable bodyguards all the time when working for her uncle?

She also liked Elizabeth, with her maple syrup accent and bubbly personality, only slightly dimmed by her years of being used as a punching bag. She made Tessa feel like a real person, someone she wanted to get to know, and not an ex-yakuza.

Alicia stomped toward the coffeemaker. "The least you could have done was start the coffee," she snipped.

Tessa hadn't lived with her sister under the same roof since Alicia hightailed it out of the house when she was eighteen. And now she'd be living with Mom *and* Alicia? She might as well draw a red target on her forehead.

She went to the living room while Alicia and Mom went

about making breakfast. Tessa's new cell phone—which Mom had gotten for her out of frustration when people kept calling the home phone—was on the coffee table, and she dialed Wings shelter.

The sooner she moved out of her mom's house, the less likely she'd turn Michael-Myers-crazy herself.

Chapter 5

The Michael Meyers case was going to kill him. Not just the ribbing he got from his colleagues about his client's name, but because the man had the organization of a monkey. In the wild.

"Abby, did the interrogatory responses from Meyers' lawyer show up yet?" Charles entered his legal secretary's office and glanced up from the documents he was reading.

Abby, normally efficient and unruffled, had a deer-in-the-headlights look as she looked at him while on the telephone with someone. "Yes, ma'am. Right away, ma'am. No, ma'am. Yes, you are correct, ma'am."

Only one woman in Charles's life would warrant four ma'ams from his Oregon-born secretary. Charles held his hand out for the telephone headset, and Abby almost hurled it at him in her haste to pass the buck.

"Hi, Mama," he said.

"Charles! Did you know that Macy's has *eight floors?*"

Alarm shot through him, and it took icy thoughts of the North Pole to keep him calm. "Really, Mama? Shreveport is really stepping up these days."

"Shreveport?" Mama's light laugh tinkled on the phone. "Charles, honey, I'm in San Francisco."

The Eagle has landed. Alert all battleships.

"Mama, you're in Union Square all by yourself?" What if something happened to her? He needed to go pick her up right now.

"Charles, you worry too much. I'm having a great time."

Sure, alone in an eight-story Macy's store with thousands of strangers around her. "Where are your suitcases, Mama?"

"Oh, I had the taxi take me to the Hilton, and I asked the bellman to hold my bags for me. Then I headed to Union Square."

"Mama, you're not staying at the Hilton."

"Well, if they didn't bother to check that before they took my bags, that's their fault now, isn't it?"

Outrageous. As always. "You're early," Charles said carefully.

"Your Aunt Coco helped me pack." The words were bitten out.

Uh, oh. "That's ... nice of her."

"That woman could skin a deer with just the sound of her voice," Mama snapped. "When she first invited me to stay, all she could talk about was the wonderful times we'd have together and how she was looking forward to eating my cooking, but in the last few weeks, it was 'Vivian, we might need your bedroom soon,' and 'Vivian, your trunks are taking up so much space in the garage.' And Charles, she had the gall to tell me my Thai-Italian fusion lobster fingers were too minty! The nerve! Why, I almost threw her precious African violet into my frying oil. *That* would have made it less minty, let me tell you."

"Mama, Aunt Coco has other strengths besides ... hospitality."

"Well, I had already planned to come out to San Francisco, so here I am!"

Charles covered the mouthpiece and told Abby, "Reschedule

all my appointments this afternoon. I have to go pick up my mama. I'll come back to the office tonight." He had to if he wanted to catch up on all the work he wouldn't be doing this afternoon. When Eddie had called Abby to make the appointment with Charles for the indoor climbing wall — without telling him — he should have said no yesterday, but he had never rock climbed, and it had only been for an hour . . .

Well, he'd be paying for it now. He'd never make partner otherwise.

"And Abby, the next time my brother calls to make an appointment with me, tell me right away."

Abby nodded, but her gray eyes reproached him gently. "You hadn't seen him in over a month because you canceled the last lunch appointment you made with him."

That's right, he'd forgotten about that. One of the senior partners had wanted to speak to him, so he'd canceled his lunch with Eddie to squeeze the meeting into his packed schedule. But really, Eddie understood, right? After all, it had been the head of Charles's practice group.

Mama's voice interrupted his thoughts. "Oh, Charles, they have a cannoli making kit! That's exactly what I need!"

She had said the magic word. If Charles had a downfall, it wasn't the beignets he grew up with; it was the cannoli he had discovered when he first moved to California. There was a great restaurant in North Beach that made the dessert, with a crispy shell, decadent mascarpone cream filling with chocolate chips, and smothered in homemade chocolate sauce. "Mama, you're making cannoli now?" He tried to keep the excitement out of his voice. At least it wasn't gumbo sushi.

"And what a fantastic espresso maker. It foams your milk for you. Excuse me, how much is this?"

He needed to get to Macy's before Mama started borrowing on next quarter's income check.

But he'd make sure she bought the cannoli kit first.

•••

"I'm here for the food," Mama told him.

"The food?" Charles followed her around Macy's, holding the things she wanted to buy and surreptitiously putting some back when she wasn't looking. "You already had the clam chowder and sourdough bread bowl on Pier 39 the last time you were here."

"No, not tourist food. Oh, this is a nice whisk." She held up something that looked like a satellite for communicating with aliens. "Do you have a whisk?"

No, he didn't. "Yes."

She handed it to him to put on top of the pile and continued down the aisle. "I want to eat the different ethnic foods in San Francisco."

He "accidentally" dropped the whisk back into the bin it had come from. "North Beach has good Italian food." And cannoli.

"And I want to take cooking classes. Oh, now I definitely need this." Mama brandished a stainless steel snail that had instead of a sluggy body, four wicked-looking circular blades.

Charles ducked. "Mama, be careful with that thing. What in the world is it?"

"An herb cutter. For mincing fresh herbs."

She handed it to him, and he gingerly took it from her. He'd have to be careful about dropping this one back on the shelf. He might slice off a finger.

"Anyway, cooking classes. I'm too late to register for the cupcake class at Sur La Table —"

"Sir La-who?"

She shook her head. "And you're part French. What am I going to do with you? Sur La Table. It's a kitchen store. Anyway, the cupcake class isn't given again until next month—"

Shucks.

"—but I signed up for the Brazilian cooking one next week." Her blue eyes were brighter than Xenon headlights.

"Mama, all next week I'm in court."

She pffft-ed away his objections. "I'll just drive to the store myself."

"In San Francisco?" He had a horrible vision of his NASCAR-fan mother going bumper-to-bumper with northern California drivers. Worse, *city* drivers.

"I'm a very good driver," she said, her eyes wide and daring him to disagree.

She wasn't a bad driver—she was a crazy driver. "You're a good driver, Mama, but parking at Union Square is something like $25 per half hour." He only exaggerated a little. Like eight times. "Maybe Eddie can take you."

"Charles, I'm not a Royal Doulton teacup. I can find my way around a city. If worse comes to worst, I'll get a cab."

Before or after being mugged? Knowing Mama, she'd give the mugger her handbag, invite him to church, and promise to cook supper for him afterwards.

"But there's another reason for me to be in San Francisco," Mama said. "I want you to help Elizabeth St. Amant."

"Who?"

"My goddaughter. She used to live in Louisiana, but now she lives in San Francisco. You used to play with her at church picnics. Do you remember her?"

"Not really." He had a vague memory of a chubby little girl with dark frizzy curls.

"She didn't change her name when she married. But the St. Amants had wanted her to marry some boy they picked out for her—his family owned a million acres of land or something like that—and when she married Heath Turnbull instead, they had a conniption fit."

"People still do that? Arranged marriages?"

"It wasn't arranged, really, but they'd been *strongly encouraging* a match since Elizabeth and the million-acre boy had been friends all their lives. Anyway, Elizabeth moved to San Francisco with her husband, but she called me a few days ago. She told me her husband Heath had hit her son."

Charles's hands dug into the cardboard of the cannoli maker box he was carrying.

"She didn't say so, but I think …" Mama looked away, her hand dropping from the shiny colander on the shelf. The two last knuckles of her right hand were abnormally swollen, and the pinky and ring fingers stuck out at odd angles, the way they'd been for fifteen years.

Charles still remembered clearly the day Daddy had broken those.

"Elizabeth had tried calling the St. Amants, but they'd cast her out when she married Heath and they refused to do anything for her. But Elizabeth's *mama's* family, the Tolberts, had been good friends with my mama's family for years. None of the Tolberts are alive now, so Elizabeth called me as the next best thing."

"What does she need? A restraining order? Divorce papers?"

"I'm not sure, but I have the number of where she's staying, and I said I'd talk you into helping her. She told me she needed a lawyer. Poor girl was crying and hysterical."

"Sure, I'll help her," he said, ignoring the clamoring in his head about the mountainous workload he had. He really couldn't afford to take on a pro bono case unless he dropped one of the cases he already had. And any of his colleagues would be only too happy to pick up more billable hours in their race to make partner.

But the bastard had hit her son. Had probably been hitting her for years. Charles wasn't going to sit around and let that happen.

He had vowed he'd never do that again.

Chapter **6**

What in the world are you wearing?" Elizabeth demanded when Tessa walked into Wings domestic violence shelter.

Tessa looked down at her dark gray pantsuit. "What? Are there creases on my shirt?"

"You look like a gangster."

Not the look she'd been aiming for. "I thought I looked professional." As opposed to the yakuza she knew, who tended to be a bit flashy.

"I guess I was expecting more *Alias* and less Secret Service," Elizabeth said. "Here, take off your suit jacket."

Good, because she didn't like how it constricted her shoulders. Tessa shrugged it off and dropped it over the back of a nearby couch. The two women sitting on the couch looked up at her and scuttled away.

Elizabeth's dark eyes flashed after them. "I don't understand why they do that every time you come in here. You watch the children, for goodness' sake."

"And they watch me when I'm with them. Probably afraid I might get hungry and start snacking on one of them."

Elizabeth laughed, then returned to studying Tessa. "Take your hair out of that bun — it's already falling down anyway."

"Oh, man. It took me forever to do it up this morning." Tessa pulled out all eighty-one bobby pins and finger-combed her straight, slippery hair. She had considered using hair spray to keep it in place but hadn't wanted to ask Alicia to borrow hers. Her sister might have given her mace instead, just for kicks.

Elizabeth frowned at Tessa's white button-down shirt. "Okay, now roll up your cuffs a little. You have such beautiful slim wrists." She sighed.

Tessa stared at them. "Really?" She had just thought they were ... well, wrists.

"I always wanted skinny wrists," Elizabeth said. "I thought I looked so disproportional."

Tessa eyed Elizabeth's hourglass figure. "Come again?"

"Look at them." She thrust her graceful hands out. "I have wrists like tree trunks. What's the point of suffering through a personal trainer to keep your figure when you can't do a thing about your man hands?"

Tessa stifled a giggle. "Most men aren't as shallow as the guys on *Seinfeld*."

"But I'm that shallow." Elizabeth winked. "Now you look better. Too bad we don't have a cute scarf we can give you to lighten that outfit."

"But I don't look like a bodyguard."

"You're only sort of my bodyguard. Until I pay you, you're my friend. So you may as well look the part."

An unfamiliar feeling washed over Tessa, something warm and liquid, pleasant but strange.

"What's wrong?" Elizabeth asked.

Tessa shook her head. "It's nothing." Plain silly was what it was.

Elizabeth gave her a stern look. "It's not nothing."

"I just … I realized I have never really been friends with a girl before."

Elizabeth's eyes opened almost as wide as her mouth. "What?"

"I've always been a tomboy. I got along better with my male cousins, and I've never gotten along with Alicia, who always criticized me. The girly-girls at school thought I was strange because I liked playing sports and being outdoors all the time, and the other tomboys didn't like how I always said what I thought. I definitely flunked tact in the school of life."

"Your male cousins—were they all, you know … mobsters?"

"Most of them are yakuza."

"They just let you hang out with them?"

"My uncle was their *oyabun*, their boss, and so they didn't mess with me because of him. But they treated me like a younger sister, and I felt like I belonged."

"Bless your heart," Elizabeth said, reaching out to take Tessa's hand.

"Hey, I may be from California, but I heard that in the South, that's an insult," Tessa said, trying to lighten the mood.

"Honey, if I wanted to insult you, I'd make sure you knew it." But Elizabeth squeezed her hand.

How odd it felt, to have this woman to talk to.

"Daniel's with the other children," Elizabeth said, "so it'll be just the two of us meeting with my lawyer." But she cast a worried look at the back door of the living area, toward the rooms where the children were playing together.

"Think of this as a girls' day out," Tessa said as she steered her toward the side exit.

"I feel guilty." Elizabeth wrapped a scarf around her head and put on a pair of borrowed sunglasses. The effect partially masked the bruise on her face. "Poor Daniel hasn't left the shelter since we came, but I'm going out for coffee."

"You haven't left the shelter since you came either, and it's not coffee — it's a meeting with your lawyer that happens to be at a coffee shop."

Tessa hustled Elizabeth into the 1981 Toyota Corolla parked in the alley next door to the shelter and after babying it through a rough engine start, they headed out toward Market Street.

"Did you buy a car?" Elizabeth asked.

"I borrowed this from my cousin Ichiro."

"That was nice of him."

"He didn't need much persuading. This is an extra car he has, it used to belong to his dad." When her uncle was in *college.*

They parked in the parking garage, and on their way to the coffee shop, Tessa kept a close eye on the cars driving past them and the people walking around them. Elizabeth seemed to be enjoying the brisk November air but cast occasional nervous glances when a man in a business suit came into view. Tessa studied him too, but he didn't even glance their way — two women out for coffee on a cloudy fall morning.

The coffee shop was only halfway full, so they ordered — Tessa paid with some cash she had borrowed from her mom — and got a seat in a corner near the back.

"I don't know why I'm so nervous," Elizabeth said. "Heath doesn't know I went to the shelter. He can't have known we'd be here today. And I don't have his son with me either."

"He might have somehow discovered you went to the shelter," Tessa said, staring hard at a gray Nissan Sentra that passed by the shop. Had she seen that car behind them on the way here? "And even though Daniel isn't with you, he can still grab you to make you take him to his son or tell him where he is."

"I feel so paranoid. If I went to the police talking like this, they'd say I was neurotic."

Tessa was the last person to want to become BFFs with a policeman, but even she thought Elizabeth should have gone there when Heath hit Daniel.

"I think that's him." Elizabeth sat up straighter as a tall man in a sharp suit entered the coffee shop, looking around. "I remember his curly hair from when we played together as kids."

"No way!" Tessa said.

"What? What'd I do wrong?"

"I mean, I can't believe it. It's the dishy rock climber from OWA."

"You've met him before?"

Dishy Climber met Elizabeth's eyes and smiled, and an unseen choir from *Hair* sang out, "Leeeeet the sun shine in!" in the tiny shop.

Then Dishy Climber saw Tessa sitting next to Elizabeth, and the smile morphed into horror.

First a cold, lonely chill squeezed her heart, then fire engulfed her limbs. What was up with that? It wasn't like *she'd* been the one to fall on *him*.

Dishy Climber trudged toward them and sat at the table next to Elizabeth, and across from Tessa. "Elizabeth? I'm Charles. Vivian Britton is my mama."

They shook hands. "This is my bodyguard, Tess—"

"She's your bodyguard?" He eyed Tessa like she was *yagijiru,* goats' innards soup, and his nostrils flared as if she smelled like it too.

She discreetly tried to sniff her armpits.

"She's much tougher than she looks," Elizabeth said. "She knows Tie-Kwayan-Do and Gee-you Jeets-you."

Tessa winced as Elizabeth's accent decimated her favorite martial arts.

Dishy—er, Charles, however, only frowned more. "She's an ex-convict, and she's involved in the Japanese mafia."

The words were like the Hiroshima bomb dropped on the table. Tessa and Elizabeth had been stunned speechless.

Then they both spoke at once.

"I know exactly what she is, and she's been nicer to me than—"

"I am not involved in the yakuza anymore, and who are you to—"

"*Sure* you're not involved with the yakuza," Charles said, "what with your uncle being head boss in San Francisco."

"If there's one thing my uncle did, it was never judging me before hearing my side of the story," Tessa shot back.

A spasm crossed Charles's (rather muscular) throat.

Tessa glared at him. "Besides which, I never tried to kill someone by flattening them like a pancake."

"My brother dropped me—"

"You're the one who fell."

"What in the world did you do to her, Charles?" Elizabeth demanded.

He looked decidedly harassed. "It was an accident."

"Then a gentleman apologizes to a lady rather than accusing her of illegal doings." Elizabeth's voice could have sliced his head off.

His mouth worked as if he'd eaten something nasty and was trying not to spit it out. Then he grunted, "Again, I'm sorry for falling on you. I hope you're okay."

She noticed he didn't apologize for wrongfully accusing her, but Elizabeth said, "See, now we're all friends. Tessa's going to protect me from my husband, and Charles is going to get me my money back."

••••

Talk about dropping a bomb. A nuclear bomb.

Years of debate in high school, top marks at Tulane, and years of experience in a courtroom, and he couldn't keep his gigantic mouth shut about Tessa Lancaster, right in front of her?

What was it about her that set his back up? He'd seen her sitting next to Elizabeth—whom he'd recognized right away, despite the purple bruise over her eye—and been stunned to see a gorgeous woman with her light brown hair curling around her shoulders, glowing in the soft light from a nearby wall sconce. She was looking at him with a sparkle in her eyes and a slight smile on her lips.

But as soon as he realized who she was, her smile faded, and the light in the room dimmed.

He hadn't been able to shake off his jitters—or stop looking at her—except by making some cross remarks.

She glared at him now, noting his non-apology. Something deep inside him had to feed her animosity, to remind himself of who she was.

Man, he wanted to kiss her.

Dork. He had to focus. "Elizabeth, tell me what happened."

She looked down at her coffee cup and swallowed hard. "You know how my family didn't want me to marry Heath?"

He nodded.

"It was mostly the St. Amants—my daddy's family. They wanted me to marry some idiot with more land than brains. So when I eloped, they cut me off. I didn't really care because I had my inheritance from my maternal grandmother, and Heath had plenty of money too."

"What does he do?" Charles asked.

"He works for a private equity firm, Stillwater Group. They've been very successful in the past few years, making investment deals with very wealthy clients. He said they were getting twenty percent returns every year."

Charles knew that those types of firms didn't need to register with the SEC and were largely unregulated. They worked with the ultra rich. Even if Heath were a minor fish in that pond, he probably made at least twice more than Elizabeth's inheritance.

"We were so happy the first few months," Elizabeth said sadly. "He was so romantic—showing up unexpectedly with roses, or to take me out to dinner. He was so gentlemanlike— he never complained about holding my purse or opening my door for me. He loved telling me what clothes looked good on me, and always told me how beautiful I was. He praised me to his friends all the time, talking about how I was such a good hostess, I made people feel welcome, I helped him do his job … although in private he would sometimes tell me if I had said something that might have sounded ignorant to his colleagues."

Tessa's brow lowered at this innocuous list of actions. Her reaction confirmed Charles's own gut instinct, that the man sounded controlling rather than romantic.

"But then, he started criticizing me more and more," Elizabeth said. "He would get suspicious if I went to the ladies' room for too long, and if I went out with my girlfriends, he'd ask if I met anyone interesting—as if I'd had some secret assignation. It got so bad that I stopped going out to lunch with friends. That seemed to make him happy for a while."

Her home sounded like a gilded cage.

"But he began getting angry with me all the time over stupid things. He'd physically hurt me—at first it was just grabbing me too hard, but he always apologized so much afterward until I forgave him. And then he started hitting me."

Under the edge of the table, Charles's hand clenched hard. His entire arm trembled with the tension in his muscles. Relax. He had to relax. He had to get a hold of himself.

Tessa reached out to touch Elizabeth's hand, and pain was written in her expression. Seven years ago, she hadn't shown any emotion in her eyes. She'd heard her sentence from the judge with a face like a stone statue.

This change, this foreign Tessa Lancaster, unnerved him.

"Heath said it was always my fault, that I had made him do it. I believed him for a time. And then after a while, I just didn't feel anything. His emotions became the only thing I felt." Elizabeth's eyes had become dull like black stones, but now he saw a spark. "Until he hit Daniel."

A sickening jolt went through him.

"It wasn't hard—an irritable backhanded thing like swatting a fly. But I saw my little boy on the carpet crying, and it just shook me up. Like I'd been sleeping and I woke up."

"How old is he?" Charles asked. His throat was tight and his voice came out sounding a little strangled.

"Three years old."

Heath had hit a boy who had just begun to walk.

"That's when you ran?" Tessa asked.

"I packed up and went to a small hotel near Union Street. I used a different name, but Heath found me that night. I took off with Daniel and just the clothes on our backs."

A woman alone with a three-year-old boy at night in San

Francisco. She was lucky she hadn't encountered someone even more dangerous than her husband.

"A homeless man saw me on the street and was saying some strange things, so at first I ran away from him because I was so scared. But then he said he wouldn't hurt us, he only wanted to lead us to someplace safe. He ... he must have seen the bruise on my face."

It covered almost the entire left side of her face, making her cheekbone puffy. The scarf she wore around her head hid some of it, and he had noticed her sunglasses on the table, which probably helped too.

"He started walking, and he kept looking back over his shoulder at us. He wasn't making much sense, but he wouldn't leave us alone until we started following a few feet behind him. He led me to Wings."

"Wings domestic abuse shelter?" He donated money to that shelter anonymously every month. His legal secretary, Abby, had told him about it.

"That's where I met Tessa."

"You did?" He had been successful in avoiding looking at her, but he turned to her now. A member of the yakuza at a shelter for abused women and children?

His disbelief must have shown on his face, because Tessa grudgingly answered, "My cellmate Evangeline got out a few months before I did and ended up there one night because of her abusive boyfriend. After she got away from him, she started volunteering there. When I got out, she told me about Wings and I started volunteering there too."

"Why?" he blurted out.

Tessa's eyes narrowed. "What do you mean, why?"

The martial gleam in Tessa's eyes made him back off. He didn't want to cause an even bigger scene than what he'd already done. *Be cool and professional, Charles. Stop acting like a Neanderthal.*

"Tessa's doing me a huge favor," Elizabeth said. "She's agreed to be my bodyguard, but she won't be paid until I can get my money back."

"Did you put it into a joint account with Heath?"

She slowly nodded. "He froze my account. I'm penniless."

"You're not penniless. California law entitles you to your inheritance plus half of everything the two of you made while you were together, and if he's making as much as he said he is, you might come out of the marriage with more than you brought into it."

"But I still need to get that money."

"I'll start the paperwork for you," Charles said. "It shouldn't be hard to get him to give you what's rightfully yours."

But Elizabeth was shaking her head. "He doesn't want this. He'll fight you. He'll try to come after me."

"We'll get a restraining order on him."

"That won't help. He doesn't just want his son. He wants to kill me."

The words seemed a bit hysterical. Sure, Heath beat her up, but the majority of abusers Charles saw weren't murderers. It was a pretty big leap from one to the other, and they didn't often cross it voluntarily. He glanced at Tessa, who also seemed confused. "Well ..." He cleared his throat. "You have Tessa to protect you. If he comes near you, just call the police—"

"No. They'll call child services to take Daniel away from me, or worse, they'll give him to Heath, because who looks like the better parent—the friendly, responsible businessman or the unemployed, homeless Southern belle?"

"Elizabeth, the police will know you're in need—"

"No, I won't trust the police ever again," she replied viciously.

Her tone surprised Charles. From Tessa's raised eyebrows, it surprised her too.

"A neighbor called the police once," Elizabeth said tightly. "Heath charmed the two officers. He even charmed the neighbor who called it in. Then he beat me and I ... I miscarried."

The rage built up in him, like a dust devil in his gut. Heath had killed that child.

"I hate the police," Elizabeth bit out. "I won't lose another child because of them."

There was a long moment of silence. He understood her anger at the police, although he knew officers who were honorable. "Can't you go home?" Charles asked. He'd be more than happy to help her move back to Louisiana.

Elizabeth's eyes filled with tears. "When I first came to Wings, I called my daddy, but he wouldn't even talk to me, wouldn't call me back. I tried my daddy's sister and brother—the entire St. Amant family wouldn't help me. My uncle told me that I'd made my bed and I had to lie in it."

The coldness and cruelty made him press his lips together. He'd known families like hers, though—stubborn, proud, and unfeeling.

"That's why I called your mama. My mama's family is gone, but your maternal grandma was such good friends with mine ..."

He couldn't imagine a family turning its back on a daughter. It was almost worse than what Heath had done to her. "We'll help you with this," Charles told her. "Consider us your family now."

The words made the tears fall faster. "Thank you so much."

A few people in the coffee shop glanced their way, then turned aside and ignored her. Tessa hesitated, then put an arm around Elizabeth as she cried.

He didn't know what to make of Tessa. She'd been interviewing for a job at OWA, now working without pay as a bodyguard for Elizabeth. And volunteering at Wings. Was she trying to go legitimate or was this some strange scheme of hers? Or maybe her uncle was putting her up to it? Had she had some falling out with her uncle, and would it cause problems for Elizabeth?

Whatever it was, he intended to keep a close eye on her. If she stepped even an inch out of line, he'd be there to rescue Elizabeth and Daniel and make sure Tessa Lancaster was sent back to prison.

Chapter 7

They were being followed.

And not by very intelligent pursuers, either.

Tessa completed a fourth right turn in a row and saw the same gray Nissan Sentra follow suit. Then again, this was San Francisco and some tourists got so lost they finally emerged twenty years later from the Lombard Street time warp.

So she did a U-turn at the next light.

The gray Nissan followed.

Her heartbeat tapped against the base of her throat. Who were these guys? How had Heath found Elizabeth? It had to have been a fluke; maybe he saw them on the walk from the parking garage to the coffee shop or the opposite direction.

Or was she just being paranoid? She'd imagined zombie attacks when she was younger—why not conjure up a car tailing them now that she was in her thirties?

"Tessa," Elizabeth said, "I feel like those ballerina dolls on those music boxes, going around and around and around. Please tell me we're just lost."

"Okay. We're just lost."

Elizabeth twisted in her seat to look out the back window, a difficult feat considering how cloudy the glass was. Tessa actually heard her swallow.

"Can you see who it is? Is it Heath?"

"If it is, the man dyed his hair black and grew a full beard in the week since you last saw him."

"So it might not be Heath."

"It could be because of me," Tessa said softly. Except that she'd been out for three months, and no one had tailed her before today.

Plus, with the exception of a rather unhinged Greek banker named Pollux, most of the people who might want to ensure she never again applied to be on *Survivor* were Asian, and this guy was definitely not Asian.

"Can you see a license plate number?" she asked Elizabeth.

"He doesn't have one on the front." Elizabeth turned back in her seat and said firmly, "We're not calling the police, regardless."

Well, she was the boss. Sort of. If she paid Tessa.

The problem was, this wasn't the best car for doing any fancy maneuvers—not with the Corolla's putt-putt engine—and because of its age and decrepitude, it also wasn't exactly the most inconspicuous car on the road, even in San Francisco's eclectic streets.

Still, she had to try something.

She signaled to make a left turn, but when there was an opening in traffic, she didn't go.

Cars behind her started honking furiously, and Elizabeth shifted in her seat. "What are you doing?"

"Relax." A wave of cars was fast approaching from the opposite direction. "And hang on."

Tessa threw it into first gear, revved the poor, abused engine, and whipped the little car into a U-turn directly in front of a black Porsche.

Elizabeth screamed and grabbed at the hole in the ceiling upholstery.

The Porsche's tires screamed too.

Tessa screamed with pure adrenaline and slammed her foot on the accelerator.

The car responded, guttering and screaming in a tantrum that would have ripped the tail lights off if they hadn't already been missing. Tessa could have sworn the mulish Corolla slowed down instead of sped up. The Porsche loomed large in her rear view mirror despite the cloudy glass.

Okay, maybe she'd timed that a little too close.

She wanted to wince but didn't want to close her eyes, expecting the sports car to ram their rear bumper—what was left of it—any second.

"Lord God Almighty!" Elizabeth shrieked.

Then with a gagging cough, the engine popped out a short burst of speed and the car hopped forward. Clouds rose up behind them—from both the Corolla's exhaust and the Porsche's burned tires.

They puttered down the avenue, safely embraced by a chorus of car horns.

Elizabeth had sunk down in her seat, one hand grabbing the top of the car, the other twisting the seatbelt. "You. Are. Crazy."

"Yup," Tessa said cheerfully. "I took an extra course of Insane. Got my PhD in Nutty."

Elizabeth began hyperventilating.

"Cover your mouth and one nostril," Tessa told her. "It'll help you take in less oxygen and raise the carbon dioxide level in your—"

"Shut up!"

"So what did you promise God?" Tessa asked, not at all offended.

"What?"

"When we were about to get slammed by that Porsche. What did you promise God if we survived?"

Elizabeth grew still, then pale. "Oh, no."

"Come on, it can't be that bad. Your firstborn son into a monastery means he'll always have job security."

"No, nothing like that. Worse."

"What?"

"I promised to give up Dr. Pepper," Elizabeth moaned.

"Oh." Tessa pressed her lips together and gave Elizabeth a sidelong glance. "Good luck with that."

Elizabeth started to cry.

••••

"Is there some crazy virus going around or something?" Rick Acker demanded as he stalked into Charles's office.

Charles looked up from his desk, not entirely surprised to see Rick but a bit confused by his ranting. "What?"

"First some psychotic driver in an ancient Corolla in front of me in a left turn lane deliberately stalls, then pulls a U-ey practically up the nose of the sweetest Porsche I've ever seen—I almost wept, I tell you—and now I hear you're giving the Butler case to Randy McDonald. Randy? Really?" Rick leaned against Charles's desk. "You're going to give me an ulcer."

"You already have an ulcer."

"That's because my eldest wants to go to Stanford instead of

Cal. Travesty. You, on the other hand, are causing me a second one. Randy McDonald?" Rick demanded.

"The only reason you don't like Randy is because he can beat you stupid at soccer."

"He didn't beat me, I had a cold."

"Every week for the past month."

"It's a long-term illness," Rick said with a sniff.

"Look, Rick, the Butler case is going to be open and shut, and I felt like an errand boy doing it."

"So now multimillion-dollar corporations are beneath you."

"They are when their CEO drops fifty large at a horse race and writes a company check."

"Sure, John Butler's an idiot, but he's only a puppet king, you know that. We're working for the Jedi High Council, not the little apprentice Jedi."

"Which means Randy McDonald will do fine. I have another case."

"It better involve lots of supermodels and Dom Pérignon." Rick gave him a hard look.

"It involves a wife-beater and an old Southern family's inheritance money."

Rick rolled his eyes. "Sounds like a Nancy Drew mystery."

Charles hadn't expected Rick to understand—the man had the compassion of Norman Bates, and might even be less sane—but he had to admit that Elizabeth's case sounded a bit insignificant compared to his normal bill of fare. And yet the Butler case had the lowest number of anticipated billable hours out of his entire caseload.

"Look, Charles, you work a lot harder than even I do and you're not a bad soccer player either, but—"

"Was that a compliment? I think I'm going a little deaf ..."

"Don't screw this up, man." Rick rose to his full six foot height so that his now serious blue eyes could meet Charles mano a mano. "You are so close to making partner."

Partner. The magic word that drove him through the early hours, through two hours of sleep a night, and two-hour meetings. Was he really screwing things up by doing this? Couldn't he just refer Elizabeth to a divorce lawyer? He knew a few. Granted, they were all as overworked as he was, but she'd eventually get her money back.

Except for her, it wasn't about the money. It was about her son. She needed to feel grounded again after being numb and adrift for so many years.

The bruise stamped on her face made his gut clench even in remembrance. He'd seen worse. And at the time, he'd been too scrawny and scared to do more than cower.

Never again.

"I'm submitting the memo for this pro bono case, Rick," Charles said.

"It'll annihilate your career. You think that taking this nothing case isn't going to hurt you in the eyes of the senior partners, but it will."

"Like the Butler case isn't a nothing case?"

"The cases involving the idiots always make you look good."

"Well then, this will make me look like Superman, swooping in to rescue the damsel."

"Yeah." Rick turned to leave. "Superman ... or Braveheart, stabbing at men with big swords."

••••

Charles felt like a circus clown.

It was his maroon button-down shirt. It was his favorite—most days, it made him feel powerful and yet understated.

But not today, and not in front of a senior partner.

Charles had received the phone call at four o'clock, and he presented himself in Mr. Greer's office promptly at 4:05 p.m.

Manchester Greer was entirely shades of gray, from his steel-colored head to his Italian leather shoes. The only spot of color was a topaz ring on his right hand.

He regarded Charles under bushy flint brows, and an arctic wind swept through the room. Why would the venture capital and private equities lawyer need to see him? He didn't have any cases with Mr. Greer—the man dealt with the big guns. What had Charles done to get his attention?

He thought of Elizabeth's case, which the pro bono coordinator had approved, but she said he needed one of the firm's partners on it. She had sent out an email to all the partners to ask if one of them would be lead on this case. Charles thought Rick would have grudgingly agreed, or one of the other newer partners in the firm. Was it possible Mr. Greer was taking him on?

No, why would he? This was far beneath him.

Then again, if he had agreed to be the lead partner on this case ... Charles stilled his suddenly racing pulse. If Greer was the lead partner for Elizabeth's case, and Charles did a good job, he'd be on the fast track to partnership.

"How do you know Elizabeth St. Amant, Charles?" The deep voice sounded like gravel chugged around at the bottom of the man's throat.

"She's a family friend through my mother's side."

Dark gray eyes pierced like a lance, trying to probe his soul, maybe draw blood and see what color it was. "And why does she want to separate from her husband?"

"He beats her and their son. He's also holding onto her funds right now."

Mr. Greer frowned and stared at a corner of his massive mahogany desk. "It's not a normal case for you."

"She's a close family friend." But how would family ties matter to a man like this, a senior partner in one of the most elite law firms in San Francisco?

"Do you think you could do a good job with this?"

"Yes, sir." He clenched his teeth. His nervousness was showing if he was resorting to "sir" like a proper Southern boy.

"I have to admit I was surprised when I saw you were taking this on."

He had to sell this. He could sell this. "My pro bono work so far has been for struggling companies, a few underdogs to generate sympathy, and one or two favors for a legislative official. This case, however, could create positive media buzz."

"Yes, that media buzz concerns me." Mr. Greer toyed with a Montblanc fountain pen, his long fingers caressing the gold finish. "You can't embarrass us, Charles."

"The media buzz wouldn't be embarrassing. On the contrary, it'll polish our sterling reputation." *Sell it, Charles.*

"That's dependent upon how you handle this." Mr. Greer gave him a hard stare. "I need to know you are going to take care of Elizabeth St. Amant."

"Sir?" What was going on? He felt like he'd been having one conversation and his boss had been having another. *Just don't act like it, dimwit. Nod and smile.*

"I'm sure you're already aware that the St. Amants are one

of the oldest and most powerful families in New Orleans," he said. "This type of service to one of their own would make them extremely grateful and bring prestige to this law firm."

The St. Amants. Mr. Greer didn't know Elizabeth's father's family had cast her off. But there was a good chance that Charles's working on Elizabeth's case would make the St. Amants grateful.

Mr. Greer almost—almost—smiled. "That's why I decided to agree to be lead partner on this case."

The magic words floated through the air. Charles would be working with Manchester Greer on Elizabeth's case.

"I expect only the best from you," Mr. Greer said. "I think we will work very well together."

It was only a formality—in reality, Charles would probably be doing most of the work and Mr. Greer would get the credit, but the tradeoff was that he'd be able to demonstrate his abilities to a man who had strong influence over the other partners in the firm. When the time came for all the partners to vote on which rising lawyers would be able to become partner, having Mr. Greer in his corner would make Charles almost a shoe-in.

"You won't be disappointed, sir."

Mr. Greer nodded, then picked up a stack of papers on his desk, signifying their discussion was coming to an end. "Oh, and whatever you do, don't give the Butler case to Randy McDonald."

Oops.

Chapter 8

The street went straight up into the sky.

Tessa peered out the front window of the Corolla at the sheer wall of asphalt. She knew Lombard Street was supposed to be the steepest street, but this had to be a close second.

And Karissa lived about two-thirds of the way up.

After the incident in the restaurant, Tessa hadn't expected Karissa to call at all, much less to ask to go to church with her, so Tessa wasn't about to balk at a vertical street now. She grit her teeth, threw the sticky clutch into first gear, and rammed it.

The Toyota coughed and stalled.

Not driving for seven years really put a cramp in her style. She restarted the car and punched it up the hill. The engine roared so loudly that she had a moment—a small moment— when she wondered if it might possibly explode into a million pieces in her face.

But the car slowly made its way up the hill until she could turn into a parking space, perpendicular to the street because it was so steep. Karissa's house, one of the Edwardian stick houses all along the street, was white with trim in shades of blue. It wasn't as nicely renovated as several other houses on the street, and the faded paint screamed "renters" as opposed to "mortgage-payers." Another clue was the four names on the wall next to the front door, kind of like an apartment house.

Tessa rang the doorbell and was immediately rewarded with pounding feet. Rapidly pounding feet. Which weren't slowing down.

Maybe she should get out of the way of the door —

She hadn't stepped aside enough when a young Asian American man swung open the door and barreled out while throwing on a wool coat. He clipped the side of her body and immediately turned with apologetic eyes. "Oh, sorry about that! I didn't see you. Are you okay?"

He was tall and stocky, which would explain why he looked so anxious about hitting Tessa's smaller frame. "I'm fine."

"Are you here to see me?"

"Only if your name's Karissa."

He grinned. "No, it's Josh. Hang on." He opened the door and called inside, "Karissa! Someone's here to see you."

"I rang the doorbell," Tessa said.

"It sticks."

"My name's Tessa, by the way."

He shook her hand with a hearty grip. "Josh Cathcart."

They heard softer footsteps from inside. Karissa opened the door, already wearing a warm winter coat and holding her purse. "Hi, Tessa! Thanks for picking me up."

"Don't thank me until Grandpa gets us to Wings." Tessa gestured to the Corolla, which she thought might have glared at her in protest at the nickname.

"Josh, I thought you were late for church," Karissa said to him.

"I didn't want to leave Tessa standing on the front porch. I'll walk you guys to the car."

"Thanks." Karissa locked the front door, and when they'd gotten into Grandpa, he gave them a friendly wave and bounded down the street, pulling car keys out of his pocket.

"He's a really nice guy," Tessa said. "I feel bad — now he'll be late getting to wherever he was going."

"Oh, Josh is always late for his church down in San Jose." As Tessa fired up the engine, Karissa said, "I'm ... I'm really glad you asked me to the Sunday service at Wings."

"You didn't go when you were there?" Tessa winced as Grandpa chugged loudly.

"No, I was only there for a night."

"Have you gone to Josh's church?"

"It's friendly and all, but there aren't many people my age there. It's mostly older couples."

There was another moment — a small moment — when they were nearing the base of the hill and Tessa wondered if Grandpa's brakes would be able to stop them at the stop sign, but the car jerked to a halt rather than sending them careening into cross traffic.

Karissa winced, then patted the dashboard. "Good Gramps."

Tessa loved how a big city always had activity — people on the streets, cars zipping here and there, shops or restaurants or clubs open at all hours. But Sunday morning seemed to have less traffic than 2 a.m., and they got to Wings domestic violence shelter in record time.

Parking, on the other hand, was like a game of Tetris. Further down the street, Tessa finally found a space and they started to walk toward the shelter.

When they were still about a block away from the renovated Victorian house, a man in khaki trousers and a polo shirt approached them with a friendly smile.

Tessa recognized him immediately from pictures Elizabeth had shown to her—Heath.

She moved in front of Karissa. His smile was friendly, but his eyes were merely neutral. That meant either deception or he wanted something from them. Either way, considering the source, she brought up her guard like a Trojan raising his shield.

"You're Elizabeth's friend, right?" he said to her as he approached.

The only way he could know that was because he saw them together the other day when they had gone to see Charles.

"You can stop right there." Tessa kept him several feet away and surreptitiously tried to look around to see if he had any friends with him. Thank goodness for Sunday morning—the streets were empty and she could clearly see two men in business suits trying to blend into the background several yards away. The gray suit of one of them was too tight across his shoulders, constricting his arm movements. The other one's pant legs were a little long, and he might be induced to trip over them.

"I'm not going to hurt you." Heath's smile had a little dimple on the right corner but the left side was higher than the right, and his cheeks remained neutral.

He was lying.

Tessa reached back to gently clasp Karissa's wrist. "What do you want then?"

"Just give Elizabeth a message for me."

"I'm not going to see her anytime soon."

Heath's expression softened to one of condescension. "I know she's in that domestic violence shelter. I'm assuming that's where you're headed?"

How did he know Elizabeth was at Wings?

"Please just give her a message."

"You can write to her yourself. The address is right on the door." She casually reached into her pants pocket for her car keys.

"Tell her I only want to speak to her."

When cows turn pink with orange polka dots. "You can call and request to speak to her inside. They allow meetings in their conference room."

He shook his head. "I don't want to risk being overheard. And I don't want to hurt her."

"No, you just left the imprint of your fist on her cheek."

His upper lip tightened for a split second. Then his eyes dropped to the ground, and he clasped his hands in front of him. "I'm sorry about that."

No, he wasn't. "Because of course, I've never heard that before."

"I really am sorry." He looked up, held her gaze. "I'm going to a counselor at another church."

"That's great." *You big, fat liar.* "Maybe in a few months, then, you can talk to Elizabeth and apologize."

"Just tell her I'm sorry. She doesn't have to see me right now." His eyes blinked rapidly. "Tell her I'm getting help because I love her so much. That's all I want you to do."

Tessa knew she'd developed a bit of cynicism after volunteering at Wings for the past three months, but she also had always had a sensitive ability to read body language that made her good at the jobs Uncle Teruo asked her to do. She'd further developed that ability when she studied psychology in prison. "You're in our way. Please move aside."

He threw his arms wide in a dramatic gesture. "If she wants to see me, I'll be right out here. I won't even come near her." More rapid blinking. "Please tell her how much I love her."

"Get out of our way, please," Tessa said with a tight jaw.

"I really mean it," Heath said. "You have to believe me."

"No, I don't," she snapped. She held onto Karissa's wrist and tried to move around Heath.

She had to admit, she wasn't really surprised when he grabbed at her arm. She jerked it out of his grasp. "Don't touch me."

"You're her friend. You can tell her you saw how sincere I am."

His complete insincerity made Tessa's shoulders tense. She wanted to smack the innocent look off his face to reveal the true ugliness underneath. She growled, "You're about as sincere as the spider to the fly."

His upper lip tightened again. "Are you calling me a liar?"

Tessa didn't answer—she shouldn't have even responded with that spider comment. Again, she tried to move around him.

"You don't walk away from me." His hand whipped out and clamped around her neck. Her muscles tensed as his fingers dug into the tendons alongside her throat.

She slammed him in the nose with the heel of her hand.

He howled—actually, it sounded more like a honk—and his hand loosened. She grabbed his hand and peeled it off her neck, twisting his wrist and entire arm in the process.

"Owowowow!" Heath's body went into acrobatic contortions as he tried to escape the painful torque on his hand and wrist.

The bodyguards started to approach. "You two stay back," she said, "or I'll twist his arm off." Not that she really could and not with this hold.

Problem was, they seemed to know that too, because Pants-Too-Long kept walking toward them.

Tessa twisted Heath's hand harder, and he shrieked. "Stopstopstopstop!"

Pants-Too-Long hesitated.

"Karissa, run," Tessa told her. The problem was that Heath's bodyguards were in between them and the shelter.

Karissa tried to circle around them, but Pants-Too-Long lunged for her.

Tessa shoved Heath aside and rushed forward. She aimed a jumping downward punch at the bodyguard's neck and shoulders, which made him flinch. Karissa darted up the street toward the shelter.

Pants-Too-Long approached her warily, but Tessa just waited for it ...

There. He reached a hand down to tug his pant leg up.

She stepped into a jiu-jitsu high kick and clipped him in the jaw.

She didn't wait around. The street was at an incline—just in case she doubted she was in San Francisco—and her thighs burned as she sprinted up the hill. Just a few more yards and she'd be able to flag down the shelter's security guards, who sat at a desk in the front room of the shelter and would see her through the bay windows.

But instead, the door to Wings opened and two of the security personnel rushed out. One of them ran to her and ushered her inside the shelter while the other one landed on the sidewalk and looked mean.

Karissa was waiting just inside, panting hard. "I told them as soon as I got inside."

"Good ... girl," Tessa panted. She thought she was in better shape than this. Since she got out, she hadn't been working out as diligently as she used to.

"I'm sorry we didn't see you guys earlier," the security guard said. "We try to keep an eye on the street to prevent stuff like that from happening. Not that it happens very often."

Tessa shook her head. "Not your fault. We were almost a block away—I don't know if you'd have even seen us."

"You were amazing," Karissa said. "I wondered if maybe he was telling the truth ... until he grabbed you."

Heath actually hadn't been that bad a liar, but Tessa had been able to tell there was an undercurrent of stress making him jittery. It caused him to make bigger gestures than necessary and to lose control of some of his facial features. Maybe he really did love Elizabeth and his emotions made him unstable. Or maybe he feared what would happen if she pressed charges. Maybe he didn't want her to divorce him for some other unknown reason, and the strain of worrying about it made him antsy.

"He's desperate," Tessa said. "It's not a good sign."

"But the woman he was talking about—Elizabeth?—she's safe here, right?"

"She should be," the guard said, "unless she leaves the shelter for some reason."

How long would Elizabeth have to hole up here? Wings wouldn't force her out, but would Elizabeth slip up and put herself in danger?

Or would Heath eventually find a way to talk to his wife, convince her he was sincere? Tessa hoped Elizabeth wouldn't listen to him, but did she still love her husband? Many wives did, despite what had been done to them.

One thing was certain—Tessa would have to tell Elizabeth, and she had no idea how Elizabeth would react.

••••

"How did that scumbag find me?" Elizabeth said.

Well, scratch that about her still loving him.

But Elizabeth chewed her lower lip as she wrapped an arm around Daniel. The little boy picked up on his mother's anxiety and sucked his thumb, clinging close to her. His brown eyes were wide as they looked at Tessa.

"I'll find out how he found you," Tessa said. "Just be careful. You should be safe here with the security personnel—after all, the shelter is designed to protect women from people who want to hurt them."

"But not people who want to kill them." Elizabeth's lower lip was red.

This was the second time she mentioned this. "Would Heath really want to kill you? It would only throw him in prison."

Elizabeth paused in chewing on her lip.

Tessa continued, "And then what would happen to Daniel? Heath loves his son, doesn't he?"

Elizabeth nodded. "He does. Even though he hit him that one time, it was because Daniel was crying and Heath was angry. Normally, Heath always enjoyed playing with Daniel and spending time with him. He became so light-hearted, like a little kid himself—it reminded me of when we first started dating."

"So you two will be safe here," Tessa said. "I'll still be around too."

But Elizabeth was shaking her head. "We can't stay here. He'll find a way to get to me."

"You're strong. You won't listen to his lies again—"

"No, Heath will get to me and kill me." Elizabeth's eyes were huge and dark in her pale face. "You have to find somewhere else for us to go."

"Somewhere else?" But where? Wings had a full security staff and places for the women and children to sleep comfortably. Tessa had a cramped house with a sulky sister, an emo teenager, and a crabby mother—their version of home security consisted of nagging an intruder to death.

Elizabeth started to cry, and she put both arms around her son, rocking back and forth. "He'll get to us here. He'll send in some woman who looks like she's been hurt, and she'll come to kill me."

Actually, if Heath really was trying to kill Elizabeth, that would be the way to do it. How chilling. Maybe Tessa was watching too much *CSI.*

"Please," Elizabeth said, "now that he knows we're here, you have to find us somewhere else to stay."

Tessa also realized that if she was going to do this, they should do this now. Heath had been chased off by the security guards, who said he went into a black Lexus with the two bodyguards. Unless Heath had set additional, different guards to watch the shelter, no one would see Tessa sneak Elizabeth and Daniel out if they left right now.

But where? Heath would be watching anyone Elizabeth knew, so she had to find her a place completely unconnected with her old life. That meant a nice hotel was out. A cheap motel had too many prying eyes and only one exit. If only Heath hadn't somehow discovered Elizabeth was at Wings—it was the perfect place for her, completely un-Elizabeth-like in real estate and company. Tessa needed to find Elizabeth another place that was just like that—a place that had absolutely no connection to a Southern belle, to her private equity firm husband, and to their social circle of other young people with new money, someplace Heath would never think to look.

Tessa immediately thought of the perfect place. And her mom was going to kill her.

"Okay, get your stuff," Tessa said.

"What stuff?" Elizabeth said. "We came here in the middle of the night from a hotel room, remember?"

Daniel removed his thumb briefly in order to say, "Slasher."

"Oh. Well, we'll have to ask Evangeline if you can take Slasher with you."

"Slasher?" Tessa asked.

"It's a pink stuffed dog," Elizabeth explained.

Ah. Perfect name.

"It used to be white, but one of the girls drew pink polka dots on it. Daniel was very upset but he still likes it."

"No one messes with Slasher," Daniel said.

Of course not. Slasher's enemies probably thought he had measles.

They left the shelter in only ten minutes.

Karissa opted to go with them. "Are you kidding?" she said. "You're more exciting than a *24* marathon!"

When asked if they could take Slasher, Evangeline glanced around to see if any of the staff was looking, then shoved the polka-dotted dog into Karissa's purse.

Tessa cased the street before letting Elizabeth, Daniel, and Karissa leave the building. There weren't any loiterers on the sidewalks or anyone sitting in parked cars. They made it to the Corolla without incident.

But Tessa took the precaution of taking a circuitous route out of San Francisco. And that's when she saw it.

The dark blue SUV had been behind them early, just a few stoplights away from Wings. When she'd done four right turns in a row, the SUV had disappeared, going straight on one of the turns.

But now, on Mission Street, it appeared behind her again.

Heath *had* arranged to have the shelter watched. They were being tailed again.

Worse, it was a team of two or three cars.

She couldn't be 100 percent sure. Maybe it was a different SUV. Maybe the driver was lost. Maybe she was being paranoid — that wouldn't be anything new.

But she'd rather drive a little crazy than lead some really bad people to her mom's house. Maybe it had been a good thing that she had gotten so skilled at losing a tail in her yakuza days.

She turned into a gas station. "Stay in the car," she said to her passengers.

Making it look like she was checking the tire pressure, she searched under and around Grandpa's frame. She didn't really expect there to be a GPS tracking device, but she wasn't taking any chances.

She also used the time to note any cars that passed the station. The blue SUV didn't make an appearance, but she committed to memory the other cars she saw.

Once back in traffic again, she spotted a maroon Hyundai, which she thought she'd seen pass the gas station. Inside were two men wearing casual T-shirts and granite-hard expressions.

She had to lose a multiple car tail in an ancient Corolla.

She signaled right and got into a right-turn-only lane, but at the last minute, darted left and cut off a businessman in a black convertible who was talking on his cell phone.

"What are you doing?" Karissa screeched as the businessman laid on his horn.

Elizabeth, for whom evasive driving maneuvers were becoming old hat, simply dug in and made sure Daniel's seat belt was tight.

The maroon Hyundai turned right. One down.

She spotted the blue SUV a few cars behind her, so she got onto the freeway and moved over into the left lane. The SUV followed.

Tessa rode on the tail of a gold Mercedes until the owner, a woman with gold earrings and gold bracelets visible where her hands rested on the steering wheel, moved over to the right lane.

Tessa then downshifted and forced Grandpa, growling and spitting, to speed up toward the next car in front of her in the lane.

"Tessaaaaa ..." Karissa said as they bore down on the white pickup truck.

She pulled right at the last minute, cutting off a green mini-van. Had she seen that minivan pass the gas station too? And actually, the van didn't lay on the horn when she pulled in front of it. Hmm, tricky ... She cut back in front of the pickup truck and zipped along in the fast lane.

Did the minivan speed up a little too? The blue SUV was by now several cars behind.

Tessa continued to push Grandpa to new feats of daring driving as she wove in and out of traffic for a mile or two. The green minivan fell further behind.

Then she cut across two lanes of traffic and exited the free-way amidst honking horns and a few squealing brakes. There was some squealing inside the car too, as Karissa covered her eyes with her hands.

Daniel giggled.

Tessa turned left at the light and slowed down as she passed under the freeway, wondering if the green minivan or blue SUV were passing above, watching to see where she turned.

She might be becoming a bit obsessively neurotic.

She quickly found the BART station she'd been targeting and screeched into a parking spot. "Everybody out of the car! Hurry!"

"Here!" Karissa thrust a clipper card into Tessa's hand. "Take them and go. I'll drive your car out of here."

"No, it's too dangerous."

"It won't be once you guys are gone."

"Watch for a dark blue SUV, a maroon Hyundai, and a green minivan."

Karissa rolled her eyes. "Like there aren't a thousand of those in San Francisco."

"Don't get back on the freeway—if you do, they'll know you're a decoy. Drive around and then head back to Wings—don't go home."

Karissa's eyes sparkled. "This is so Jason Bourne! See ya."

Tessa hustled Elizabeth and Daniel toward the rapid transit station and used hers and Karissa's clipper cards to get them past the fare gates. They nipped into a train just before the doors closed.

Seven trains later—including transfers from BART to Caltrain to light-rail—they arrived in San Jose Japantown. Tessa checked her watch—maybe Mom would be gone to her job by now. She was a hostess at Oyasumi, one of Uncle Teruo's restaurants in Palo Alto, and Sundays were busy days for them for both lunch and dinner.

Just her luck, Mom was about to head out the door when Tessa walked in with Elizabeth and Daniel.

"Mom! Hi!" Tessa pasted on an exuberant smile and hoped Mom's sense of Japanese politeness would prevent her from complaining and arguing until later when they were alone. "This is Elizabeth and her son, Daniel. They need a place to stay so I said they could take the sunroom for a few days."

Chapter 9

"Mom, it's only temporary."

"When have I heard that before?" Mom groused over the mobile connection.

Tessa got off the bus near the San Carlos Motel off of Union Street and in the noise of the bus chugging away from the curb, she had to shout into her cell phone, "It's only until I can find another place to hide them. I want to keep Heath off balance."

"So keeping your family off balance is fine? What if Heath manages to follow you to our house?"

"He'd have to find me first. He doesn't even know my name. Wings isn't going to give him any information about me or Elizabeth — they're very careful about stuff like that." Added to that was the fact she was the best out of all her yakuza cousins at spotting and getting rid of a tail. But Mom didn't have to know about that fascinating ability.

"Knowing your luck, he'd manage to go to the only grocery store in the entire Bay Area where you happen to be shopping, or something ridiculous like that. And then you'll bring more trouble to your family. You're certainly not going to win any Daughter of the Year awards."

As if she'd ever? What with working for her mob boss uncle against Mom's wishes and then suddenly coming back from prison penniless, she figured she'd forfeited any parental brownie points. "Please, Mom, Elizabeth's desperate. You saw the bruise on her face, and I thought we did a good job cleaning up the sunroom in the past couple days."

"I have to admit, her fried chicken last night was good."

Tessa couldn't speak for a moment. The concession had been grudging, but for Mom to admit someone else's cooking was good was like being knighted by the Queen. "I thought so too," Tessa said in a neutral voice, but inside she was shrieking, "Good? It was flippin' awesome!" The crust had been crispy and flaky. Colonel Sanders had nothing on Elizabeth St. Amant.

She entered the squeaking glass door to the small motel. A pitted wooden counter almost entirely hid a balding head sitting on a low chair behind it.

"Mom, I've got to go. I'll call you later."

"We are not done talking about this."

Tessa hung up with a sigh. They'd talked about it every single time Mom got her alone for the past two days. You'd think they'd talked it to death by now, but Mom liked beating dead horses. Maybe she thought the problem would go away if she mentioned it ad nauseam. At least she hadn't been rude to Elizabeth or tried to get them to leave. In fact, she'd played with Daniel this morning and chatted comfortably with Elizabeth.

Tessa fought a twinge of jealousy that her mother, who had only disapproved of her all her years growing up, was so kind to a perfect stranger. Even now that Tessa was trying to go legitimate, her mother didn't seem to treat her very differently.

Tessa approached the counter. "Who works nights here?"

"I do." The man had a beak of a nose that reminded her of

Gonzo from the Muppets. And he had as much—or rather, as little hair as Gonzo too. But unlike Gonzo's wide friendly eyes, this man's were narrow and bulgy like a lizard.

"A week or so ago, a man came—or maybe he came with several men." Tessa showed a picture of Heath.

The man's eyes remained flat, emotionless. Giving nothing away.

"They asked about this woman." Tessa flashed a picture of Elizabeth.

A flicker, but it was so subtle, it could have been the indifferent fluorescent lights on the ceiling.

"I'm not a cop."

"I could have figured that out, lady." The eyes gleamed with a film of slime covering the irises.

Tessa realized she'd automatically fallen into the stance she usually adopted when talking to people on behalf of her uncle— neck high and chin up, confidence falling off her shoulders like a robe. She had flexed her muscles, the strength coursing through her limbs like buzzing electricity, waiting to be unleashed.

She had become yakuza again.

But she wasn't yakuza any more, and this wasn't yakuza business. Did that count? Was she still wrong to regress into this persona, if it got her what she wanted?

She didn't know. She didn't know who she was anymore.

She had to not show weakness. She had to uphold her pride or she would never get what she wanted. She leaned against the counter, but kept her shoulders straight. "What did these guys ask you about this woman?"

"Which time?"

"They talked to you more than once?"

"I can be persuaded to remember."

Tessa dug into her back pocket for the cash she'd stashed there—cash she'd guiltily taken from her mom's purse. She'd needed the money right away, and her cousin Ichiro hadn't answered his cell phone. As soon as she got a hold of him, he'd lend her the money to pay Mom back—Itchy owed her more favors than he could repay in this lifetime.

She slapped a twenty on the counter, but kept her hand on the bill. "Convince me of how much your information is worth."

He eyed the denomination with distaste. "More than that."

"That's for you to prove to me."

He sighed. "They came twice. Once before the woman bolted, and once after."

This man had enabled Heath to find Elizabeth? "The first time, you told them she was here?" Tessa kept her voice low and spoke slowly to hide her anger.

He nodded. "The second time was right after she'd gone, he was upset he hadn't found her."

"Is that it?" Tessa started to turn to go, leaving the twenty dollar bill.

"No, it's not it." The twenty on the counter disappeared as the rat snatched his piece of cheese. "I told him to talk to Junie on the corner, because he sees everything that happens. Junie would know what direction your lady friend went."

"And Junie is who?"

"Homeless guy at the corner of Union. He'll be there by now. He works a corner a few blocks away in the mornings, and this corner in the afternoon and evenings. Hey, don't I get any more?" he asked when Tessa started to leave.

She stopped, turned, and leaned over the counter to get in his face. "You might have if you hadn't given up a young woman and a three-year-old boy to a slimeball and his thugs. Be grateful I didn't turn your nose into a coat hook, Gonzo."

"Who?"

Junie was indeed at his corner, holding a sign up for drivers caught at the light to read while waiting. His beard showed streaks of red under the dirt, and he flashed a knowing smile with lots of black teeth as Tessa approached. "I have a feeling I can do something for you rather than the other way around."

"These guys asked about this woman a few days ago." Tessa showed him the pictures. "What'd you tell them?"

"It depends on how much you're going to donate to the Junie Foundation."

She tossed a twenty into the upended hat at his feet, but he sneered at her. "Gonna take more than that, lady."

She didn't have much money, and she didn't know who else she might have to bribe. "I don't have any more I can give you."

"Then you ain't getting nothing."

"I gave you a twenty."

"The Junie Foundation thanks you kindly."

Her hand snapped out and grabbed his ear, which was slick with oil and dirt.

"Hey, hey, hey!" He winced and tilted his head toward her. "No cause for that."

"I want the information you gave those guys."

"No, you didn't give me enoug—"

She twisted his ear, and he swallowed his protest. "She ran up Van Ness toward Lombard."

She screwed his ear a tiny bit harder. "No she didn't, Junie." Tessa actually didn't know if he was telling the truth, but figured it wouldn't hurt to press him a bit.

"Okay, okay, she went down Green."

"Is that all you told them?" Junie's ear was getting more and more disgustingly slick as his sweat mingled with his ear wax.

"That guy gave me another fifty bucks for this infor— owowow! Okay, okay, I saw Calypso talking to her. At least, I think it was Calypso. It was dark, and it was pretty far down Green. Looked like Calypso was running after her."

Elizabeth had mentioned a man who ran after her, who then led her to Wings. "Who's Calypso?"

"Weird guy who's usually hanging out at Laguna and Harris, but for some reason he was on Green that night and went after the woman and her kid."

"Thanks Junie." She let go of his ear and scrubbed her hand against her jeans. She'd have to wash them tonight to get Eau de Junie off of them.

She asked a street performer on Laguna where Harris was, and dug out a few coins to toss into his guitar case. This trip was getting more expensive than she expected.

She spotted Calypso right away because he was the lanky African American man shouting at no one in particular on the street corner.

"Because the meek will inherit French fries!" he proclaimed to a passing motorcycle. "And four sips of Dr. Pepper will fix your leg right up!"

Calypso smelled way worse than Junie, and his hair was in long, white-speckled dreadlocks. His eyes fixed on Tessa as she approached, and they were wide and child-like.

"Howdy, partner? You done ride Buzz Lightyear to the Chrysler building and back to buy a Happy Meal but I was playing my saxophone with James Earl Jones."

"That must have been quite a concert," Tessa said.

"We roooooockin' down the schoolhouse with Mozart and chocolate tea."

Elizabeth had said that a man told her he wouldn't hurt her and wanted to lead her someplace safe—could that really be Calypso? "I heard you helped this lady a few nights ago." Tessa showed Elizabeth's picture. "If that was you, she and her little boy are really grateful to you."

"My little man was flying with his wings and eating cotton candy."

Wings—meaning he'd led them to Wings shelter? If anything, Calypso apparently liked his food. "Did you talk to this guy?" She showed him Heath's picture.

He blinked rapidly and frowned. "Darth Vader and Ronald McDonald weren't sharing the Kit-Kat."

"You don't like him, huh? You got good taste."

"Blessed are the merciful, for they shall receive mercy." Calypso reached out and touched her hand briefly, softly. For a flash of a moment, his eyes were focused on her.

Then he removed his hand and shouted, "Hallelujah! Christ the Lord is eating Oreos."

Tessa winced as he used his outside voice barely two feet away from her eardrum.

Well, it didn't look like Calypso talked much to Heath, if at all. Not that Heath would have even understood him. So then, how did Heath know Elizabeth went to Wings?

"Did this guy talk to anyone else about the lady and her son?"

"No can do, and a belly of rum. Yo, ho, yo, ho . . ." he sang.

"This guy was at Wings shelter, and I'm trying to figure out how he found out she was there."

"Arrr, matey. Polly want a cracker."

This was impossible. Calypso was completely unintelligible.

She sighed. "Well, thanks for helping, Calypso. And thanks for leading Elizabeth to safety—"

Calypso grabbed her hands, his face tense. His breath, smelling like cat poo, washed over her as he said, "Aye! Avast, Captain! Yo, ho, a pirate's life for me ..."

What? "Pirates of the Caribbean?"

"Yo, ho ..."

"Captain Jack Sparrow?"

Calypso started jumping up and down, but his hands were still firmly grabbing hers and she bounced with him. "Who's Captain Jack?" she asked.

He abruptly released her and started walking rapidly in the opposite direction. After a few seconds, he turned to look at her and shouted, "Somewhere over the rainbow with lemon drops."

So she, uh, followed the yellow brick road.

People looked strangely at her, a woman following a homeless man, who absolutely *reeked*, and she often couldn't avoid being downwind from him, but Calypso strode with purpose, not looking to the right or the left.

After several blocks, he broke into a run and then launched himself at another homeless man sitting on a low wall behind a bus station. The two of them tumbled onto the sidewalk in a heap of dirty clothing, and one of them lost a holey Keds that flew past Tessa's head.

Calypso fought like he talked—after pushing the man to the ground, he smacked his ear, then tried to pull off his sock.

"What are you doing, man? Crazy." The other man shoved Calypso off him and stood up.

Calypso grabbed his ankle and tried to bite it, but the man yanked his ankle away. "Stop it!"

"Why does he want to hurt you?" Tessa asked.

"Beats me." The man ran his hand through his matted hair, which was so dirty that Tessa couldn't tell what color it was supposed to be.

"Are you . . . Captain Jack?"

The man grinned, pushing back his shoulders and puffing out his chest. "Arr. I like that. Maybe I'll start calling myself that. Captain Jack."

Calypso had gotten to his feet and stood glowering at Captain Jack. "Arrest the dude I kiss on the cheek."

Judas—betrayer? Did Jack betray someone—maybe Elizabeth? "Did you talk to him?" Tessa showed the picture of Heath.

Jack's face became blank. "Maybe."

Tessa pulled out another twenty and waved it enticingly.

"Yeah, I might have talked to them."

"What did they want?"

"Some lady."

"You knew something about her?"

Jack looked away toward the busy street. An older Asian woman was walking toward the bus stop, but upon seeing Jack, Tessa, and Calypso, who was still glaring at Jack and who had also started drooling, she turned and walked away.

"What'd you tell them, Jack?"

"I'm not talking for just a twenty."

"I could just let Calypso keep beating you up. He'll eventually hit you somewhere that hurts."

Jack frowned. "He smells like cat poo."

As if Jack smelled like a bed of roses. "What'd you tell them?"

"Nothing. I showed them the house she entered the other night."

"You saw her?"

"Who didn't see her? Calypso was talking to his invisible friends all the way there."

"So after you saw a woman and her little boy enter a *domestic violence shelter*, you led a man who was looking for her right to it?"

Jack shrugged. "What's the problem?"

Tessa closed her eyes and looked away. It had been bad enough Junie had blithely told those men about Elizabeth and her son, but Junie hadn't known what those men wanted with Elizabeth. Jack, on the other hand, had seen Elizabeth enter the shelter—might have even seen her bruised face—and still told a man and his bodyguards where to find her. No wonder Calypso wanted to pound his face into the pavement.

Tessa turned and started walking away.

"Hey, what about my twenty?"

"Did you hear me promise you anything? You're lucky I don't punch your lights out for what you did."

"I didn't do anything, lady," Jack snarled.

She had been prepared for Jack to try something, but even as she reacted to Jack's hand reaching out for her, Calypso dove at him like a raven. "He was wounded for our transgressions!" he shouted as a flailing fist caught Jack in the jaw.

"Ow!" Jack stumbled backward, his knees wobbling.

"Nice left hook, Calypso," Tessa said.

"Expel the wicked from among you," Calypso said. But he backed away.

Jack leaned against the bus stop, his hands slightly raised in front of him, his eyes unfocused.

"Thanks for helping me," Tessa said to Calypso. "Can I buy you some hamburgers from McDonalds?"

Calypso suddenly rose to his full height, which brought him

at Tessa's eye level. His face had become serious, his eyes intent and focused. He again took Tessa's hands. "But whatever was to my profit I now consider loss for the sake of Christ."

His voice was deeper than normal, spoken in a soft voice that rang with reverence, as if he were reading Scripture at a Sunday church service.

Tessa was shocked. What had happened? This was kinda freaky.

Calypso continued, "What is more, I consider everything a loss compared to the surpassing greatness of knowing Christ Jesus my Lord, for whose sake I have lost all things. Remember that."

Calypso then turned and walked away.

Chapter **10**

Tessa walked into her mom's house and was attacked by paper cranes.

Actually, she only collided with streamers of paper cranes hung over the doorway, but it sure felt like an attack. Sharp paper beaks jabbed her in the eye, and when she yelled, "Hey!" she inhaled a paper tail into her open mouth.

"Tessa, this is so much fun!" Elizabeth gestured to her to join them in Mom's living room, where she, Daniel, Alicia, Paisley, and Mom were gathered around the coffee table. Colored squares littered the floor and the table.

"Tessa," Daniel said, and held out to her a crumpled silver paper that looked vaguely like a rock. With ears.

"Wow, Daniel," Tessa said, "that's a great ... uh ..."

Elizabeth mouthed "frog" to her.

" ... frog. In fact, that's the best frog I've ever seen. What's his name?"

"*Her* name is Freddie, and she's Slasher's girlfriend," Elizabeth said with a roll of the eyes. "You can blame your niece for that one."

"I didn't mean to," Paisley said with wide eyes. "The name just popped out."

"Come join us," Elizabeth said.

"No," Alicia said quickly, "this is too girly for Tessa."

A sensation like cold water trickled over her shoulders, her arms, her stomach. Alicia had said the exact same thing when Tessa was twelve and she'd come home from hanging out with her male cousins to find Mom teaching Alicia to fold paper cranes.

Mom had said, "Oh, that's true."

Tessa had left the house and gone to Aunty Kayoko. Uncle Teruo had been out, so he hadn't witnessed Tessa's valiant attempts to hide her tears.

Aunty Kayoko had gotten out the best origami paper she owned—large squares thickly strewn with pink and red flowers and highlighted by gold gilt, bought in Kochi Prefecture on a trip to Japan. She made one paper crane for Tessa, but instead of being right side out, she made it with the white underside on the outside.

"Your femininity is inside," she'd told Tessa, "just like the beautiful pattern is on the inside of this crane. Other people can only see it if they get close enough to touch it and handle it."

Then she taught Tessa how to make the cranes herself, with the pattern on the outside, on the expensive imported paper. Tessa worked hard and only went through a couple dozen of the beautiful sheets, and Aunty Kayoko had praised her.

Tessa had never told her mom or her sister. She hid the inside-out paper crane in her drawer, and when she'd gone to prison, she had asked Aunty Kayoko to find it and mail it to her. The crane had eventually been tucked into her Bible, where it remained even now, with a few tear stains from when she'd taken it out on the day of her aunt's funeral.

At hearing Alicia's words, Elizabeth's fine dark brows rose as she looked at Tessa's sister. "*What* are you talkin' about?" Her accent had become even thicker and she had slowed down her words, for a change. Her tone made the question sound like a finely veiled insult.

Alicia drew herself up, raising a pointed chin. "Tessa is a tomboy through and through. You can barely get her to wear makeup to a job interview."

"Tessa doesn't need makeup. She has flawless skin," Elizabeth fired back.

Tessa was speechless. She'd never before had a girlfriend stand up for her to her family. When working for Uncle Teruo, and even in prison, she'd always had to fight her own battles. It was what she'd needed to do within the yakuza, where women weren't often respected, and again in prison. While she'd argued with Alicia countless times, it was completely different to have a stranger tell Alicia about Tessa.

And Alicia didn't like it either, apparent from her flushed cheeks and prim mouth. "All I'm saying is that *throughout our childhood together*, Tessa has never been interested in feminine things." Meaning, *I've had many more years of observing my wild woman sister than you have, Scarlett.*

Elizabeth casually looked away with the air of a woman humoring a crazy person. "Well, I'm sure you'd know, since even with your own *girly* friends, you would have been so *close* to your tomboy sister. She must have spent so much time with you."

Tessa gaped at Elizabeth. She met Mom's eyes, which were also wide with surprise. Mom strode into the breach. "Er ... Tessa, you don't know how to fold paper cranes, do you? Why don't we teach you too? It's a good thing for a Japanese girl to learn."

"I already know," Tessa replied.

"You do?" Alicia asked. "Who taught you?"

She hesitated. It would be embarrassing to them, and as much as Alicia criticized her and Mom neglected her, she didn't want to do that to them, not in front of Elizabeth. "One of the aunties."

"Who?" Alicia demanded.

Well, she asked for it. "Aunty Kayoko." The yakuza *oyabun's* wife. It was like having the First Lady teach a niece how to do laundry—implying something lacking in that niece's family. And the *oyabun* would know it.

Alicia stiffened and her face grew pale, but she shut her mouth and said no more. Mom's eyes fell to the crane on the table in front of her.

Oblivious to the embarrassment of Tessa's family, Elizabeth held up a crane. "This is the most lovely paper. And folding cranes is so soothing."

"Japanese believe that if you fold a thousand cranes, your wish will come true," Tessa said.

"Sit down and have some tea." Elizabeth pointed to a teapot on the table. "Unless you're too *girly* to sit with us girls." She slid a pointed glance to Alicia, whose lips disappeared in her face, but didn't reply. "So what did you do today?" Elizabeth asked.

Tessa told her about finding out how Heath discovered her, but she didn't tell them about the disturbing Bible verse Calypso had quoted to her. "I bought a couple Happy Meals for Calypso, and also some crackers and peanut butter, but when I went back to his street corner to give them to him, he didn't seem to recognize me, even though he'd beaten a guy up for me only twenty minutes before. But he did thank me."

"Disturbed man," Mom said, shaking her head. "The kind of people you interact with, Tessa."

"I didn't seek him out because I want to marry him, Mom," Tessa said.

Mom shuddered at the thought.

"I also laid a few false trails in San Francisco for you," Tessa said to Elizabeth.

"False trails?" She rubbed the top of Daniel's head, and he jerked his head to get her to stop.

"It was actually kind of fun." Tessa ticked them off on her fingers. "I opened an account for you with Wide World Travel Agency, and gave them your information so they could pull up all your frequent flyer points for all the different airlines you've flown. I gave them a bogus address at a motel in San Francisco."

"But Heath will go to that motel like last time, ding dong," Alicia said.

"The clerk will have no idea what he's talking about, and Heath will either think the guy's clueless or well bribed. He can't bust down every door in the motel, ding dong."

Alicia made a conceding gesture.

"I also called Pacific Real Estate to get them to run credit checks on you in Canada and Mexico."

"But I don't want to go to Canada or Mexico."

"But Heath doesn't know that. I started processes to open a bank account for you in Vancouver, and I got the Barnes and Noble cashier to pull up your membership card number for me when I was at the store today and bought a book on living in Canada."

"They just did it for you?" Alicia was appalled. "You didn't have to show any ID?"

"I was very charming to the cashier, and made a big deal

of searching through my wallet for my card and not being able to find it, and he was happy to search on the computer for me when I gave him 'my' name. Oh, and I also bought a DVD on Canada too."

"With what money?" Mom demanded.

Tessa felt her face flame. "Sorry, Mom, I'll pay you back as soon as I get in touch with Ichiro."

"No, I'll pay you back," Elizabeth insisted, "as soon as Charles gets my money for me."

Mom gave Elizabeth a warm smile. "Oh, no, don't worry about it. I don't mind at all."

Tessa actually felt like the color green — a slimy, scaly, sickly green. Mom was just being hospitable, teaching Elizabeth to fold paper cranes and not begrudging her the money Tessa had spent. She gave herself a shake both mentally and physically to get it to go away, but a sharp talon still pierced something soft in her chest.

"So now, if Heath searches for you or hires a P.I., they'll find you planning to jump ship to Canada. They'll keep their eyes on World Wide Travel, waiting for you to make your plane ticket."

"While I'm holed up here in San Jose," Elizabeth said. "You're so clever!"

While doing all this, Tessa had thought to herself that she was being rather clever, but now, with Alicia and Mom barely looking up at her, it didn't seem as brilliant as she'd first thought. "Well, it'll buy you a few days. I'm going to be looking for a safe house for you."

"Oh, you can stay as long as you like," Mom gushed to Elizabeth.

"You're so kind to us," Elizabeth said.

That green, nasty feeling washed over Tessa again.

"I'm sorry the sunroom is so small and so bright in the mornings," Mom said. "I thought about taking the room-darkening shades from Tessa's room, but it wouldn't be enough to cover all the windows."

She should be used to this, being last in her mother's thoughts. She had caused her mother a world of pain and humiliation when she went to prison. She had embarrassed her sister and caused a tarnish on her niece's reputation at school to have a convict for an aunt.

But it still didn't make it hurt less.

"If Tessa moved out, we could put you in her room," Alicia said.

"If Tessa moved out," Tessa snapped, "it would be because Elizabeth didn't need a bodyguard anymore, which also means she wouldn't need to hide here with the three of you."

As soon as she said it, she heard how petulant and ugly it sounded, but she couldn't take the words back.

Alicia didn't notice — obviously because anyone living with her would have no cause for complaint. Mom looked vaguely sad, maybe at the prospect of losing such a nice houseguest.

But Paisley flinched and looked back down at the crane she was folding.

Tessa felt contaminated. She needed to get away from her sister, from her mom, from the patterns of behavior she had with them that she still fell into even though she was supposed to be a new creation in Christ. They would all be better off without each other.

If she was supposed to be so different, why was it more and more apparent that she was still the same person?

••••

The irony was killing her.

An ex-convict—no, even better, an ex-yakuza, asking a lawyer for money.

Well, technically it was his client asking for the money, but since Elizabeth was pretty much under house arrest, it would be Tessa spending all of Charles Britton's borrowed cash.

They took light-rail to the train station and headed to San Francisco. While they were on the train, Tessa remembered the Toyota Corolla. Karissa had texted her to tell her she got a ride home that Sunday, but the car was still parked outside Wings.

They got off at the San Francisco train station and Tessa called her cousin Ichiro at a pay phone.

"Hello?"

"Itchy, it's Tessa."

"Are you done with my car?"

"Like you're even using it. I need another favor."

"Oh, so paying insurance on a car I'm not even driving so that my cousin can ride around the Bay Area isn't enough?"

"Do you have another set of keys for the car?"

"No. Aw, man, did you lock yourself out?"

"No, I didn't. It's good you don't have a spare set of keys because I want you to break into the car."

"What?"

"Pretend like you're casing the cars on the street and then steal your car. It's being watched and I want it to seem like a random theft."

"Like anybody's going to believe I'm going to voluntarily steal a 1981 Toyota Corolla?"

"Well ... pretend like you're a vintage car buff."

"If I'm a vintage car buff, I would have enough money not to need to steal a car."

Itchy was being unreasonably logical. "I don't care what you do, just steal the car. And if you're followed, lose them. Don't let them track you back to your house."

"Tessa, who did you tick off?"

"Nobody—"

"'Cause I kind of like my head where it is, you know?"

"They're not going to chop off your head—"

"And I like having all my fingers and toes."

"They won't cut off your fingers—"

"If they're not dangerous, then why do I need to steal my own car?"

"It's a guy who beat up his wife, and I kind of helped her, and so he might be watching my car."

"*My* car."

"Your car. Whatever. Can you do it for me?"

He sighed. "What if I get caught?"

"Your name's on the vehicle registration and insurance, so how is that a problem?"

"Oh."

Tessa could almost hear Itchy thinking.

"Okay, fine," he said. "You better hope I even remember how to boost a car."

"Like you didn't just do it last week."

"Hey, how did you know about that?"

She hadn't, but knowing her cousin, it wasn't hard to guess. "The Corolla's parked somewhere near this address." She gave him directions to Wings, then hung up.

Next, she dialed Charles Britton's assistant and handed the phone to Elizabeth. "Hello, Abby, this is Elizabeth St. Amant. How are you doing?" The Southern charm poured off of her like fairy dust.

"Oh my, and she's only nine years old? She's as sharp as her mama ... You better watch it, in five or six years, you'll have to beat the boys off with a stick ... I would love to talk to Charles if it's not too much trouble."

Most of Charles's clients would have to leave a message, but for Elizabeth St. Amant, Charles's legal secretary gave her an, "Oh let me patch you right through."

"I think I need to go to charm school," Tessa said.

"Honey, all they do is make you walk around with a book on your head," Elizabeth said. "Oh, hello, Charles.... Oh, he's fine. I'll have to have you meet him sometime, right now he's with—" She cut off as Tessa made a slicing motion with her hand across her throat. "Oh, I think I'm not supposed to say who Daniel's with. Anyway, I have an eensy teensy problem. I need some cash, but I promise I'll pay you back when I get my money back." She named the sum Tessa told her she needed, and Tessa could hear Charles's "What?!" through the earpiece of the phone.

"Really, Charles, there's no need to yell.... No, I'm not going on a shopping spree, I need it for ..." Her eyes silently questioned Tessa.

"Disposable cell phone," Tessa said.

"Disposable cell phone," Elizabeth chirped into the phone.

"Paying for your current safe house."

"Paying for my current safe house." She whispered to Tessa, "Good idea, your mom will appreciate the extra cash."

Tessa thought about what else she needed. "Bribes—no, don't tell him that. Um ..."

"Brib—er, I mean ..."

Tessa could hear Charles demand, "Is that your bodyguard? Let me talk to her."

Elizabeth handed the phone to Tessa with an apologetic expression.

"What do you need bribe money for? And what do you mean, 'safe house'? Isn't she at Wings?"

"No, Heath found out she was there. And I borrowed money so that I could lay down $40.75 to get that information, thank you very much. Hence, bribes."

"So where is she now?"

"Now, we're at the train station. And do you really think I'm going to tell you over the phone where she is?"

"Paranoid much?"

"I think we were followed. Twice."

"Like I said, paran—"

"The first time was after we'd met with you. They had followed us from Wings. I made four right turns in a row and was followed by the same gray Nissan Sentra."

A short pause, then a conceding grunt.

"Then I was accosted outside of Wings on Sunday morning. Heath wanted me to give Elizabeth a message."

"What did he want?"

"His words were remorseful but his body language wasn't. Then he tried to grab me, and his goons tried to attack me."

"Elizabeth's okay?"

Elizabeth? "She wasn't with me, but yes, I'm fine, thanks for asking."

"Considering who you are, I pretty much assumed you'd be okay, Xena."

The remark should have annoyed her, but there was a thread of humor in his voice that made her almost crack a smile. And yet, his comment also told her that he respected her abilities. It reminded her of how Kenta had made her feel. She shook off the old memory.

"When we left Wings, we were followed by two, maybe three cars. I had a friend drive my car back to Wings while I took Elizabeth and Daniel on BART."

"You're pretty sure you lost them?"

"Yes."

"I guess you're not paranoid then."

"With flattery like that, I'm surprised the girls aren't all stalking you on Twitter."

A pause, then he said, "I'm sorry I called you paranoid. I should have known that with your skills, you wouldn't cry wolf."

His apology paralyzed her. In the world she had lived in, no one apologized. Men never apologized to women. Her mother or sister had never apologized to her. No one apologized for anything in prison.

But this man — this stranger — had apologized. For not trusting in her judgment. She didn't know how to react. She didn't know what to say. She didn't know what to feel.

So she ignored it. She coughed, then said, "So can you get us the cash? We'll pay you back once Elizabeth gets her money."

"Sure." Suddenly he was all business too. "Since I'm her lawyer, she'll have to promise in writing that she'll repay, but it'll be fine. How do you want to get the money?"

"An ideal place would be a restaurant where you can get a table in the back. I know they followed me and Elizabeth, but I don't know if they saw you with us and followed you too. If they did, they might be watching you. I want to meet in a place where they can't see you meeting us."

"There's a restaurant a few blocks from my law firm that will give me a private room in the back. I've done that for some high-profile clients." He gave her the name and address.

As she hung up the phone, a thought came to her—would Heath have bugged Charles's phone? Would he have the means to do that? Was he desperate enough to get Elizabeth and Daniel back that he'd hire someone to do that?

She could only hope they weren't walking into a trap.

Chapter 11

This lunch at Lorianne's Café was going to cost him more than normal.

With an obscene stack of cash in an envelope in his pocket, Charles entered the first floor portal to the restaurant, which was just a small foyer with an elevator. Lorianne's, an upscale restaurant serving California fusion cuisine, was on the second and third floors of the building, which suited the understated entrance, adorned only by valets in black suits.

He got off on the second floor and it was only a few feet to the reception desk. "Charles Britton, party of three," he said.

"Two of your party are already here," the hostess said. "Follow me, please." She led him up a short flight of stairs to the third floor, which was entirely composed of private dining rooms. They passed two walnut-paneled doors and entered the third door on the right.

Tessa and Elizabeth sat at the small table, but Elizabeth was looking forlornly at her glass of amber-colored ice cubes. Tessa had a mischievous gleam in her eye which transformed her — she reminded him of a woodland sprite in the production of *A*

Midsummer Night's Dream that he'd seen at the Curran Theater a few months ago — graceful, saucy, sexy.

No, his thoughts shouldn't be going there. He forced a smile as he approached them both, but Elizabeth only offered a half-hearted hello, then sighed and stared at her glass again.

"Did you want a refill?" he asked.

"No."

"Then why the long face?"

Tessa giggled, a sound he would never have expected to hear from a woman who'd had such a fearsome reputation on the streets of San Francisco. "She's keeping a promise to God," Tessa said.

"It was made under extreme duress," Elizabeth said tartly. "I think it shouldn't count."

"Extreme duress? What happened?" Charles asked as he sat down.

"I was almost killed because my bodyguard thinks her aging car belongs in the Indy 500."

"Hey, Gramps did the job and we lost the tail," Tessa said.

"Gramps?" Charles asked.

"My 1981 Corolla. I call him Grandpa because he's old and crotchety."

"He's even older than you," Elizabeth told her, "and after the way you abused him, can you blame him for protesting?"

"What exactly happened?" Charles asked.

"It involved squealing tires and the most awful burned rubber smell and my life flashing in front of my eyes," Elizabeth said.

"I made a U-turn in front of a wave of traffic to try to lose the tail," Tessa clarified. "And it worked, because I am magnificent and my car has unseen depths of character."

"And what was the promise?" Charles asked.

Tessa giggled again and Elizabeth groaned. "I promised God I'd give up Dr. Pepper if he got us through alive."

"Good Lord Almighty, I wouldn't make that promise even if Aunt Coco were threatening to move in with me." Charles glanced at the glass. "What were you drinking?"

"Coke. And it's not the same thing. I'm so depressed."

"She's had four of them," Tessa said.

"Four? How long have you been here?"

"About ninety minutes."

At that moment, the waitress came to ask Charles if he'd like anything to drink, and with a wicked glance at Elizabeth, he ordered a Dr. Pepper.

Elizabeth glared at him. "You're evil."

"I assume I'm paying for lunch, so it's my prerogative."

Tessa burst into laughter. It made her eyes turn into glittering amber stars, and he watched the long column of her throat as she tossed her head back.

Her laugh brought Elizabeth out of the doldrums a little, and she sipped noisily at the last drops of her Coke.

"I'm sorry, but I'm legally required to have you sign a document promising to pay me back." He slid it across the table at Elizabeth with a pen. "Why did you arrive so early?" he asked as she signed it.

"I wanted to make sure we got here before Heath might," Tessa said. "I didn't want him to see us entering the restaurant."

"Do you really think he'd find out?" Her paranoia was getting a bit out of control.

Tessa shrugged. "It's better to be safe than sorry."

"You're taking a lot of precautions." He slipped the signed document back in his briefcase.

"I have a …" Tessa hesitated, and the uncertainty in her face made her seem years younger.

"What is it?" he asked.

She shook her head. "It's nothing."

"No, tell us," Elizabeth urged.

"I just …" Tessa rubbed the condensation on the side of her glass of soda. "I think what Elizabeth said at our last meeting was right. I have a feeling in my gut that Heath doesn't just want his wife and child back."

Elizabeth tensed, and while Charles was leaning toward agreeing with Tessa, he didn't want Elizabeth to become too alarmed and emotional, so he said, "I'm sure it's nothing sinister. He's probably just persistent. Men who work for private equity firms are driven and focused. They have to be for their jobs."

Elizabeth's lips firmed. "Now, don't go trying to sugar coat things for me. What convinced you?" she asked Tessa.

"I mean, he had us tailed. Twice. And the second time, with three cars. That's a level of professionalism you don't see very often. He has hired some very high class guys to find you, and that just doesn't seem like the actions of a man who only wants his wife and son back. He wasn't into anything shady, was he?"

"I wouldn't know," Elizabeth said. "I don't know anything about his job, just that he made a lot of money. I barely know what a private equity firm is."

"It basically means he invests people's money for them," Charles said. "With some firms, it involves millions of dollars from very wealthy, private investors."

Elizabeth frowned. "Is it legal?"

"There are some firms perfectly above board, and some who work in the shadows."

"Just like any company," Tessa said.

She probably knew a lot of illegal businesses herself. He kept forgetting that when he saw her like this, like one of Elizabeth's friends.

Tessa asked him, "Have you contacted Heath yet?"

"No, I'm getting the paperwork together. I'll do it this week though."

The waitress interrupted them with Charles's Dr. Pepper and a refill of Elizabeth's Coke. Elizabeth ordered a crab and lobster salad and Charles ordered his favorite, the buffalo burger, anticipating the cannoli for dessert.

Tessa only had half a turkey sandwich and a small salad.

"Not hungry?" Charles asked.

Tessa shrugged. "I'm on the job. I don't eat heavily just in case."

Charles caught Elizabeth looking at his Dr. Pepper like she'd just run the Badwater Ultramarathon in Death Valley. He made a point of taking a slurp and she glowered at him.

"So tell me about those two tails," Charles said.

She told him about the gray Nissan — with interjections from Elizabeth about Tessa's maniacal driving — and then about being accosted outside of Wings.

"I had picked up a friend, Karissa, for church, and we parked a couple blocks away — "

"Church?" The word burst out of him before he could stop himself.

The look she gave him was inscrutable. Not calm, but not emotional either. Waiting, wary, but at the same time proud. "Yes," she said. "Church." She enunciated the word, almost like a challenge.

"You ... you go to church now?"

"I became a Christian three years ago," she said evenly.

A Christian? A Christian yakuza? Was this the reason for the changes he'd seen in her the last time they'd met? Was it really possible?

Was her faith real?

Was this woman, this murderer, now his sister in Christ?

His world tilted for a moment, then righted itself. No, it couldn't be. He'd seen this before—men who came to Christ in moments of stress, only to go back to living their old lives with their old morals a few years or even months later. And half his old youth group from his church in Louisiana had gotten into some sort of trouble—teenage pregnancy, drugs, jail. Tessa might be the same, reverting back to her old ways or getting herself in deeper trouble.

Or maybe this was a real change, the kind only Jesus could bring about.

Tessa Lancaster, a Christian? He couldn't wrap his head around it. He cleared his throat. "So, um, you were going to the church that meets at Wings?"

She told about Heath getting a little physical, and then about being tailed as they drove away from Wings.

"I made sure they didn't follow us," Tessa said. "You should probably watch yourself too. I don't want something to happen to you because I didn't warn you, even though I only have suspicions and no proof."

Again, his world tilted—Tessa Lancaster being concerned for him? Well, he was her client's lawyer, and she wouldn't get paid unless he did his job. "You're at a safe place now?" Charles asked.

Tessa nodded. "She's at my mom's house in San Jose."

Ayumi Lancaster? He had a hard time believing she was happy about that. "That's, uh ... going well?"

He caught a flash of a grimace on Tessa's face, but Elizabeth said, "Oh, Tessa's mama is the nicest person. She loves Southern cooking, can you believe it? And she taught us to make paper cranes the other day."

"I laid a few false trails in San Francisco for Elizabeth," Tessa said. "If Heath is searching for her, he'll think she's going to Canada."

Despite what he knew about her, he had to admire her abilities and sense of responsibility. He couldn't entirely trust she wasn't still working for her uncle, but she was doing a thorough job protecting Elizabeth ... who was again staring at his Dr. Pepper. With a sigh, he shoved his glass toward her and she started sucking it down.

The waitress brought their food and Elizabeth asked about his family.

"Mama's living with me in San Francisco now," he said.

Elizabeth swallowed her bite of salad. "When I talked to her a week or so ago, she was still in Louisiana."

"She moved, um ... rather suddenly."

Elizabeth tilted her head as she thought. "She told me she was living with ..." Her eyebrows rose. "Oh. Coco Britton. That explains it."

"You know my Aunt Coco?"

"Not personally, but my mama talked about her a few times. A *very* few times." To Tessa she said, "She's like your sister, Alicia, but on menopause."

"Oh." Tessa nodded sagely.

Tessa's sister? It seemed strange to think of her having a regular family with dysfunctional relationships. For some reason, he had assumed all her family were involved with the yakuza and working together like an efficient family business. Maybe he should have paid more attention to *The Sopranos*.

"My mama had a sister like your Aunt Coco," Elizabeth said. "My Aunt Pearl. She'd try to dictate to every one of us kids which carpets we could walk on—and that was in *other* people's houses."

Tessa laughed. "My aunts are much more meek. But all of us cousins tend to be a bit more wild."

That was an understatement. Charles gave a soft snort.

Tessa skewered him with her gaze. He returned it, a slab of granite. She wasn't about to intimidate him like she did other people for her uncle.

Then she spoke slowly, "How do you know about my cousins?"

And he realized his mistake. Most of her cousins, like Ichiro, peppered numerous police reports but had been kept out of the media, especially considering the lack of evidence against them. Only someone who saw those police reports would know exactly how wild her cousins were.

Elizabeth glanced from one to the other, confused by the tension between them. "What's going on?"

"At first I thought you'd just followed the media coverage of my trial," Tessa said, her voice cold and even. "But if you know about my cousins, that means you know things about me that you wouldn't have been able to find out unless you'd unsealed court documents."

Elizabeth now looked at him with chin raised, requiring an answer.

"You don't remember me," Charles said reluctantly.

"From what?"

"Your trial."

There was only a subtle shift in her features—blood leeching from her lips, a single pulse at her throat.

"Charles, you were at her trial?" Elizabeth demanded. "And you didn't say anything?"

"Since you didn't remember me, I thought it was best."

"You weren't one of the prosecutors," Tessa said.

"I was just out of law school and serving as the judge's law clerk."

"Law clerk?" Elizabeth's brow wrinkled.

"I did research for the judge, helped him understand the facts of the case."

"That's how you know about me—you researched me for the judge," Tessa said. "You researched ... everything about the case." It wasn't a question.

Unspoken—maybe for Elizabeth's sake—was, "Including my mob boss uncle." Charles found the condensation ring on the table fascinating.

"It's probably best we not talk about my trial," Tessa said.

"But Charles is a defense lawyer now," Elizabeth said. "He's on your side, right?"

"Is he?" Tessa asked, giving him a steady gaze, her eyebrows raised.

"Charles, you should have been upfront about being at Tessa's trial from the beginning," Elizabeth said.

Him? What about the ex-yakuza, ex-convict she had hired?

Then again, Tessa had been upfront—about her past, her current situation, her conversion to Christianity. She hadn't hidden who she had been.

He just wasn't entirely sure who she was now.

"I'm sorry." He spoke directly to Tessa. "I guess I was just embarrassed at meeting you. I'd been at your trial when it hadn't been open to the public, so I know things about you and your family most people don't."

She nodded, a short jerk of her chin, but she didn't look at him, instead staring at her hands folded on the table in front of her.

He didn't blame her. She had a powerful uncle and he was a lawyer. How could she know Charles had no interest in using her to get incriminating evidence against Teruo Ota?

She couldn't. And he couldn't honestly say he wouldn't take any information he happened to hear straight to a federal prosecutor.

Charles reached in his pocket and withdrew the envelope of cash, and then slid it across the table deliberately to Tessa, not Elizabeth. "Before I forget." And that's all he said. Nothing about making sure she took care of Elizabeth. He actually wasn't sure if he trusted her, but in some strange way, he trusted her warrior's code and knew she wouldn't let Elizabeth down. He didn't understand it himself.

Tessa eyed the money, then looked up at Charles, her dark eyes unreadable. But he thought he saw a flash of green in their depths.

Elizabeth cooed and picked up the envelope. She winked at Charles. "Pardon me while I step out to Union Square ..."

"You need a babysitter, not a bodyguard," he teased her.

And the rest of the meal went smoothly; the tension dissipated, at least on the surface. He convinced them both to try the cannoli for dessert, and Elizabeth declared she'd found a new love.

Tessa didn't smile at him again.

Chapter 12

"This is all your fault!" was the first thing Alicia said when Tessa picked up the phone.

The accusation was like a glass of lemonade thrown in her face—startling and stinging. "What's my fault?" she demanded.

Tessa's voice made Elizabeth look up from where she was playing with Daniel on the living room floor.

"Everything!" The crack of hysteria in her voice clued Tessa in to the fact that Alicia was even more high-strung than normal.

When she listened closely, she could hear Paisley sobbing in the background. Tightness gathered just under her breastbone. "What happened?" Her tone was still tense but she tried to soften it by speaking low and slowly.

Alicia didn't answer, which always drove Tessa stark raving *nuts*. She listened to the symphony of Paisley crying and Alicia wailing for a full two minutes while Elizabeth alternated between playing Slasher-the-valiant-pink-dragon with Daniel and shooting Tessa what-in-the-world-is-going-on looks. Tessa gave her I-don't-know looks back.

Suddenly in the background she heard an aggravated voice shout, "What you do, lady? *Aiee,* poor *didi* ..."

Alicia raised her voice to shriek, "What did *I* do? This is a hazard! You should be sued!"

The slam of a car door, then the sounds of two voices arguing over each other with fighting words like, "You hit my *didi*" and "Your stupid monstrosity" and "You in big trouble" and "You don't know what trouble is, mister."

Finally she heard Paisley say, "Mom, give me the phone.... Hello? Aunt Tessa?" She sounded small, but her voice didn't wobble.

"Paisley, what happened? Are you two all right?"

"We're ..." She took a deep breath, and her voice was steadier as she continued, "We're fine. Mom got into a car accident."

"Is anyone hurt?"

"No, we're fine. Mom hit a ..." She gulped.

An 18-wheeler? A tractor? A dump truck?

"... a Fat Burger Boy."

Tessa rattled a finger in her ear. "What did you say?"

"You know, those big Plexiglas boys in front of the Fat Burger restaurant, the ones wearing a sombrero and a kimono and wooden shoes."

Oh, that's right.

Elizabeth tugged at Tessa's sleeve, and Tessa mouthed, "Auto accident," and gave her a thumbs-up to show they were okay. Elizabeth nodded and sighed in relief.

The argument in the background had ended, and Tessa could hear Alicia's heaving sobs that sounded more frustrated than traumatized, punctuated by an occasional, "It's all her fault!" She also heard what sounded like a solid kick to a piece of Plexiglas, followed by an "Ow!"

Tessa relaxed a little. Alicia must be okay if she was attacking shattered Fat Boys. "How's the car?" she asked Paisley.

"The front bumper looks like it's frowning, but other than that I think the Fat Boy got the last fry in the Happy Meal."

"I don't think he's happy with you mentioning his competition."

"He can't be happy anymore about anything," Paisley said dryly. "His entire head is gone."

"Did your mom call her auto insurance adjustor?"

"No, she called you first."

"Check in her wallet for her insurance card."

She could hear all the gigantic brass buckles clanking as Paisley rummaged through Alicia's purse — Alicia had a neurotic thing for buckles.

"I got it."

"Call the number on it and let them know what happened. You're probably also going to have to get the car towed. Does she have AAA?"

"I don't see a AAA card," Paisley said.

"Oh." Tessa didn't have AAA anymore.

Then Elizabeth tugged on her sleeve again. "I have AAA," she said.

And they were flush with cash. "Paisley, where are you?" She took down the address then told her, "Call the insurance adjustor. Elizabeth and I will come as soon as we can to pick you up and help you get the car towed."

Tessa called a cab company and had the driver pick them up a few blocks from her mom's house. Within twenty minutes, they were being dropped off at Fat Burger. Luckily, Alicia had chosen to assault a fast food restaurant nearby their home as opposed to across the Bay Area.

"What took you so long?" Alicia demanded, tottering toward them on her pumps. "It's all your fault!"

Tessa knew Alicia had just been through something terrible, she was probably worried about Paisley, she didn't handle stress well—a gross understatement—and Alicia worried about the money to fix the car and the Fat Boy now that she had started divorce proceedings. But Alicia's habit of always accusing Tessa was wearing her down, and Tessa found herself responding the way she usually did.

"Brilliant driving, Dale Earnhardt."

Alicia's eyes were jade spikes. "What are you talking about? And *this*—" she swung her arms in wide circles to encompass the headless Fat Boy "—is all your fault."

"Excuse me, but *this*—" Tessa swung her arms in identical circles at the Fat Boy "—was caused by *this*—" She swung her arms to include Alicia's dented SUV "—which was driven by *this*—" she swung her arms in a giant circle to frame the picture of Alicia's figure.

Only then did it register to Tessa that her sister was in a business suit. She dressed up just to pick up her daughter from school?

"I knew you'd be completely insensitive," Alicia said. "You're making jokes while your niece is in hysterics." She flung a hand out toward Paisley, who was leaning against the car and braiding a lock of her straight brown hair.

"Yes," said Tessa. "I can see she's practically incoherent."

"I talked to the insurance adjustor, Aunt Tessa," Paisley said without looking up from her braiding. "Her name was Linda Teng and she was really nice. She talked to the restaurant owner and got his information. She says it shouldn't be a problem to cover the cost of *didi*, here." She jerked her head toward the headless statue.

"Didi?"

"The restaurant owner's name is Bobby Wong. He calls the Fat Boy *didi*, which Linda told me means 'younger brother.'"

"Well, that's appropriate."

"Are we done talking about statue nicknames?" Alicia said acerbically. "Where's the tow truck?"

Elizabeth handed Daniel over to Paisley, who promptly showed him Fat Boy's head on the ground and got him to start bopping him on the nose, while she called AAA and got a tow truck.

"It's all your fault," Alicia said to Tessa while they waited.

Okay, this repetition was going beyond Alicia's typical It's-Tessa's-fault-just-for-existing sort of rant. "What do you mean, it's my fault?" Tessa braced herself—after all, she was asking for it just vocalizing the question.

"If stupid *you* hadn't been doing all those stupid jobs for Uncle Teruo, stupid Duane wouldn't have had any grounds to sue for custody."

Tessa clenched her teeth at the excessive use of the word *stupid*, but by judicious intake of oxygen, let it slide. "How can he sue for custody?"

"He said that since I was living with my sister, who had been accused of murder and gone to jail, I was an unfit mother to expose my child to such a questionable influence."

"So him living with his stripper girlfriend is a better influence?"

"Your memory is like a strainer—he left the stripper already. He's with an airline attendant now."

"So it's better to expose a thirteen-year-old to a stewardess dressed in whipped cream?"

"Rather than an ex-convict?" Alicia snapped. "What do you think?"

What could she say to that? Despite Alicia's normal level of unreasonableness, Tessa couldn't deny that her conviction had deeply impacted so many more people than just herself.

"He's only doing this to annoy me," Alicia said. "His girlfriend can't stand Paisley."

"That's 'cause the last time she left her bra hanging in the bathroom, I punctured her water cups," Paisley called from Fat Boy's head.

Tessa and Elizabeth both stifled their laughter.

"You're not supposed to be listening," Alicia shot back.

"Then stop talking like I'm not here," Paisley retorted.

"You muzzle that attitude, missy, or you're grounded," Alicia said.

Paisley pouted, but kept her mouth shut.

"I was driving, but I was so upset when I got the phone call, it was like I went blind," Alicia said, and her voice cracked.

That twist in her sister's voice caused a twisting in Tessa's gut. Regardless of Alicia's complete lack of common manners toward Tessa, Alicia really did love her daughter, and Duane wouldn't have had a leg to stand on in this custody battle if not for Tessa's past involvement with the yakuza and her incarceration.

"And that stupid statue jumped in front of me," Alicia said. "The next thing I knew, I had some Chinese man yelling at me that I hurt his poor *didi*. How am I supposed to know what *didi* is? At first I thought he was upset I had disrupted the place's *feng shui*."

Tessa eyed Fat Boy's sombrero, dented on one edge, which rolled near his wooden shoes. "I don't think Fat Burger cares much about *feng shui*."

"And now I'll have to pay the insurance deductible. How am I supposed to raise a daughter while dealing with Duane the moron and trying to pay a deductible with money I don't have?"

"You might get that job you interviewed for today, Mom," Paisley said.

Hence the business suit. Tessa should have guessed. "You went for an interview today?"

"Do you think I dressed like this just to pick Paisley up from school? Of course I had an interview," Alicia snapped, but then she rubbed her forehead with her fingers. "I can't even apply for a ground-level biologist position. I'll be lucky to get a lab cleaner position that pays absolute dregs."

Tessa wanted to say, "Trust in God to take care of you," but the words glued her mouth shut like a lump of saltwater taffy. On second thought, her atheist sister's raging temper might make her spit the words right back at her.

But Tessa did send a quick prayer heavenward. *Jesus, please help my sister find a good job. Please take care of her and Paisley.*

And she heard a weird, strange answer in her head: *Don't I always?*

Somehow, that voice calmed her and enabled her to say, "I can pick Paisley up from school for you, if that'll help with your interviews and any job you might land."

"Fine." Alicia crossed her arms and didn't look at Tessa.

Her gratitude was truly overwhelming.

Then again, she hadn't expected it. Knowing how Alicia typically treated her, if she'd said, "Thank you," Tessa would have been more likely to faint dead away.

But Paisley caught her eye and gave her a grin. Things had been awkward between them for the first three months after Tessa got out, since her last memory of the girl had been of a rowdy six-year-old, but she was starting to like her niece, who seemed to have Tessa's adventurous spirit and the determination of a nicer version of Alicia.

She hadn't been very Christlike in her interactions with her sister, and of all her family, she didn't want Paisley to get the wrong impression of how Tessa's new faith had changed her— or not changed her, as the case might seem. This might give her a chance to connect with her niece better and also start exercising that love she seemed to be utterly and completely lacking when it came to her family. She had pink cloud-framed visions of explaining the gospel to her niece and having Paisley come to Christ amidst a choir of angels singing in the background.

Okay, well, maybe not.

But she could at least become a good enough aunt that Paisley wouldn't be ashamed to bring her to school for Aunty Day. Did they even have Aunty Day?

Oh, and all this while protecting Elizabeth and Daniel from a man who might or might not have hidden motives for tracking them down.

No sweat. She could multitask.

Chapter 13

For Tessa, finding a good safe house was like finding a good man — she was just too picky.

"You didn't like any of the seven places you visited?" Elizabeth asked as they got off the train in Menlo Park. "No, Daniel," she said as her son tried to hop back into the train.

"Slasher wants to ride again." He shook the polka-dotted dog so that it became a pink blur in his hand.

"Slasher doesn't want to go on the slide?" Elizabeth said.

He pondered this earth-shaking decision before saying, "Slide first, then train."

Tessa casually looked at all the people who had exited the train, but she was reasonably sure they hadn't been followed. She'd had them exit one of the light-rail trams at a station partially hidden from the street so they could take the next train, and she had kept a close eye on all the passengers and passing cars. She had basically looked for people doing what she would have done if she had to tail someone. "It's a short walk to the park," she said.

"Good. He's antsy after being on the train for so long. So what was wrong with all of the houses?" Elizabeth asked as they started walking.

"One place had a nosy neighbor who looked out her window and called no less than four people while I was looking at the house. The woman must know half the Bay Area. All I need is for her to tell the wrong person about her new neighbors and Heath would find us."

"Okay, and what about the others?"

"Three of them didn't have good escape routes—it would be too easy for a couple men to trap us in the house. That's the reason I don't like hotel rooms or apartments—all you need is one man on the fire escape and one on the elevator and your only other option is jumping out the window."

"He'd probably like that." Elizabeth raised a sardonic brow at Daniel, who was doing running long jumps alongside them.

"The other places weren't in safe enough neighborhoods. I also don't know what kinds of connections Heath has, or whatever private investigator he'd hire would have, and seedy neighborhoods attract snitches."

"I wish we could stay at your mom's house," Elizabeth said. "It doesn't seem like such a bad place to hide."

"It's actually not bad. Mom and Alicia both don't have many visitors at home, it's a quiet neighborhood, and it's completely unrelated to anyone you knew in San Francisco."

"But we're putting your family in danger," Elizabeth finished her thought for her.

"I just worry that eventually Heath will track down who your mysterious friend is, find out my mom lives in San Jose, and connect the dots."

"How would he find out? Wings wouldn't tell him about you, would they?"

"No, they have a strict policy about that. They certainly don't give out information about women who stay there, but they also don't even give out the names of staff or volunteers because some of them also came from abusive relationships. Still, he only has to get a picture of me and show it to the right person to get my name."

"You didn't tell Charles you're looking for a new safe house for us," Elizabeth said.

Tessa blinked. "It didn't really occur to me that I should. I mean, I don't think he could really help us."

"I guess not. I wouldn't think he has lots of shady connections he can ping."

"I wouldn't really need him to ask shady connections. I just need options."

They made it to the park and Daniel went crazy on the Tots playground while Elizabeth watched him and Tessa watched everyone else.

Then Elizabeth's new disposable cell phone chirped. "Oh, it's Charles."

A second later, Tessa's new disposable cell phone also rang. She recognized the number. "Itchy, finally. I called you three hours ago."

"I didn't know it was you, because you called me from a different phone number," her cousin said. "Usually I have Darth Vader as your ringtone."

"Haha, very funny—"

"I wasn't kidding."

"Listen, I need to borrow the car again."

"Now? I'm watching the Giants game," he whined.

"I told Alicia I'd pick Paisley up at school today, so I need the car."

"Can't it wait? It's top of the ninth, tied game."

"If you'd called me back earlier, you could have gotten me the car and been back in front of the game by now."

"You're my little pita bread, you know that?"

"I know that's not a compliment, Itchy."

"Where are you anyway?"

"I'm at Burgess Park in Menlo Park. It's going to take you at least forty-five minutes to get here."

"Sixty minutes — this is the Corolla, remember?"

"Which means you need to get your butt off the couch now."

"Aw, Tessa ..."

"Fine. Do *you* want to explain to Alicia why I couldn't pick her daughter up on time?"

Tessa could almost see Itchy's mouth puckering. "Fine, fine." He hung up without saying goodbye.

Elizabeth also hung up her phone call and said, "Charles is coming."

At the same time, Tessa said, "Itchy's coming."

They stared at each other for a beat.

Tessa's heart rate jumped to marathon pace. "Charles is coming here?"

Elizabeth squeaked, "Itchy's coming here?"

"Well, it might not be a bad thing ..." Tessa said.

"Think about this. Your old gang mate yakuza cousin meeting straight-laced Charles."

It would be Tessa's luck that Itchy would start talking about someone he whacked last week. "You're right. They can't meet each other."

Elizabeth winced. "Charles is bringing my godmother too."

"*What?*"

"I haven't seen Aunt Vivian yet, and she said she wanted to meet you."

Tessa covered her eyes with her hands. "This is getting worse and worse." Tessa's old gang mate, yakuza cousin meeting straight-laced Charles *and* his straight-laced mama—it would be like matter and anti-matter. Kaboom!

"When are they getting here?"

"When is he getting here?"

Tessa checked her watch. "He'll probably stay to watch the end of the Giants game."

"Charles said they're in Palo Alto, so they'll be here in only twenty or thirty minutes."

"Maybe they'll miss each other."

Tessa whipped out her phone. "I'll tell Itchy he can finish watching the game." But Itchy's phone rang and rang, and then went to voicemail. "He's not picking up." He was probably tired of talking to Tessa and figured it wasn't important. Tessa sent a text message but again, Itchy may not read it, especially if he was either watching the game or on his way.

A part of her was curious to meet Charles's mother. Considering the enigma that Charles was, she wondered what his mom was like to have raised someone like him.

At the same time, she wasn't stupid enough to let hotheaded Ichiro anywhere near Charles or his mother. Talk about oil and water. Or more like honey and wasabi.

She waited with Elizabeth, dutifully keeping an eye out to protect her client, but feeling antsy. Then Elizabeth started waving at a silver sports car entering the parking lot.

And Tessa fell in love.

••••

She wouldn't stop staring at his car.

Charles would be lying if he said he wasn't at least a little flattered by the starry-eyed look in Tessa's eyes as she circled his car, running her hands over the silver lines, catching her fingers in the four intertwined circles of the Audi logo. It was only an R8, not the most popular sports car model, and certainly not the most expensive, but he loved the look, the lines, and how it handled—it fit him.

And it apparently caused car-lust in Tessa. She was practically drooling on his windshield.

"She certainly appreciates her cars," Mama said from the passenger seat as he opened her door and leaned down to unbuckle her seatbelt. "I like her already."

"That's Tessa, Elizabeth's bodyguard," Charles said.

"I know that," Mama said. "Elizabeth told me all about her."

"*All* about her?"

Mama stood up. "All. She sounds nice and spicy."

"Mama, she's not a bowl of etouffee."

"No, she's wasabi."

"What? That sinus-clearing green stuff you fed us that one time?"

"Yes. She's perfect to liven up ..." His mama slid a glance toward him, "cold fish."

Mama must be talking about one of her exotic dishes that Charles could do without. What happened to the days of baked ham and cornbread stuffing?

"You certainly like your cars," he heard Mama say in a louder voice, as she put out her hand to shake Tessa's. "I'm Vivian Britton."

Tessa tore her eyes away from the Audi to shake Mama's hand, and her face broke into a wide smile. She had a faint dimple on the left corner of her mouth that made his kidneys turn to jelly. "I'm Tessa, Elizabeth's bodyguard. My cousins loved their cars, and since I hung around them, I started appreciating nice cars too."

"Charles does like this sports car," Mama said.

Tessa's gaze flickered from her to Charles, since he was standing beside his mama, and something she saw in his face made a faint flush rise to her cheeks. Then she blinked and returned her attention to Mama.

"Goodness, you're so pretty," Mama said. "You don't look like you could squash a spider, much less defend yourself against a two-hundred-pound man. Is it all that kung fu?"

Tessa laughed. "I don't know kung fu. I do mixed martial arts."

"Mixed martial arts? You certainly don't look very Asian."

Charles was ready to sink into the ground. Then again, there weren't that many Asians in Louisiana, so maybe she was indulging in curiosity.

Tessa took it in stride. "I'm only half Asian. I'm half Japanese."

"Oh, that's right, what with your uncle and all. What was your father? German?"

"English, Scottish, and a little Italian." There was a slight tightening around her mouth as she talked about her father's ethnicities.

Charles knew Wayne Lancaster had left the family when she was ten, but he had never thought about how that might have affected her. He'd been focused only on what she'd done after he left — becoming more deeply involved in her uncle's business, hanging out with her cousin Ichiro and other yakuza.

"You're certainly a pot of gumbo," Mama said with a warm smile.

And Charles witnessed Tessa unfolding like a flower to the sunlight under his mama's smile. Lots of people melted under Mama's charm, but he never thought someone like Tessa would respond to her that way.

"So I hear your uncle is Teruo Ota, the yakuza mob boss,"

Mama said with bright, inquisitive eyes. "What was it like, working for him? What kinds of things did you do for him?"

Good gravy, because Mama was so transparent about her own life, she assumed everyone else would be too. Tessa had stiffened in shock, and a red haze of embarrassment was rising from her neck.

"Mama, I'm sure Tessa doesn't want to answer that." Charles reached out to take his mama's hand from where it still clasped Tessa's, and his fingers brushed Tessa's.

He didn't feel any jolt of electricity or bolt of lightning, but boy did his head spin for a second like a perfectly thrown football.

"Charles, that's very presumptuous of you," Mama protested. She pulled her hand away from him, breaking his contact with Tessa's fingers too, and he dropped his arms to his sides. The spinning sensation faded away.

"I didn't mean to be," he said, "but Mama, I'm pretty sure Tessa doesn't want to get in trouble with her uncle by telling you things she shouldn't."

Tessa gave him a look full of gratitude, and that spinning started again with his head. Must be an inner ear infection or something.

"Oh." Mama's blue eyes grew wide. "I didn't realize that. I'm so sorry, darling." She raised a hand to touch Tessa's cheek.

Tessa froze at his mother's touch, but for some reason, it reminded him of when he and Eddie had been fishing at a stream and a fawn had stumbled out of the woods only a few feet away from them. They hadn't breathed, hadn't moved a muscle, their eyes riveted to the soft golden body, the slender feet picking their way through the rocks, the delicate muzzle bending to drink.

Then Mama's hand fell away—the fawn nimbly leaped back into the thick trees—and the moment was gone.

Elizabeth had gathered Daniel from the playground and now stood nearby waiting to greet her godmother. Mama opened her arms wide to enfold both of them. "Elizabeth, you've grown so beautiful! And this is your little boy?"

There was an awkward minute of silence between him and Tessa. He wasn't about to apologize for his mama—he loved her exactly how she was, and he'd give his life to protect her. But she was ... Mama.

He had opened his mouth to say something inane when Tessa suddenly stiffened. To Charles's eyes, she seemed to grow taller and wider even as she stood there, glaring at a truly decrepit Toyota Corolla that had entered the parking lot.

No, she wasn't looking at the Corolla, she was looking at the sleek Lexus that followed behind it. A tall, handsome Asian man sat behind the wheel, wearing expensive sunglasses.

And suddenly he realized who it was. One of the yakuza.

He went on high alert. Why were they here? Had Tessa called them to come? Was she still working for her uncle despite her newfound faith?

And did Charles have to do anything to make sure his mama would be okay?

He didn't realize his hands had bunched into fists until Tessa laid gentle fingers on his wrist.

"It's okay," she said in a low, tense voice. "I'll take care of them. Stay here with your mother and Elizabeth." Her eyes turned to him then, amber chips in a fierce, determined face. "I won't let them come near," she promised. Then she hurried to meet them.

He realized he believed her, he trusted her words, spoken

with stone-hard resolution. He wasn't sure why he trusted her, but he did.

He approached Mama and Elizabeth and said in a low voice, "Why don't you two go to the playground?"

Elizabeth saw the tall Asian man, wearing a very modern-cut business suit, getting out of the car, and she grabbed Daniel, who'd been about to dart away. "It was just supposed to be Itchy."

"What?"

"It was only supposed to be her cousin Ichiro who came. He's letting Tessa borrow his car. I don't know who that other man is."

That's why Tessa had been so surprised, and so wary.

"Will Tessa be all right?" Mama asked. "He's terribly mean looking, don't you think?"

He looked like a Japanese version of the Terminator, except in a very classy suit. Ichiro had gotten out of the Corolla and he was just as Charles remembered from the files he'd looked at seven years ago—short and stocky, with deceptively sleepy eyes. He wasn't known for high intelligence, but he had a mean streak that made people fear him. Today, he dressed in hip, flashy slacks and a fashionable shirt rather than the heavy leather jackets he used to wear.

Tessa wasn't comfortable or casual with the two men. Her shoulders were thrust back and her chin up, but there was tension knotted across her upper back. She spoke to the one in the suit, and it was obvious Ichiro deferred to him as well.

"Don't leave her alone with them," Mama told Charles.

"I'm sure she can take care of herself." But he didn't like how they outnumbered her. Tessa was tall for a woman, yet next to the two men, she looked petite and fragile.

"Stay here," he told them.

His car was idling at the entrance to the park green, so he went to park the car in the lot. The two men had parked on the other end of the parking lot, near the fountain, which was turned off for the winter, but the lot curved around the fountain with more stalls on the other side, although they were partially hidden by the stand of trees ringing the fountain. Charles found a stall there and parked the Audi.

At that moment, a couple of teenagers in low, muscle cars entered the parking lot, their music blaring from open windows, and Tessa and the two men moved closer to the fountain.

Charles could hear every word as it carried over the smooth concrete to his parking spot on the other side of the fountain, but sitting in his car, he was partially hidden from their view by a redwood tree.

"I had to talk to Jun," the tall man was saying, "to assure him we weren't trying to set up competition against him."

"Jun knows who I am," Tessa said. "I don't understand why he'd think I was trying to move into his territory."

"He's paranoid," Ichiro said with a shrug. "He's been dealing drugs for longer than most *because* he's paranoid."

"Kenta, how did you find out I was in that neighborhood to begin with?" Tessa asked. Her voice wasn't belligerent, but it wasn't just idly curious either.

Kenta—Charles remembered the name. One of Teruo's captains.

"The house you were looking at a few days ago is next door to a woman who plays Mahjong with Jun's aunt," Kenta said. "She talked to the aunt, the aunt talked to Jun, Jun went to Mits, Mits came straight to me."

Mits—Kenta's younger brother, if Charles remembered correctly, and another of Teruo Ota's men.

"Why were you looking at a house?" Kenta asked. "And in that neighborhood?"

"I'm looking for a new safe house for my client."

Where Elizabeth was now wasn't safe enough. Why hadn't Tessa told Charles that?

"Your uncle could have found you something," Kenta said.

Tessa shook her head and looked away. "He offered but I said no. I want to keep Elizabeth away from all that."

She had refused her uncle's help? For Elizabeth's sake?

"Are you suddenly too good for us?" Ichiro demanded.

Tessa gave him a hard look. She had absolutely no deference to her cousin, in contrast to her politer tone with Kenta. "She's been through a lot and I don't want my connections to cause problems for her. She's got enough."

"You're turning your back on your family?" Ichiro said doggedly.

"I went to jail for my family," she snapped. "Don't you dare accuse me again."

"It looks to me like you're choosing her over us now." Ichiro craned his neck to look at Elizabeth, who was still with Mama near the playground.

The two women were watching Tessa, but when Elizabeth saw Ichiro looking at them, she pulled Daniel closer to her.

"Then again," Ichiro said in a different voice, "I would probably want to spend time with her . . ."

In a blink, Tessa had shoved her forearm into Ichiro's neck and backed him against the fountain's edge. He sat down hard and teetered over the empty basin.

"You stay away from her," Tessa said in a voice as calm and sharp as a sword blade. "Believe me, prison didn't make me softer."

Ichiro glared at her but fear creased the edges of his eyes.

Kenta laid a firm hand against Tessa's shoulder, and she released Ichiro immediately. He grabbed the edge of the fountain to get his balance and sat there pouting.

Charles wasn't sure what to think. This was a side of Tessa that he hadn't seen before. He'd known about her ruthless abilities, but had never witnessed them until now.

Now he knew why most men didn't want to cross her.

Tessa and Kenta moved a few feet away from the fountain. "Keep him away from my client," Tessa said. "She and her boy are under my protection, and they're my responsibility now. I take that very seriously."

He nodded. "I understand." He touched her arm in a gesture that seemed more intimate than just casual acquaintances. "Ichiro's just angry because it seems like you're distancing yourself from us."

"I am." She raised her chin to look him square in the eye. "I explained this to you in my letter, Kenta."

He looked away.

"I became a Christian. This is not my lifestyle anymore."

"It's hard to understand," he said. "You're turning your back on so much. And . . . you're turning your back on me."

Charles went still. He'd never considered Tessa had any type of romantic relationship with any of her uncle's men, but it would make sense that Teruo would only give his niece to someone he trusted.

And yet Tessa had chosen God over this wealthy, powerful man. Over her uncle too. An uncomfortable twisting in his gut made him fidget in his seat. These weren't the actions of a woman only playing at being Christian.

As she looked at Kenta, there was pain and regret on her

face. She opened her mouth, hesitated. Then said, "I wouldn't willingly hurt you if this didn't mean a great deal to me. This changed me, Kenta."

"You are changed," he said in a neutral voice.

Her eyes fell, her mouth tightened. "I'm sorry." Charles saw her mouth move more than he heard her.

There were several long seconds as they stood there in silence.

"Let me help you," Kenta said. "I can help you find another safe house."

Tessa grew very still. Her eyes were heavy as the temptation weighed on her. But then she slowly shook her head. "I appreciate the offer, but I can't. This doesn't involve you. It shouldn't involve you."

Kenta looked over her head in the direction of the playground. "Are you trying to protect me too?"

A small smile peeked from the corner of her mouth. "Maybe. But it's mostly for Elizabeth's sake. She doesn't know anything about this world, Kenta."

"That's probably for the best." He reached into his pocket and drew out his car keys. "I shouldn't have surprised you today. I told Ichiro not to tell you I was coming, but I didn't realize you were with your client."

"I would never be unhappy to see you," she said, but her tone was a bit automatic. Charles had seen her anger when Kenta had driven into the parking lot behind Ichiro.

Kenta reached out then, and the tips of his fingers touched the edge of her jaw, the corner of her mouth.

For a brief moment, her eyes closed, she turned her cheek toward his hand . . .

Then she pulled her face away and faced him with head high, expression serene. "Thank you for speaking to Jun about

me. I'm sorry for causing you any inconvenience or embarrassment."

His hand fell away quickly, almost as if he hadn't touched
her at all. "It was no trouble," he said. He hesitated a moment,
then said softly, "If you ever need help, please call me."

Tiny muscles in her face tightened, as if she were trying to
hold back from saying something. "Thank you."

He strode away, and Ichiro hastened to catch up with him.

"Itchy!" she called after her cousin. "Keys."

He reached in his jacket pocket and tossed them to her with
a bit more force than necessary, then followed Kenta and got
into the Lexus.

Tessa strode back to the playground.

Charles stayed where he was until Kenta left the parking lot,
and then he got out to join the others at the playground.

Tessa's eyes widened as she saw him. He could tell it was on
her lips to ask where he had been, but he could also tell that a
part of her didn't want to know, and she closed her mouth and
went back to listening to his mama.

"Charles, Elizabeth was just telling me how Tessa is looking
for another safe place for them to stay until you can get her husband to stop harassing her. Why don't they stay at your house?"

"My house?" Charles choked.

"Your house?" Tessa choked.

Mama looked at the two of them as if they were both Dumb
and Dumber. "Why not? Elizabeth is my goddaughter and her
family has always been close to my mama's family, so it is our
honor and duty to help protect her."

Mama's wording was a bit melodramatic, but it was exactly
what she would feel duty-bound to do for any of her godchil-
dren. Charles had a fleeting uncomfortable thought about what

his coworkers might think when they found out that his pretty young client was staying at his house, even though his mama was there with them and the young woman in question was his mama's goddaughter. It was definitely allowed for an attorney to house a client, but it might raise eyebrows if they found out the extent to which he was getting personally involved with his client.

"Plus Charles's house has plenty of room and it's in a gated community," Mama continued. "Heath will eventually know Charles is Elizabeth's lawyer, if he doesn't already. And Charles has a panic room."

Tessa's eyes narrowed thoughtfully. "You do?"

He'd forgotten about it. It was more of a glorified storage room right now. "It came with the house when I bought it."

"I think it's a wonderful thing to have, what with all your big clients," Mama said. "Who knows if any of them might hold grudges if you lost a case?"

Let's hope it never came to that. "I'd have to make sure it still works."

"Oh, it does," Mama said. "I tried it out yesterday."

A knot suddenly twisted in his neck. "Mama, it calls the police department when it's activated."

"Well, how was I supposed to know that? But the officers were very nice. I promised them I wouldn't do it again unless it was a real emergency."

"I think that's a wonderful idea," Elizabeth said. "I'd feel ever so much safer with a panic room."

"But Mrs. Britton—" Tessa started.

"Vivian, darling."

"Vivian, it might put you in danger. I told Elizabeth that I'm not sure what Heath is really up to."

"Oh, Elizabeth told me about that. And she told me how

you've been so vigilant in trying to find a place you can defend so you can take care of her. Well, since Elizabeth trusts you, *I* trust you to keep me and Elizabeth and Daniel safe, and I trust my son, here" — she threaded her arm through his — "to quickly get Elizabeth's money back for her."

And that was that, in Mama's mind.

"So Tessa, you come look at Charles's house and see if you like it."

Tessa opened her mouth, glanced sideways at Charles, then said, "Sure, Mrs. Brit — er, Vivian. Why don't I talk to Charles and arrange things?"

They moved a few yards away while Mama played with Daniel on the playground slide.

"I'm sorry," Tessa said. "If this isn't what you want, I completely understand."

Her sensitivity in speaking to him seemed so at odds with how she'd manhandled her cousin only a few minutes ago. Who was the real Tessa — the beautiful woman looking up at him with her green-flecked eyes, or the tough fighter who'd been able to subdue a man fifty pounds heavier than herself?

And yet, he realized he was even considering this *because* he'd seen how she carried herself — how she'd be able to defend Elizabeth, Daniel, and his mama.

"Do you think you could keep them all safe?" he asked her.

She met him with openness and honesty. "I'd do my absolute best. The question is, is my best good enough for you?"

The real question was, could he trust her, with her background, in his house and protecting his mama? And she knew that was the real question too.

Seven years ago, he'd seen reports of the assaults and murders Ichiro was suspected of. She'd been close to Ichiro, although

Charles knew that with the intricacies of the yakuza, because she was female, she wasn't officially part of her uncle's group. However, she did things for her uncle and she had a fearsome reputation on the streets.

Back then, she'd been tough, mysterious. Favoring all black leather like Ichiro, she'd seemed more male than female. People had said she was even more ruthless than her cousin, more subtle, definitely smarter.

But now, even her appearance had changed. She seemed softer, although there was that edge and wildness to her that seven years in prison — and her new faith — hadn't quite rubbed away. She seemed more feminine. More appealing — although his mind shied away from the admission.

She'd agreed to help Elizabeth even when she wasn't able to be paid. She'd kept her cousin away from Elizabeth too, and she was giving him an out now, when she could have just taken advantage of his mama's generosity.

Her integrity stared him in the face even as her amber eyes met his. So far, she hadn't given him a reason not to trust her . . .

Yet.

"Why don't you come by today to see the house?" he said. "You can decide if it'll work for you."

She betrayed herself with a flicker of her dark eyelashes. He had surprised her.

"All right. I need to pick my niece up from school in an hour, but after that, we can look at your house."

Doing soccer mom duty? Tessa continued to throw him for a loop.

"What time works for you?" she asked.

"I took the afternoon off to take Mama to a doctor's appointment."

"She's okay?" Her cheeks became rounder, younger, with her concern.

"She's fine—she said she wanted to meet her new doctor here in California *before* she had to come to her for any type of emergency. I think she just wanted a good gossip with the doc. Then she dragged me to a new restaurant at the Stanford Shopping Center."

Tessa's smile was small, but it made him want to reach out and touch her jaw, her lip, the way Kenta had. He closed his fingers into a fist, then released them.

"How do we get to your house?" she asked.

He gave her directions. One insane side of him wondered what she'd think of his house. The other side of him felt like he was letting a wild tiger into his home.

Chapter 14

All for the sake of a pink dog named Slasher.

Tessa walked into the front door of her mom's house to find Mom sifting through a dusty box.

"Oh, I'm glad you're here," Mom said. "After you all left, I found some old clothes. Do you think Elizabeth would want these for Daniel?" She held up a powder blue shirt with a fuchsia and lime-green flower in the center.

"Uh ..."

Tessa tried not to grimace at the shirt, but Mom must have read her expression, because she pursed her lips together and dropped the shirt back in the box. "Well, I'm only trying to be helpful. I don't know why I kept all these old children's clothes in the first place. Although these are so cute." She picked up a pair of tiny jeans.

Trying to be helpful, Tessa began to say, "Now those might ..."

But then Mom flipped them over and exposed the embroidered sparkly yellow and green fairy on the pants pocket.

Scratch that.

"Do you have a box of my old children's clothes? There might be stuff that would, uh, fit Daniel better than Alicia's old clothes."

"Oh, I didn't keep any of those. Most of them had holes all over the place. You were so hard on your clothes, Tessa."

Tessa turned away before her face betrayed her feelings. True, she'd been a typical tomboy and she'd run her clothes to shreds, but somehow Mom's choice of not keeping any of her things while keeping Alicia's clothes pricked at her. She wasn't competitive with Alicia in that sense, but it seemed her family took pains to point out how different she was from them.

And different had always been lonely for her.

"You all certainly packed up quickly," Mom remarked. "I barely had time to say goodbye to Elizabeth and Daniel before you hustled them out the door."

"I wanted to get them into the new house so you'd have more space here." Tessa had purposefully neglected to mention being tailed a couple times ... and attacked outside of Wings ... and in possible danger. She didn't really want to think how Mom would have responded to that information, and it didn't matter now that Elizabeth and Daniel were moved out.

"Well." Mom paused, then said, "That's very thoughtful of you, Tessa."

Tessa savored the echo of the words for a moment before she replied, "Thanks, Mom."

"I didn't really mind having them here," Mom said.

"Yes, well, Alicia did."

Mom looked up from the box and met Tessa's eyes squarely. "Well, it's not her house, is it?"

Tessa blinked. "I guess not."

Mom went back to idly sorting through the box. "It was nice having you here too."

A tingling passed all over Tessa's skin. She wasn't sure what to say. How to react. How to feel.

"Are you sure you need to stay with her?" Mom asked.

"It's only until Elizabeth has her money and is safe from Heath."

Mom looked thoughtful. "I think I'll still get those room-darkening shades for the sunroom. Then you can move in there and I'll use your room for a craft room."

And just like that, the world righted itself and went back to normal. It was as if the surreal moment hadn't happened.

"Mom, did you see Slasher?"

Mom frowned. "I don't watch those horror movies."

"No, I mean Daniel's pink dog. He calls it Slasher. Elizabeth thinks he left it here this morning."

"Oh, that was a dog? It looked like a six-legged cow."

Yeah, Slasher was looking a little ratty.

"I saw it in the spare bathroom."

Tessa found Slasher twisted in a floppy heap beside the toilet. Hmm, maybe she should have Elizabeth wash him. She put him in a plastic grocery bag and headed out the door. "See you, Mom."

She was glad Alicia was out somewhere. Her sister had tried to command the move this morning like a brigadier general, which was a bit hard considering Mom kept hustling here and there with things to give to Elizabeth—an extra toothbrush, a few of those Japanese candies Daniel liked, a pair of quilted house slippers in case where she was going had cold floors.

Tessa was only about eight blocks from Mom's house when she saw the gray Nissan Sentra driving toward her.

Same deal—no license plate on front, Caucasian man with dark full beard driving. Except this time he had two other men in the car with him—in fact, the same two men who had been with Heath outside of Wings.

The car passed Tessa going in the opposite direction. She tried to look away quickly, but the driver saw her.

And pulled a fast three-point turn in the narrow residential street.

Tessa downshifted and tried to speed up, but Gramps wasn't having any of it. The engine roared, but the speedometer only wavered up by a few lines.

Wham! The entire car jumped forward as the Sentra rammed her from behind. Her head knocked into the steering wheel as the force threw her forward and the seatbelt dug into her belly painfully, but Gramps kept going. Her pursuers couldn't hit her much harder because they didn't have enough room to accelerate and really ram her good.

Wham! Another hit. Gramps started gagging.

She needed to make it to a heavier traffic street so the Sentra wouldn't have as much room to maneuver. Only another block . . .

The gray car loomed large in her rearview mirror for a moment, then disappeared toward her left blind spot.

He was going to do a PIT maneuver.

"Oh, no you don't." She started swerving back and forth so that he wouldn't be able to get into the right position to hit her left rear corner and send her spinning out.

Bam! The contact sent her body skidding sideways on the seat, her abdomen sliced by the seatbelt. The street in front of her windshield jumped sideways as the car began to spin out.

She hit the brakes and cranked the wheel to the side to try to perform a J-turn and combat the spin out, but she wasn't a stunt driver. The car skidded out of control and crashed sideways into a tree planted on the edge of the street.

Her head rang with the rattling the impact had done on her brain. She fumbled with the seat belt, then the door handle.

They would come for her. She had to get out of the car.

She had barely gotten to her feet when a fist collided with her cheek.

Owowowowow!

"That's for the last time we met," a deep voice growled.

She opened a bleary eye and recognized Pants-Too-Long. His jaw was still discolored from the kick she'd sent into it.

"Hey!" a distant voice cried out.

"Stay back!" Pants-Too-Long warned the bystander.

Stay back, she repeated in her head. She didn't want to have to try to protect any innocents. No collateral damage.

But the person's interference gave the throbbing in her face a few precious seconds to subside, and she could see and think more clearly when Pants-Too-Long looked back at her.

Two other men ranged around them, but not too close—the driver stood to her left, a rangy man who only looked large and intimidating because of his full, dark beard, but who was actually a bit scrawny up close. The other man she also recognized from the incident at Wings, and again, his gray suit jacket was too tight across his shoulders, which would constrict his arm movements.

She sagged back against Gramps, dropping a little lower to the ground so that Pants-Too-Long had to bend down toward her.

Off balance.

Her hands darted upward to the back of his head, her forearms resting against his collar bones, and she snapped his head downward just as she brought her knee up. His jaw collided with her femur in a soft *crack*, and his unconscious body slid downward.

She didn't wait for him to hit the ground. Since Beard Papa was so close to her, she turned toward him and aimed a hook at his liver, just under his ribs. He gave a soft, "Oof!" and curled inward. Then she sent an uppercut elbow to his jaw. He staggered back.

Jacket-Too-Tight came in with a wide, wild swing that was a little slow. She stepped into him so his fist landed in the air behind her shoulder and wrapped both arms around him in a grappling embrace that brought him off balance. She did an underarm hook take down to drop them both to the asphalt.

He threw a few elbows at the air around her head, and she scrambled to get behind his body. She sliced the blade of her forearm under his chin, closing off his carotid arteries in a rear naked choke. He tried to twist out of her grip but she had locked her legs around his upper thighs. In four seconds flat, he had passed out.

In the long breath she took after he had gone limp in her arms, she noticed that her heart pulsed against her breastbone, but wasn't racing. Good to know she wasn't completely out of shape from her street fighting days.

She jumped to her feet. Pants-Too-Long was out cold, and Beard Papa wasn't unconscious, but he was rolling and groaning in pain on the ground.

"Are you okay?" A tall blonde-haired woman came running up to her.

"I'm fine." Speaking was painful because of the swelling already rushing into her cheek. "I'm sorry about your tree."

The woman gave it a look of utter distaste. "It's not my tree, and when I petitioned the city to remove it, they refused, so I really couldn't care less."

Jacket-Too-Tight gave a soft moan.

"Go get in your house," Tessa told the woman urgently. "Lock yourself in. Don't talk to these guys."

The woman was already backing up. "I'm calling the cops. You better get out of here too."

And Tessa suddenly realized — they had been coming to find Elizabeth at Mom's house. Was Mom okay?

She staggered to Gramps and got in. Before she turned the key, she sent God a short prayer. *Please, Lord, please let it start.*

The engine coughed, sputtered, groaned … and started chugging.

Thank you, Lord!

She eased forward. The wheel alignment was hopelessly off and the car pulled to the left, but she drove it back to her mom's house, checking for a tail and eyeing all the cars she passed on the street.

"Mom!" She fumbled with the front door but it was locked. That was a good sign, right? She unlocked it and stumbled into the house.

"Did you lose your ke — Oh my goodness, what happened?" Mom had been making her way to the front door but now halted at the sight of Tessa's face.

"You're okay?"

"Of course I'm okay. Why?" Then she gasped. "Whoever did that to you was looking for Elizabeth, weren't they?"

"Is that Tessa?" Alicia's voice came from the back of the house.

Oh, no.

Her sister's annoyed face — really, what other expression did she have in her repertoire? — appeared from the back hallway and grew even more annoyed as she saw Tessa. "You were brawling again?"

"No, I wondered what it would feel like to slam my head into a lamppost. What do you think?"

"You couldn't stay out of trouble even if you tried."

"Whoa, Aunt Tessa, can I touch it?" Paisley's expression was alight with curiosity and maybe admiration.

"Paisley!" her mother said.

Paisley hunched her shoulders but still snuck awe-struck looks at Tessa.

"I need you all to go to Uncle Gordon's just for a few days," Tessa said.

"Absolutely not," Alicia said.

"Ooh, I like Uncle Gordon's house," Paisley said.

Mom pouted. "But I've got the TiVo set to record *Man vs. Wild*, and Gordon doesn't have cable."

Both Tessa and Alicia stared at their mother. "Mom, really?" Alicia said. "Tessa's telling us to uproot and all you can talk about is reality TV?"

"But Bear Grylls is a hottie."

Paisley coughed but Tessa thought she stifled a giggle.

"It's only for a few days," Tessa repeated. "Mom, Uncle Gordon's house is even closer to your work."

"And how do you know they won't try to hurt her at work?" Alicia said.

Tessa leveled her a look. "I doubt only the most stupid thugs will try to attack Mom at her brother's Japanese restaurant."

"And what about us? Of course you wouldn't spare a thought for your sister and niece."

Tessa was about to retort that her sister never spared a thought for her, but Mom interjected with, "Alicia, your name isn't on the title so they don't even know you're living here."

Both sisters were shocked into silence by their mother's uncharacteristic reply. Usually it was Tessa or Alicia trying to be logical to their emotional parent.

Tessa recovered first. "You want to make sure Paisley will be safe, right?"

"Uncle Gordon's dog Scratch is a Boxer so he at least looks mean," Paisley said, "even if he is kind of a marshmallow."

Alicia frowned at Tessa, but she told Paisley, "Go pack your overnight bag."

"Cool." She headed back to her room.

"It's just like you to bring danger to your family," Alicia spat, then turned toward her own bedroom to pack.

Tessa expected some similar vitriol response from her mom, but she only said, "Elizabeth and Daniel are okay?"

"They're fine."

Mom nodded and laid a hand on Tessa's arm. "She's your client, so she's your responsibility." Her mother's hand was heavy and yet soft at the same time.

"I'll keep them safe, Mom."

"I know you will." Mom looked away, as if she couldn't say the words directly to Tessa's face. "I married your father to escape your uncle's world, not to have my younger daughter be fully embroiled in it from the age of sixteen. But even though I didn't like what you were doing, you were always responsible with what your uncle gave you to do."

Tessa didn't know what to say. She knew her mom never liked the choices she'd made, but she also never knew her mom saw anything remotely admirable in her younger daughter.

"I'll go pack," Mom said, but then she turned back and grabbed Tessa's hand. She drew her daughter in close and said in a deep, serious voice, "Will you please make sure my TiVo doesn't erase *Man vs. Wild*?"

••••

"Oh my goodness!" Vivian exclaimed.

"Tessa, are you all right?" Elizabeth asked.

"I hope the other guy looks worse," Charles said.

Tessa walked into Charles's house and handed Slasher to Daniel, who was the only one who didn't notice the shiner over her right eye.

"Let's get some ice on that," Vivian said.

"Oh, and you're bleeding a little too," Elizabeth added.

"So did you fight off all fifty of them with just your pinky?" Charles asked.

To be honest, Elizabeth's and Vivian's fussing made her uncomfortable, and Charles's quips made her feel more in control of the situation. No one had ever really fluttered over her when she got injured—usually it was from sparring with her cousins or other yakuza, and if she couldn't patch herself up or walk away with her head high, she'd lose the ounce of respect she'd fought hard for, a woman in their man's world. And other times, it had been herself sneaking into her mom's house late at night, or years later, coming home to her empty condo. No gentle fingers probing her cuts or laying a soft, towel-wrapped bag of ice over her eye. She felt awkward, clumsy, and three years old.

Then again, it wasn't exactly the worst feeling in the world either.

"Did they come for us?" A horrified look came over Elizabeth's face. "Did they come to your mama's house? Is she all right?"

"They saw me in my car a few blocks from Mom's house. We, er ... had an altercation and I left them to the tender mercies of a lady dialing the police department."

"But they hurt you," Elizabeth said. "My past keeps hunting me and hurting you."

And Tessa realized that she and Elizabeth were more alike than she realized. Elizabeth's past — Heath — was hunting her just as Tessa's yakuza past hunted her. "It's okay. They didn't hurt me very much, and I didn't tell them anything."

Charles was staring at her, his humor set aside now, and she couldn't quite interpret his look. Admiration and wonder, disbelief, anxiety, a hint of wariness.

And intensity. It spilled over the edges of his gaze, pulling at her with its strength. Just like that powerful moment between them at the park, after Kenta had driven away, there was a sense of the deep well of his passions, normally covered tightly by his businesslike veneer. And more than that, there was the sense of his passion for *her* — the burning attraction between the two of them.

No, she was just feeling ghosts of Kenta's regretful affection for her. Even before her arrest, their relationship had been close and yet distant. He had been one of her uncle's closest *kobuns*, years more mature than his age, and she'd been the *oyabun's* unconventional niece. A useful niece, but not a marriage trophy. She would see moments in Kenta where he'd act as if he wanted to draw closer to her, but something held him back. She had respected that.

And after she'd become a Christian in prison, she had written to him to tell him, and he hadn't visited her again. She had known then that the one man who had wanted to reach past her tough outer shell was lost to her, and she may not ever find another man who was her equal, or who would even want her.

This *thing* with Charles was just … a rebound, especially after seeing Kenta again today.

But she couldn't deny right now how she felt, almost as if the air were shimmering between the two of them.

It was worse when Vivian bustled off to make some poultice she claimed would clear the swelling right up and leech out the discoloration, and Daniel demanded attention from Elizabeth.

Charles came up to her, his hands in his pockets as if to keep himself from reaching out to her. She loosely clasped her arms around herself, wanting him to reach out to her.

"I'm sure you've had worse." A faint smile deepened the dimples on his cheeks.

"I'm sure I have. I just don't remember at this moment."

That intense gaze again, the shimmering air. She couldn't breathe, as if the temperature had suddenly shot up to 115 degrees and 80 percent humidity.

And then his hand came out of his pocket and he reached up to touch her cheek—her good one.

He had touched her before—his fingers had grazed hers at the park, when Vivian had been holding her hands. It hadn't been melodramatic, but she'd noticed the feel of his skin against hers, even for that brief moment.

But now, the pads of his fingers sent a shiver through her. Her skin tingled with fire where he touched her, and she could feel the heat from his palm. Her heartbeat started to gallop. She wanted to turn her face into his hand, so she could feel the length of his palm against her jaw.

This was too much like Kenta's touch today. Then, she'd had to remind herself of her faith, of her reason to distance herself from him.

She had even more reason to keep away from Charles.

With a sharp indrawn breath, she pulled away from him, took a small step back.

A flame in his eyes cooled, like a gas light dying, and his hand dropped away.

Sanity returned. She didn't want to be attracted to Charles. She couldn't, because of who she was and who he was. They were all wrong for each other. She wasn't working for Uncle Teruo anymore, but she also couldn't antagonize her uncle by getting romantically involved with an attorney like Charles — honest, upright. Uncle Teruo would say she couldn't be sure Charles wouldn't take any information he might happen to find out about the Otas and send it straight to a federal prosecutor. While she didn't condone her uncle's illegal activities, she also wouldn't be the means of his arrest — he was her uncle. She loved him, and he had done everything for her.

Charles seemed to be realizing the same thing. He twitched his shoulders back under his crisp long-sleeved shirt, looked at her hair, her chin, her left ear. He cleared his throat. "I'm glad you're all right."

"I don't know anything about legal proceedings, but I have a feeling Heath isn't going to roll over for you."

Charles glanced at Elizabeth, playing with Daniel on the plush carpet of his wide living room, which was already decorated with some of the toys her mom had given to Daniel. "I'll probably hear from his attorney soon."

"A man who sends those three guys after his wife — not even coming himself — has a different agenda."

"We could be wrong. He could just be intense."

The word jumped out at the two of them.

"We'll see, I guess," she said.

He looked her in the eyes, his brilliant, clear blue gaze that she wanted to drown in. She couldn't look away.

"We'll see," he repeated after her.

But she knew he wasn't talking about Heath.

Chapter 15

He'd really thought it would be over with just a nasty-gram or two.

Charles stared at the lawyer sitting across from him. "You've got to be joking."

Heath's lawyer fit every expectation Charles had of the kind of man a wife-beater would hire—he looked like a snake oil salesman. His pencil-thin moustache, his pinstriped suit with a slightly nipped-in waist, even his flashy black-and-white patent leather shoes, which Charles expected him to prop up on the conference room table at any minute. The hand rubbing the edges of his stack of documents was covered in heavy gold rings with the occasional flash of diamond or ruby.

"The burden of proof is on you, Mr. Britton," Dan Augustine said. His voice was as oily as his slicked back hair. "The money Mr. Turnbull is holding is his own, and none of it belongs to Ms. St. Amant, unless you can prove otherwise."

"He is illegally holding on to her inheritance money."

"Mr. Turnbull has already attested to the fact that all that money was spent years ago on a vacation to Italy," Mr. Augustine said.

"And I have already asked you for documentation and receipts. I have yet to see them."

"We have thirty days to respond to your document request, and time's not up yet."

And he'd be unlikely to give Charles the information by the deadline. Typical stall tactic. It would force Charles to file a motion to compel, which would take up more time.

"My client is currently looking through his files," Augustine said, "but he has already mentioned that he may no longer have those receipts."

"And the bank statements?"

"Again, they may have been shredded."

Sure they were. The man's teeth were black with his lies.

"In the meantime, we're serving a deposition notice for your client." Mr. Augustine slid the envelope across the table.

Deposition? This was unusually early — and very aggressive — for Heath's lawyer to require Elizabeth to appear before them for questioning. "No, we haven't gotten the information we requested yet."

Mr. Augustine cocked an eyebrow. "That's not our problem."

Charles gave him a smirk. "*You* have thirty days to respond to our request for documents. *We* have the prerogative to object to your deposition notice."

Mr. Augustine sighed and raised his eyes to the ceiling. "We offer several times and dates as options. Don't be unreasonable." He gave Charles a nasty look. "We could file a motion to compel."

"Go right ahead. It'll take even more of your precious time. But my client is not appearing in your offices anytime soon. Unless, of course, you can get us the information we asked for and release her inheritance money to her."

"We're back to square one. We're not obligated to do anything for you until you can prove that money still exists."

"The money belongs to my client and Heath Turnbull is holding her funds illegally," Charles said through gritted teeth.

"Then prove it." Mr. Augustine stared him in the eye, his black gaze triumphant and condescending.

"It's not a matter of proof. It's a matter of illegality bordering on grand theft."

"If that's an accusation, Counselor, then back it up with something more than hot air." Mr. Augustine rose to his polished feet and straightened his black silk tie. "We're done here."

As his pinstriped back left the conference room, Charles's hands rose to strangle the air, imagining Mr. Augustine's scrawny neck instead.

"Was he for real?" Rick poked his head into the room. "He looked like he walked straight out of a Spaghetti Western."

"Dealing with him just added twenty billable hours to this pro bono case."

"Only twenty? He's probably betting his colleagues he can take forty."

"What colleagues? Men like him are Lone Rangers and they eat their mates."

Rick blinked. "Mixing your metaphors, dude."

"Heath is worth a hundred million. This would have been a drop in the bucket. Why won't he be a good boy and just roll over?" Charles groaned and buried his forehead in his hands.

"What made you think he would?"

"Because I researched him. He's never had a lawsuit against him from a big firm, so I should be as intimidating as Godzilla to Tokyo. But nooo, he has to send his slimy lawyer in here to tell me Elizabeth's money is gone and all his cash is held up in private equity investments so he can't give her a dime. And of course he won't sign the divorce papers."

"Come on. I know you didn't really think he'd sign those papers without a little bit of a bar fight first."

"But the terms are in his favor. Elizabeth refuses to take a dime from him. All she wants is her inheritance money back. She's letting him keep everything else. She doesn't even want child support because she's got an obscenely large trust fund set up for Daniel from some American royalty uncle somewhere."

"The last time I believed a financial report at face value was in 1993. He's probably up to his eyeballs in debt."

"He's not in debt. Since his lawyer hasn't yet given me the discovery, I had to dig for the info myself, but the man just paid off his Lamborghini."

Rick pouted. He was still paying off his Jaguar. "I'm still right. I know you probably only looked at his personal financials because you have a limited number of billable hours, but think about Heath's business. A small private equity firm? Doing well in this economy? That didn't scream, 'Only possible in the dream world of the Matrix' at you?"

"So you're saying I'm going to need to go digging in the trash."

"Like Luke and Leia in the trash compactor," Rick said cheerfully. "I'm surprised you haven't done it before now."

"Until today, I didn't think I needed to."

"And that is why you are not yet ready to face Darth Vader, young Skywalker."

Charles eyed him with irritation. "Let me guess. You watched the Sci-Fi channel all weekend and they ran both a Star Wars and a Matrix marathon."

"I also watched a Clint Eastwood marathon on A&E," Rick said.

Charles rose to his feet. "I'm going to leave before you start quoting Josey Wales."

"Oh, I forgot to tell you at the meeting this afternoon, Greer wants a report on the Imperion case—you know, the one where you actually have a paying client?"

His gut felt like it was a sinking stone in a pond of decaying muck. He had been neglecting the Imperion case in favor of Elizabeth's.

Rick read his expression. "Going that well, huh?"

"Peachy."

"Yeah, well, glad it's you and not me." He flashed a completely unsympathetic grin and left the conference room.

The truth was Charles had thought this would be easy. He had envisioned he might have to file a complaint and publicly embarrass Heath a little, but the case wouldn't take more than a few billable hours.

But he'd spent too much time on Elizabeth's case this week after being contacted by Heath's lawyer. Normally he'd spend those hours working on his non-pro bono cases, racking up billable hours to regular clients in his race for partner.

But now it looked like he would need to spend even more time on this. And with Heath's lawyer stonewalling him, coupled with what Tessa had told him about the attack on her a few days ago, it all pointed to something deeper and darker under the surface.

But what?

The only way to find out would be to dig.

The other option would be to let Heath see his wife and throw Elizabeth and her son to the dogs, and he wasn't about to do that.

He had always been strict about his billable hours, strict and honorable to his firm. They set a limit on the number of pro bono hours he could bill. Any other time he took was on his own dime, but if it took time away from the firm's other clients, he had to prioritize.

Except Elizabeth didn't have time. If men were really after her and Daniel, he needed to find out quickly what was going on to keep them safe. He needed to help her because it was the right thing to do.

He thought about Tessa, and how she had told Kenta she was responsible for Elizabeth and Daniel. Kenta had said he understood.

The problem was that Charles didn't think his firm would be the same way. And what would that mean for him and his dreams?

He needed to make partner. Just the thought of not achieving it caused a primeval twisting in his gut, an anguish deeper than logic or words. This drive came from a dark place inside him where he never went, a place forged with blood and pain.

He could do it. He could stay within his billable hours for Elizabeth's case, or if not, work even harder so that it didn't impact his other cases. He would impress Manchester Greer with his abilities. He could do it if he set his mind to it. He just needed to focus.

If he dug deep enough, he could do this. And if he had to, he would fuel himself with that dark place.

He would make his father's legacy work for him for a change.

••••

Tessa was so bored.

Elizabeth had played for hours with Daniel, and now the two of them had passed out in their bedroom, leaving Tessa with no one to guard and nothing to do. Maybe it was the adrenaline rush of dealing with Heath's men and now the letdown of not even having a dog to walk.

She exercised on Charles's exercise equipment and decided that if it had a kitchen, she'd be happy to live forever in his exercise room; it was that full of awesomeness. She fixed herself a protein shake with his cyborg-like blender that did everything except pour itself down her throat for her.

After a shower, she was reduced to circling Charles's living room, being nosy. Except he had exactly four pictures on his fireplace mantle and a dead fly on his windowsill. Not exactly high entertainment.

Vivian glanced up at her from where she sat on the couch knitting, with the Food Network on the large screen plasma TV so that she could see every pimple on Rachael Ray's nose — not that Rachael Ray had any, darn her. Vivian had been a bit disgruntled earlier when she wanted to make Tessa's shake for her, but had understood completely when Tessa confessed she wanted to play with the blender's 237 buttons and Porsche-size motor.

"It's these acrylic carpets," Vivian said.

"Excuse me?"

She gestured with her knitting needle to Tessa's feet. "You can wear a hole in that acrylic carpet with only a thousand paces. Now real wool carpets, you can pace over them until the cows come home and they won't show a single wear spot."

Guiltily, Tessa sat next to her on the sofa and watched Rachael add bacon, butter, cheese, and cream to some hot dip for bread, aka "The dip I spit out of my mouth as soon as the camera angle moves, because otherwise I'd fall dead with a coronary right in front of millions of viewers."

Vivian sighed, then said, "I am hereby taking pity on you."

"What?"

Vivian slid her needles out of the scarf she was knitting and proceeded to pull the yarn out, dismantling it.

"What are you doing? Did you make a mistake?"

"No." She pulled the crinkly yarn out in long sweeps of her arm. "You're going to do this."

"Pull the yarn out for you?"

"No, knit."

"Oh, no, I don't knit."

"Of course you don't. I'm going to teach you."

Tessa eyed the yarn, which had rich jewel tones. And suddenly, she had a flash of memory—red, pink, and gold origami paper, and Aunty Kayoko's fine dark eyes and slender hands.

She couldn't remember a woman teaching her anything the way Aunty Kayoko taught her to make paper cranes. She couldn't remember mattering to someone so much that they'd take the personal time.

When her grade school classmates had taunted her with her uncle's reputation and she got into fights—embarrassing Alicia with the number of times she got sent to the principal's office— her uncle had cared enough to send her to martial arts schools. When her birthday rolled around, her mom had cared enough to buy her a cake—although she always got white cake, mixing up Tessa's preference for chocolate and Alicia's preference for white. When she had earned enough from working for her uncle and had wanted to buy her own condo, Uncle Teruo had set her up with his own real estate agent and mortgage broker.

But as for sitting down with her, investing time and their physical presence ... only Aunty Kayoko had done that.

Until now.

"First, I'm going to teach you the knitted cast on," Vivian said.

An automatic assault rifle had felt more comfortable in her hands than these two sticks and length of string.

"You're strangling the yarn, darling," Vivian said. "I would almost think you had unresolved anger issues."

"I do," she said baldly as she tried to insert one needle into a loop that was so tight it was practically glued to the other needle.

"I'm sure you really do love your sister, deep down."

"I do get angry with Alicia, but my anger issues are with my father."

Vivian blinked. "Your father?"

"He left us when I was ten and Alicia was thirteen." There, she got the needle through the loop.

"Good, now throw the yarn over the needle ... You're rather calm and open for someone with anger issues."

"My counselor in prison said that the fact that I could talk about it without emotion meant I have deep-running emotion about it. That didn't quite make sense to me, but whatev—rats!" She lost the yarn off the tip of the needle.

"Well, I'd be angry if my daddy left me. And at ten, I'd be old enough to remember it and be hurt by it."

"I do remember. And I was hurt. But now ..." She paused as she maneuvered the needle tip back through the loop, pulling the yarn through as well. "... now, I kind of feel numb. There!"

"Good job." Vivian smiled and laid a hand on her knee.

Her touch, her smile, reminded Tessa of a favorite fuzzy brown sweater she used to have. Alicia hadn't liked the color and so she gave it to Tessa, and the soft, lofty yarn had felt like angel's wings against her skin. She'd worn that sweater until it had huge gaping holes.

"I don't think numb is always a bad thing," Vivian said. "It just means you're not yet ready to deal with things, and when you are, well, then it'll all come out. It might even be refreshing."

Tessa shrugged.

"And maybe it happened to you for a reason," Vivian said.

"My cellmate Evangeline told me that once, but I don't see what reason there could be."

"Don't you? Paisley just lost her father."

She couldn't believe she hadn't made the connection before. Maybe because she so rarely thought about Dad. "But what could I do for her?"

"What do you wish someone had done for you when your daddy left?"

She thought back to those days. She expected to feel a pang, but she really felt nothing. She remembered drifting around the house, no dad to laugh with, to wrestle with, to go hiking with. "I guess I wanted someone to spend time with me. So, I could spend time with Paisley, except what would we do? I don't know the first thing about doing hair or makeup or—heaven help us—talking about boys. I suppose I could teach her jiu-jitsu," she joked.

But Vivian said, "That's a good idea."

"Teach my niece mixed martial arts moves? Alicia would have a cow." But actually, knowing Paisley's adventurous nature, she might enjoy it.

Vivian shrugged. "You never know until you try."

"It might be fun, but ..." She shook her head. "Alicia and I already have such a rocky relationship. I think this would only make things worse. Things were never smooth between us even before Dad disappeared."

"Do you think your uncle had anything to do ... oh." Vivian

stopped, her cheeks pink. "There I go again. I promised Charles I wouldn't ask you awkward questions."

Tessa had been touched by how Charles made an effort to not let the conversation drift into murky waters, and to voluntarily shift it if it did. He respected her position as her uncle's niece. It was almost as if he were protecting her—a strange sensation, because she hadn't had many people in her life who protected her. She always took care of herself.

"I did ask my uncle once if he had anything to do with Dad's disappearance," Tessa said softly. "He said he hadn't been involved in it at all."

"And do you believe him?" Vivian asked shrewdly.

"I don't know. Considering his position, he may not have told me the truth."

And did she really want to know? Mom had always denied Dad had any involvement in the yakuza, but it seemed he left so quietly, quickly. She had woken up one morning and he was gone.

"If he hadn't left though, I don't know that my uncle and I would have gotten so close. Even before Dad left, Uncle Teruo sent me to martial arts schools because I was getting picked on at school, but after Dad was gone, Uncle got even more involved in my life."

And what would her life have been like, if that hadn't happened? She wouldn't have gone to prison. She wouldn't have met Elizabeth or Vivian either. Or Charles. A part of her squeezed uncomfortably at the thought of never meeting Charles.

"You have to believe that God had his hand over you despite everything that happened to you," Vivian said. "He wanted you to find him, even if that meant you'd only find him in prison. And don't you think that might have been worth it?"

Tessa remembered first accepting Christ. It was as if she'd

been color blind all her life and suddenly could see all the colors around her. She hadn't even realized the burden over her until it was suddenly lifted away. The one thing she had thought over and over was, why hadn't she done this before? Why had she wasted so much time?

"Yes," she said. "Yes, it was completely worth it."

"And now, you're protecting people like Elizabeth and Daniel," Vivian said. "I think that's a noble calling."

"Noble? With my past?"

"But your past is past. You can't help it. But you can walk forward in the newness of Christ—in newness of purpose, pleasing Christ."

Newness of purpose. She liked that. "I don't know for sure what my *purpose* is. I know I should try to control my temper with my sister and be nicer to my mom, and I haven't been doing that very well."

"Trust me, patience with family takes time, even for those of us who've been around longer than you," Vivian said dryly. "Your sister should meet my sister-in-law Coco ..."

At that moment, the doorbell rang, and Tessa sat up, her knitting falling to the floor. "Were you expecting anyone?"

Vivian shook her head. "Maybe it's FedEx?"

"Charles didn't tell us he was expecting a package."

If Tessa were a team of people about to storm a house, she'd have people covering the major exits, which would include the large French doors leading from the living room. The glass was covered by shades, so Tessa moved to the wall on one side of the door and cracked the shades. All she saw was Charles's side garden, an intimate grotto with a wooden bench and a trickling fountain, empty.

Tessa next moved to the front door and peeked out the peephole. She saw a young man, a few years younger than Charles, but with the same riot of curls — more bleached blond than golden brown — and that distinctive Roman nose.

She asked Vivian, "Does Charles have a brother?"

"Oh! Eddie!" Vivian beamed. "Naughty boy, he was supposed to call before coming over. I told him all about you."

"All?" But Tessa opened the door.

"Hi!" Eddie beamed, dimples flashing exactly like she would guess Charles's would if he ever cracked a real smile. "You're Tessa? I'm Eddie, Charles's brother. Hiya, Mama."

Tessa let him in and Vivian wrapped him in an embrace. He was several inches shorter than his brother, although stockier in build. She also realized she recognized him. "You were at OWA. You were the employee who dropped him."

"I didn't drop him, he fell," Eddie quickly said. Then he winked. "He probably wanted to meet you. I could have told him easier ways to meet a pretty girl than landing on her head."

Despite herself, she felt warmth creep up her neck at the compliment. If Charles had this kind of charm, she'd have fallen head over heels regardless of her uncle's disapproval.

"You don't look dangerous," Eddie said. "Charles said you knew 101 ways to maim me with a pen cap."

"I don't make a habit of maiming everyone I meet."

"So can you teach me some moves?" He did a Bruce Lee *Enter the Dragon* impression that nearly clocked her in the nose.

"Eddie, what would you need to know fighting moves for?" Vivian raised her eyebrows at him.

"You never know, Mama. I might need to fend off a jealous boyfriend."

Vivian's eyes narrowed. "If you're stealing boys' girlfriends, you deserve every beating you get."

Eddie laid a hand on his heart. "I'm hurt at your lack of sympathy, my own mother."

"I'm appalled at your lack of morals, you tomcat."

Eddie leaned close to Tessa. "I think I need to know some fighting moves to protect me from my own mother."

This bantering both amused and saddened her. Why couldn't she have this kind of friendly relationship with her own family? What was wrong with them? With her?

"I could always not feed you, you bottomless pit," Vivian said.

"You already tried to do me in last week with that spicy Thai curry. I thought my tongue would shrivel up in my throat."

Vivian turned her nose up at him. "Wimp."

Eddie threw an arm around Vivian and gave her a smacking kiss on the cheek. "There's my loving mama."

Vivian gave a grudging smile. "For that, I'll fix you a snack. How about I try this new recipe I found for Mexican-Irish-fusion spring rolls?"

Eddie gulped. "How about cheese grits instead? Tessa, have you had Mama's cheese grits?"

"I haven't had cheese grits ever."

Vivian's eyes widened and her mouth dropped open. "Ever?"

Tessa pointed a finger at her own chin. "Half-Japanese, remember? Father left when I was ten, raised by a Japanese mother and uncle? I can make a mean *sukiyaki*, but cheese grits … what are grits anyway?"

Vivian shook her head. "You poor deprived child. You should have told me sooner. You need good Southern cooking to make your life complete." She turned and headed to Charles's massive kitchen.

Eddie suddenly slammed into her with a quick bear hug.

"Thank you," he said, his voice breaking. "You have saved our family. I thought she'd never cook real food again."

"You mean she doesn't usually go for all this … challenging cuisine?"

"We rue the day we got her cable and she started watching the Food Network. One time she tried to copy the entire six courses she saw on *Iron Chef.* The secret ingredient was oysters." Eddie shuddered. "She even made the dessert — oyster ice cream."

Blech. "How … creative. But her Vietnamese *pho* noodles last night were pretty good."

"That's because she took a class in Vietnamese cooking at the local community center last week. Before that, she was working off of internet recipes and substituting fish sauce with ketchup."

"I'm not a gourmet cook, but even I know that's just wrong."

"You are now an honorary member of the Britton family," Eddie said. "Until you have eaten every Southern dish known to man."

"Or I get sick of you all," Tessa said with a smile.

"Impossible. And you will never want to disown us after you've had Mama's biscuits and bacon gravy."

She had never felt this way before — part of a family unit. A real family, not the dysfunctional jumble her own family was. A family that made her feel welcome and included. A family where she mattered.

And what would she do when this job was over? When she had said goodbye to Elizabeth and Daniel and no longer had any reason to speak to Charles or Vivian again?

The thought made her stomach freeze. She wrapped her arms around her middle.

Things would go back to the way they were, she supposed. She just wished that thought didn't seem so bleak.

Chapter 16

Heath Turnbull's private equity firm had saved Charles's delicate stomach.

Specifically, the research into Heath's firm saved Charles's stomach. Because if he hadn't had the excuse of needing to stay at work late to look over some documents and search the online databases, he would have had to come home to partake of Mama's glorious new creation, something that sounded like Maw Paw Dough Foo.

"You just made up that excuse about work, didn't you?" Eddie accused him on the phone around seven o'clock.

"You're at the house already?" Charles asked.

"I just walked in the door and the pepper in the air is making my eyes water."

"You're being a good son. Such a valiant sacrifice of your stomach lining in the name of familial love." Charles sat at his desk with a massive *mojado* burrito in a Styrofoam container in front of him. Another burrito sat on the corner, waiting for Rick. The smells of rich enchilada sauce and cheddar cheese wafted in the air.

"How did you know Mama's *mapo doufu* was going to be spicy?" Eddie demanded.

"I googled it quickly on the computer when Mama called me this afternoon. As soon as I saw Szechuan and chili sauce, I remembered I had to work late tonight, shucks."

"Man, I wish I'd done that." Eddie coughed. "She just added another gigantic red pepper to the wok."

"I hope you brought the antacids," Charles told him cheerfully. "I'm eating Mexican food tonight."

"You dog. *Mojado* burritos from the Burrito Factory?"

"Yup." He smacked his lips.

"You're sick and twisted. You're getting too much enjoyment out of my pain and suffering."

A knock at his office door and Rick walked in.

"Gotta go, Eddie."

"Can you call Mama and tell her you need my help tonight?" Eddie pleaded.

"You can't leave Tessa to face Mama's cooking alone."

There was a significant silence on the other end of the line.

"And Elizabeth and Daniel," Charles hastened to add.

"Mama made Daniel chicken nuggets. Maybe I can steal some. Oh!" Eddie's exclamation was higher pitched and positively beaming.

"What is it?"

"Mama made cannoli," Eddie gloated.

"What? Cannoli?"

"Charles is missing his cannoli," his brother sang.

For a moment, Charles's heart sank. He might have been willing to brave his mouth on fire for some cannoli ...

No. His tongue would be too numb with pain to even enjoy it. "Bye, Eddie." Charles hung up.

Rick had settled down in the chair across from Charles and grabbed the Styrofoam container with his burrito. He used his plastic fork to cut off a huge bite and stuffed it in his mouth. "Mmm."

"You act as if your wife doesn't feed you." But Charles took an equally large bite of his burrito. The melted cheese wrapped around the flour tortilla, melding with the perfectly seasoned Spanish rice, fajita-spiced beef strips, beans, and salsa.

"My wife hates Mexican food," Rick said. "I only get this stuff when you bribe me to work late."

"Is that why you're always helping Rodriguez with his extra work?"

"Two words: homemade tamales."

Charles set down his burrito container. "Brought your laptop with you?"

Rick groaned. "I can't eat first?"

"You can eat and do database searches at the same time."

Charles looked into Heath's bank account records, which he'd subpoenaed, and realized Heath really didn't have much in his joint account with Elizabeth. It looked like it was just enough for living expenses or the occasional shopping spree. He deposited money into the account every few months.

"Most of his money is tied up in private equity investments." Rick tapped at his laptop, his feet propped up on the edge of Charles's desk. "His money could be tied up for years."

"It doesn't look like he can get a hold of any large sum of money quickly."

"You'll need a hacker to find out about his offshore accounts or any accounts he hasn't disclosed. Because you can't tell me he doesn't have them." Rick peered at him over the top edge of his computer screen.

"I found something," Charles said as he searched through one of the comprehensive databases the firm subscribed to.

"One of the major investments of Heath's firm isn't doing well."

"If he's got a lot invested in that himself, this entire divorce might be about money after all."

"Yeah. Maybe he needs his wife's money, or he's already used it without her permission. Maybe he can't divorce her because he needs the money?"

"Wait, I found an article," Rick said. "There's a rumor Still-water Group is about to make a new deal. Lots of money."

"Enough to save the firm?"

"Ten times that."

"Who are the investors?"

"Doesn't say. Very hush-hush."

A sudden knock on the door made Charles look up from his computer. "Manchester."

The senior partner stood in the open doorway. "I'm glad you're still here, Charles." His eyes fell on Rick lounging in the chair.

Rick immediately dropped his feet from the edge of Charles's desk. "Sir."

"Rick's helping me with some research," Charles said.

Mr. Greer eyed the half-eaten burritos and shook his head. "You and your Mexican food, Rick."

"Can I do something for you, sir?" Charles said.

"I hear you're fighting Augustine's motion to compel for the St. Amant case." His gray brows had settled lower over his eyes.

"It's insane that they're issuing a deposition notice so early, and that they're trying to compel us to produce our client for testimony. We haven't even gotten the documents we asked for."

"I know Dan Augustine," Mr. Greer said. "Idiot. I guarantee you that if you agree to the deposition, Augustine will blow it. You'll learn more about his case from his questions than he'll learn from Ms. St. Amant's answers."

He hadn't seemed like an idiot when Charles spoke to him. "Still, I'd like more time to research the company before we let Augustine at my client."

"The company?" Mr. Greer said. "You mean Stillwater Group? Why?"

Charles would have thought it was obvious. "It's an asset and Turnbull is fighting us over money."

"That's just Augustine blowing smoke. Turnbull's firm is doing ..." He gave a slight shrug. "Okay."

He obviously knew about Heath's company, Stillwater Group, and since Mr. Greer typically worked with venture capitalists and private equity firms, Charles asked, "Have you ever worked with this firm before?"

Greer's face grew slack, and he paused before answering. "I think I worked with a few members of this company back when they worked for another private equity firm, now defunct. However, I haven't worked with Stillwater Group in particular."

"Have you heard the rumor about the new deal they're about to make?"

Mr. Greer frowned deeply. "Lots of rumors. No way to know what's true and what's not. But we can safely guess it's a very big deal going down—maybe already a done deal—with a lot of money at stake." Mr. Greer shook his head. "Turnbull's only a small fish at Stillwater. I highly doubt this has anything to do with his divorce."

Charles wasn't entirely sure. When he considered the lengths Heath was going to in order to get Elizabeth back—or maybe shut her up permanently—it seemed to point to something more at stake than Heath's marriage or pride. However, he couldn't prove anything concrete. Even Tessa mentioned that she couldn't prove anything definitive with the two tails. But being attacked near her mama's house by two of the same men who were with Heath seemed to show how serious this all was.

"This is all highly irregular—" Charles started to say, but Mr. Greer interrupted him.

"Yes, it's unusual to have a deposition this early, but the only one who would be losing out would be Augustine. When does he want to have it?"

"He's been leaving messages, wanting it done in the next week or two." The man's pushiness bordered on urgency. Typically, it took a month or two to schedule a deposition because of the lawyers' schedules.

"Then just schedule it," Mr. Greer said. "Get it over with. What'll happen is that Augustine will give something away in his own words—he always does."

"I'm a bit concerned for my client's safety. It's another reason I've been fighting the deposition."

"Safety?" Mr. Greer looked almost affronted. "What makes you say that?"

"Ms. St. Amant's bodyguard has said there's been some … suspicious activity around her client, and most of it points back to Mr. Turnbull."

"Well, if she has a bodyguard, then she should be perfectly safe at the deposition. However, I commend you for your caution."

Mr. Greer turned to go, but turned back at the doorway to say, "I must confess, I've been extraordinarily pleased with your work on this case, Charles. I'm sure Rick will agree with me that you display all the intelligent and diligent qualities of a partner of this law firm." He almost smiled.

Then he was gone.

For a moment, Charles was a scrawny seventh grader again,

playing on the school football team. The only reason he'd tried out was because his father had forced him to, saying he was too weak and needed toughening up.

He'd run out, looking over his shoulder, but not expecting the quarterback to throw to him ... and suddenly the ball had landed in his hands.

He'd frozen. He couldn't believe it. Not just that the quarterback had thrown him the ball, but that he'd actually caught it. Then he'd registered the screaming crowd—of twelve people— and he'd run as fast as he could toward the goal line. It was the first and only touchdown he ever made.

He felt like that now.

Rick looked stunned. "That was completely surreal. Was that really Manchester Greer? Not his evil twin brother?"

"I would think an evil twin brother would fire me, not compliment me."

"Compliment? *Compliment?* That was practically a promise you'll make partner if he has any say in the matter—and oh, since he's one of the firm's biggest rainmakers, he can practically pick the new partners himself. What did you do to get on his good side? Did you slip happy pills into his coffee or something?"

"Is it so impossible that I might actually be doing a good job?"

"Since your IQ is a half step above Bert and Ernie, yes."

"Let me guess. *Sesame Street* marathon this past weekend?"

Rick groaned. "Last night. My youngest was feeling nostalgic. I haven't been able to get 'Rubber Ducky' out of my head all day."

By tacit agreement, they went back to work, because even though Manchester Greer thought he didn't need to research

Stillwater Group, Charles didn't want to go in to the deposition unprepared.

The deposition nagged at him. Tessa wasn't going to like it. Most likely it would be at Augustine's law offices and they'd probably insist Tessa leave the room when they conducted the interview with Elizabeth.

Charles admitted he didn't like it either. It didn't seem safe for Elizabeth. But Mr. Greer had ordered him to agree to the deposition, and he was technically the lead lawyer on this case.

And after Mr. Greer dangled that carrot in front of Charles tonight, could he really afford not to do as he was told? He'd been at Pleiter & Woodhouse for almost eight years. If he didn't make partner soon, he never would. And he hadn't worked this hard, driven himself this hard, not to achieve his dream.

The memory of the football game flashed in front of him again. Despite his touchdown, his team lost the game. Even after the touchdown, all his dad said was, "I'll believe it's not a fluke if you can do it again."

But he hadn't.

The memory dragged at him and tangled his soul like a weighted fishing net. He shook it off and concentrated on his computer screen.

He was *this* close to a second touchdown. He wouldn't screw it up.

Chapter 17

"Eddie wants to do what?"

Tessa was surprised at the disbelief in Charles's voice. "Become a mixed martial arts fighter."

"Eddie? Happy-go-lucky Eddie?" Charles changed lanes as they drove toward Mr. Augustine's law offices off of Geary Ave. "You really think he has the . . . aggressiveness to do this?"

"The sport requires more than just aggressiveness." Tessa watched the cars around them. As far as she could tell, they hadn't been tailed. "It requires skill and quickness and strategy."

"Eddie has all that?"

"From what I've seen when Tessa is teaching him, Eddie's pretty good," Elizabeth said from the backseat.

"He's very quick and he has good form," Tessa said.

"He's not very tall," Charles said.

"In mixed martial arts, height doesn't guarantee a win," Tessa said. "A shorter man can take down a larger one and subdue him. It's skill, not size."

"Maybe I should learn mixed martial arts," Elizabeth mused. "I could learn to protect myself instead of relying on you and Tessa."

"Well, for today, stay close to me." Tessa turned to Charles. "I don't like this deposition thing at all. At *all*."

"Your objection is noted, Counselor," Charles said dryly. "For the hundredth time."

She knew she was like a dog with a bone, but she didn't care. "Elizabeth shouldn't be forced to do this when it puts her in danger."

"I tried explaining it to you but your eyes started crossing—"

"You need to take English lessons."

"You need a hearing aid."

"Children . . ." Elizabeth chided from the back seat.

Tessa shook her head. "You couldn't have simply refused? Fought him? Paid a fine or something?"

Charles opened his mouth, then closed it. "It's complicated," he said. "It's a legal procedure. It'll be over soon."

"And you're positive Heath won't be there?" Tessa asked, with a glance at Elizabeth in the backseat.

"It was the one thing I insisted on before agreeing to this deposition," Charles said. "If Heath is there, we're walking straight out."

At that moment, her cell phone rang. Tessa recognized the number—her sister. Should she answer? She was working. But what if it was important? Besides, she had an excuse to hang up right away. "Hello?"

"You're teaching your niece to punch people?!" Alicia demanded.

"It's mixed martial—"

"It's violence! All I asked you to do was watch Paisley for one afternoon while I went to that job interview, and I come home to find out you had her spar with a grown man. How do you know he wasn't a pervert?"

Tessa had a hard time following Alicia's strident voice because she was still trying to keep track of the cars around them. "Eddie's not a pervert. He's Charles's brother. He came to Charles's house for his normal mixed martial arts lesson and Paisley was the one who wanted to spar with him." Tessa actually thought Paisley had developed an instant crush on Eddie, but wisely refrained from telling Alicia that.

Paisley had taken to mixed martial arts with gusto. A tentative suggestion on Tessa's part had turned into a full hour of learning a few grappling moves and punches. She'd felt like a real aunt to her niece.

"You are not to teach her any more of that stuff," Alicia said.

Tessa could hear Paisley in the background protesting, "Aw, Mom, but it's fun!"

Tessa kept her eye on a red Hyundai behind them, but it turned into a parking garage. "Don't you want her to know how to take care of herself?" The years of being bullied and picked on in school because of her uncle's connections had been painful. Only after Tessa had bloodied a few noses had people left her alone. She didn't want Paisley to have to endure the same taunting and teasing.

"I don't want her to be getting into fights because her aunt makes her think she's invincible," Alicia said.

Tessa said, "Paisley wouldn't get into fights—"

In the background: "Mom, I wouldn't get into fights—"

"You got into plenty of fights," Alicia said to Tessa.

"That was different."

"No, it's not. And Paisley's my daughter, not yours."

What could she say to that, really? It was true. Tessa's dreams of bonding with her niece over an armbar or elbow chop dissipated.

"No more fighting lessons, Tessa," Alicia said, and slammed the phone down.

Well, that was that.

"That's too bad," Elizabeth said behind her. "Paisley was rather good too."

Tessa glanced sideways at Charles. What did he think about her teaching a thirteen-year-old mixed martial arts? Was he like Alicia, thinking it was too violent for her?

"I'd expect Paisley to be good at it," Charles said in a mild tone as he turned into a parking garage. "She's got her aunt's genes."

His words made a fluttering warmth blossom in her chest, but she had to damp it down in order to do her job. "Slow down, I want to see in between the cars."

Charles slowed the car to a crawl.

Tessa craned her neck and scanned between the parked cars. She wasn't about to allow Elizabeth to be attacked in an underground parking garage that didn't even have a security booth.

Charles maneuvered his Audi into a parking space and cut the engine.

Elizabeth fumbled with her seatbelt. "Get me out of this car. Charles, you couldn't stick a hamster in this back seat of yours."

"It's a sports car, not a minivan. And the alternative was Gramps."

Elizabeth sighed but stopped complaining. Tessa would have put her in the front seat, but in order to protect her, Tessa needed to be the first person out of the car, and she needed a clear view all around them as they drove.

This deposition worried her. According to Charles, it was just an interview with Elizabeth in front of a court reporter who would record the interview, but since Heath's lawyer had ordered it, they had the say in where it took place. Tessa didn't like not knowing the building and rooms they were walking into.

This dark parking garage was her first obstacle. She held a hand out to make Elizabeth stay in the car while she looked around. No one in sight. She hadn't seen anyone as they drove in either. The elevator up to the law offices was only a few short meters away.

"Let's hurry." She hustled Elizabeth from the tiny car, through the garage, and into the elevators as fast as she could.

"That's a creepy garage," Elizabeth whispered. "It reminds me of all those thriller movies where the hero gets jumped."

"I'd rather be vigilant than sorry." Tessa's bruise from the attack had faded until it was easy to disguise with makeup, which Elizabeth had helped her apply this morning. It was strange to have a girlfriend do up her face. Tessa had felt like she was fourteen again, except Elizabeth was a much nicer playmate than cranky Alicia.

"Elizabeth, you're sure you don't know anything about Heath's business?" Charles asked, probably for the twelfth time, as they rode the elevator to the lobby. "Do you have any idea—even a hunch about what they might want to talk to you about during this deposition?"

Elizabeth rolled her eyes. "I could tell them exactly how many dinner parties Heath gave last year since I was hostess for all of them, but I never spoke to any of his clients about anything but current events and pop culture. I mostly chatted with their wives."

"And you don't remember speaking to anyone in particular who wasn't in that stack of photos I had you look at?"

Elizabeth put her hands on her hips and glared at him. "Charles, do *you* remember every person you ever met?"

He looked sheepish and stopped interrogating her.

Getting them through the lobby was stressful with all the people walking around. Tessa prevented anyone from getting too close to Elizabeth, but it required some fancy footwork and a bit of aggressive manhandling and body blocking. Soon they were heading up to the fourteenth floor where Mr. Augustine's offices were.

The furniture was flashy and expensive—modern shapes, smooth leather. The receptionist languidly rose from her chair and told them, "Follow me."

The first thing Tessa noticed when they entered the conference room was the large windows. Also, the conference table wasn't in the middle of the room, but slightly off center. The court reporter's station had been set up to the side, and it was obvious where Elizabeth was supposed to sit, right beside a large window with a neutral background behind her and a video recorder set up in front of her. The court reporter entered only a few seconds after they did and headed to her station.

Tessa didn't like that window. The view was magnificent, showcasing several beautiful San Francisco buildings around them, but it was too open. It left Elizabeth too exposed.

Was this just her being uber-paranoid again? Did she really think someone would try to set up a sniper to shoot her client here, in this law office? And a sniper was a far cry from her teen paranoia of a world-wide virus breakout that would send the world into an apocalypse.

But this meeting had been set up. It had been known Elizabeth would be here in this room at this time. Tessa had to act on her instincts and her favorite mantra: Better safe than sorry.

A man with midnight black, slicked-back hair entered the room. His very presence seemed oily and made Tessa want to wipe her fingers on her dress pants.

Charles, standing beside her, tensed. Tessa could tell, even under his suit jacket, that every muscle in his shoulders, back, and arms were rock hard.

This must be Mr. Augustine.

"Sit right here, Ms. St. Amant," he said immediately, pointing to the seat in front of the window.

But Tessa grasped Elizabeth's wrist to stop her.

The court reporter's seat was in a spot not as exposed because of a weight-bearing wall that broke up the architecture of the large windows. Tessa had been about to order the woman to move, but she remembered Vivian and Elizabeth's easy charm. She tilted her head and gave a wide smile to the woman just like Elizabeth would have done. She said, "Would you mind terribly if we switch your chair with Elizabeth's? She's a bit sensitive to light." She even added a slight eyelash flutter.

The court reporter looked up at her, smiled in return, and said, "Why, sure."

"No," Mr. Augustine protested in a strangled voice.

Everyone looked at him. His Adam's apple was clearly visible over the top edge of his white collar and his tie looked a little tight.

"Why?" Elizabeth asked.

"We're videotaping this," he said. "We'd have to move the backdrop."

"It's not heavy. I can move it," Charles said.

"We need the light," Augustine insisted.

While he and Mr. Augustine wrangled, Tessa and the court reporter switched the seats and adjusted the backdrop, which really didn't need to be moved more than a foot. She admitted she felt a little silly, but she did her best to stay back from the large window and not appear in it for more than a second or two. After the chairs and backdrop were arranged, Tessa brought

Elizabeth forward from where she'd been standing near the door and settled her in her seat in the safer zone behind the weight-bearing wall, out of sight from either of the two large windows.

Mr. Augustine belatedly recognized Tessa's presence. "What are you doing here? You need to leave."

"I'm her bodyguard. I'm not going anywhere."

"She's not going anywhere," Charles growled. His tall figure next to her made her feel sheltered.

"This is a deposition—" Mr. Augustine started.

Charles cut in, "There's no rule that says she can't be here. I already mentioned to you that we fear for my client's safety. You assured me every precaution would be taken."

"We have, so she doesn't need to be here." Mr. Augustine's voice was a bit higher pitched than it had been earlier.

"Your job is to know the law"—*although not necessarily to uphold it*—"but my job is to think of every dangerous possibility," Tessa said. "What if you're an undercover assassin and you attack my client in the middle of the interview?"

Mr. Augustine choked, then tried to laugh. "That's absurd."

"Or what if there's a sniper just outside that window? I'd rather be here if he starts shooting."

Mr. Augustine turned white and pasty, and Tessa could almost smell the fear suddenly wafting from his armpits. He glanced nervously at the windows—no, specifically the right window, the one where Elizabeth's chair had been positioned.

The court reporter also looked out the window where she now sat, then stared hard at Mr. Augustine. She picked up her seat and moved closer to Elizabeth.

"So you see, I'm not going anywhere." Tessa thrust out her chest and tried to look intractable.

Mr. Augustine began to fidget. "Fine!" he spat out, and made his way to where Elizabeth and the court reporter sat. Except the only space now was directly in front of the window.

He sat some distance away from the glass and looked at Charles with a baleful eye. "Are you just going to stand there?"

Charles's mouth tightened but he grabbed a chair and set it next to Elizabeth.

It was one of the most boring things Tessa had ever sat in on. Sitting along the back wall away from both of the windows, she found her mind wandering and had to fight to stay awake at some parts.

Charles had an intent look on his face as he observed, a mixture of confusion and suspicion. Mr. Augustine asked some very stupid questions, even by Tessa's standards. He must have sounded asinine to Charles. It was almost as if the lawyer hadn't prepared for the interview.

"So you lived with your husband?"

"For five years."

"In your apartment?"

"Condo."

"With your son?"

It looked like it took a massive exertion of will for Elizabeth not to roll her eyes. "Yes, after he was born."

"Were you involved in any of his business?"

Tessa leaned forward and noticed Charles did too.

"Not at all," Elizabeth said.

"Did you meet any of his clients?"

"Yes, and their spouses."

"Did you talk about business?"

"No."

Mr. Augustine blinked. "Er . . . what did you talk about then?"

"Well, let's see. *American Idol, The Amazing Race, Real Housewives of Fiji* ..."

There was a Real Housewives of Fiji?

Elizabeth coughed. "May I please have some water?"

"I'll get it for you." Tessa got up, using the opportunity to stretch her legs. She poured a glass from a carafe on the corner of the conference table and walked to where Elizabeth was sitting to hand it to her.

She had to pass in front of one of the windows.

Her steps slowed. Her heartbeat slowed. The sound of Elizabeth's voice became muted and indistinguishable. She glanced out the window at the buildings across the street, loft apartments built over the storefronts. Easy to get into. Easy to set up position on a rooftop.

For a moment she stared out that window, wondering if she was being too daring to taunt him. Wondering if he were even out there.

Then she was handing Elizabeth her glass of water. Tessa was just being melodramatic ...

But she noticed Mr. Augustine let out a breath, as if he'd held it while she walked in front of the window. The pulse at his neck beat wildly. He saw her watching him and looked away quickly, pinching his lips together. His pencil moustache twitched.

Tessa passed the water glasses and carafe on her way back to her seat, and an imp on her shoulder prompted her to snag an empty glass.

As she sat, she leaned down and laid the glass on the floor. Then she sat up and tilted her chair on its back legs. With her boot heel, she nudged the glass directly under the chair leg.

She leaned back as far as she could without bonking her

head against the wall, then brought the chair down sharply on the glass.

Crack!

The noise was louder than she expected—probably because the glass was cheap and thin—and it rang through the conference room like ... well, like a gunshot.

Elizabeth started. So did the court reporter.

Mr. Augustine, however, yelped mid-sentence and jumped a few inches in his chair.

Then he bolted toward the conference room door, shrieking and covering his head with his notepad, and escaped the room.

The four of them looked at each other for a moment in the silence that followed his dramatic exit. Then Charles stood. "Well, he left his own deposition. We're done here."

The court reporter shrugged and started packing up.

"Do I have to come back?" Elizabeth asked.

"Nope," Charles said cheerfully. "He can only issue a deposition notice once per witness, unless we agree otherwise, and we're not going to do that."

They made their way through the building's lobby, which had less people milling around than when they arrived, and got into the elevator to head down to the parking garage.

Just before the doors closed, a hand shot through in the opening and the court reporter squeezed into the elevator. "Thanks." She smiled at them as she nipped into the elevator with a small satchel. Charles pushed the button for the garage again, and the doors slid shut.

Had Tessa been wrong about the sniper? Mr. Augustine's reaction to the broken glass had been a bit hysterical, but maybe he was just a very nervous personality. Now all her precautions had seemed overkill, her wariness bordering on psychotic.

It was as the elevator stopped in the parking garage level that she remembered that in Mr. Augustine's offices, the court reporter had arrived only a few seconds after them, but Tessa hadn't seen any cars enter the garage while they'd been down here. And they hadn't exactly dawdled on their way up.

At that moment, Charles turned to the court reporter with a confused look on his face. "Where's your equipment?"

The court reporter slammed her hand into his throat.

He doubled over in pain, choking.

The woman brought her other hand out of her suit jacket. Tessa used both hands to grab the woman's wrist, and she twisted a gun out of her grip. The woman jabbed a fist at Tessa, who deflected it, but the movement made her drop the gun. She heard the clatter somewhere on the elevator floor behind her.

Tessa couldn't get her other arm up fast enough to block another blow that caught her in the side of the head. Pain exploded in front of her eye, and she was dimly aware of Elizabeth's footsteps running out of the elevator. Tessa grabbed at the attacker but only caught empty air. She heard the court reporter running after Elizabeth.

Tessa blinked her eyes rapidly to clear the stars and ran after them. The woman had a wicked-looking switchblade in one hand, and it slashed downward at Elizabeth's back when Tessa was still just half a step too far away to stop her. Elizabeth gave a short squeal and stumbled and fell.

Tessa launched herself at the woman and they both crashed into the ground a few feet from Elizabeth. The sound of metal skittered across the concrete — the attacker had lost the knife.

The woman squirmed under Tessa's body and launched her lithe form after the knife. Tessa bore down with her weight and aimed a few punches to the woman's head. The hand reaching for the knife faltered, and Tessa stretched out with her longer reach to grab the switchblade.

For a moment that seemed like an hour, she gripped the knife in her hand and eyed the woman's exposed jugular vein right in front of her. Her arm wanted to descend and slice that vein, but something in her mind stopped her, made her hesitate. This hadn't happened in a long time—since before her arrest—but this moment was like the last time, and the time before that. The temptation to take a life, and the hesitation that stopped her.

Saved her.

Tessa threw the knife away—removed the temptation—but the court reporter took advantage of her hesitation and slammed an elbow back into Tessa's bruised eye.

Tessa felt the blow through her entire body. Worse, it made her slide off the woman's body.

The attacker rolled to her feet.

Still blind with pain, Tessa tried to force her unresponsive limbs to leverage herself up.

The assassin kicked her in the gut, but Tessa had expected it and had tightened her stomach muscles, muting some of the blow. But not enough. She couldn't get her diaphragm to move, to draw in air.

She had to get on her feet quickly. She couldn't stay here on the ground, vulnerable. She had to protect Elizabeth.

Suddenly, her palms resting on the concrete registered footsteps approaching only a second before Charles launched himself at the woman. He'd taken off his shoes—smart man—and took her unaware.

However, the attacker wasn't surprised for long. After his great running take down, Charles tried to pin her to the ground, but she aimed solid blows to his gut and liver area that made him grunt with pain. She kicked him off of her.

But as she rolled to her feet, headlights blinded them all as a car entered the parking garage and drove down their aisle. The car stopped and the driver opened the door to stand and shout at them, "What's going on?"

The court reporter took off running.

Elizabeth ran toward the car. "I'm on the phone with the police, but could you please call the building security? We were attacked." She sounded okay despite the slice the assassin had aimed at her.

"Tessa!" Charles was stumbling toward her.

She rose shakily to her feet. "Are you all right?"

"I'm fine. Are you—?"

She didn't give him a chance to finish. She grabbed the lapels of his suit jacket and pulled his head down to kiss him.

Chapter **18**

She felt like she was floating in a bathtub of sage soap bubbles, melded with that male musk that was distinctly Charles. His expensive cologne was only a spicy thread, like a scent that had wafted into a room from somewhere else in the house.

Charles's lips were warm and firm despite the fact she'd surprised him. After a second, his arm snaked around her waist and pulled her closer to him. He kissed her back, deeply, almost reverently, as if he'd been dreaming of this for a hundred years. His kiss was delicious and decadent, like the sweet, rich cannoli he'd ordered for them at that restaurant for lunch.

But he wasn't from her world and she'd never belong to his. She shouldn't do this. What was she doing?

She pulled away from him, reluctantly. But his arms wouldn't let go and still held her tight.

She met his eyes. It was like diving into a warm Jamaican sea. The current was his arms, tightening around her. He dipped his head to kiss her again ...

She grit her teeth, squeezed her eyes shut, and pushed away

from him until she had the safety of two feet of space between them.

Then she turned and walked away.

••••

She'd kissed him.

He hadn't wanted to let her go.

He was dumber than a duck.

He watched her walk toward Elizabeth and the other man in the car, when suddenly police lights colored the walls with red and blue. Two cars entered the parking garage and shone bright spotlights on the four of them.

As soon as the light landed on Tessa, the shouting started.

"Hands on your head! Get on the ground!"

The doors to the cars opened and the officers pulled out their weapons, aiming them at Tessa. They approached her slowly, shouting all the while.

The man in the car—their Good Samaritan—looked startled and confused. Elizabeth, on the other hand, jumped in front of Tessa and started screaming, "What are you doing?"

Charles approached them, also shouting. "You're making a mistake."

"Sir, stop right there," an officer ordered him.

"I'm an attorney, that's my client."

"Sir, stop right there. I won't tell you again."

Obeying the shouted orders from the police, Tessa was dropping to her knees slowly, her hands on her head. By now Charles was close enough to see that her eyebrows were raised in resigned disgust.

Elizabeth refused to move from in front of Tessa, increasing her decibels and her annoyance. "Stop being so ridiculous!" Finally, an officer grabbed her by the arm and pulled her aside like a recalcitrant child.

Tessa remained handcuffed in the backseat of a police cruiser for a good long while even after Elizabeth and Charles explained what had happened. All of Elizabeth's Southern charm had vanished, replaced by Louisiana ire.

"Are ya kiddin' me?" she kept repeating to the police officers, until one of them, an older man with grizzled hair, asked her if she'd like to join the yakuza in the backseat of the car.

Elizabeth shut up but glowered at them all.

They finally had to release Tessa when it was obvious they'd get in trouble if they didn't.

After the police reluctantly removed her handcuffs, she approached Charles where he stood next to Elizabeth, whose back was being dressed by a paramedic. The paramedics had already looked at Charles's bruised throat and probed his aching gut where the court reporter had punched him, but proclaimed him fine.

"Are you all right?" Tessa asked Elizabeth.

"No, I'm not all right," she snapped. "I'm so annoyed."

"She's fine," Charles told Tessa. "She might end up with a scar, but she doesn't need stitches from the cut."

Tessa nodded but didn't look at him.

He felt a bruise on his breastbone — maybe the attacker had hit him there too.

The paramedic finished and Elizabeth stood up from her seat on the vehicle's bumper. There was an awkward moment when the EMT looked at Tessa, fear in his eyes but feeling obligated to look at the bruise on her face.

She waved him off, and he couldn't hide his look of relief.

"You should get that looked at," Elizabeth objected. "You're getting bruises on top of bruises."

"At least give her some ice," Charles commanded the EMT, who gingerly offered the bags to Tessa before scurrying away.

She slapped the ice on her face and rolled the one eye he could see. "Poor kid probably would have a heart attack if he had to treat a yakuza."

"But you're not a yakuza," Elizabeth said hotly.

"But the only ones who care about that are yakuza," Tessa said. "He probably thinks I have twenty guns stashed in my ..." She looked down at her white silk blouse. "... somewhere."

"If you didn't inspire so much fear, Xena, the police might not have wanted to book you on sight," Charles said.

"They're probably not even going to look for that court reporter," Elizabeth groused. "I didn't get her name. Did you?"

"Kristin Miller, but who knows if that's her real name. They have to investigate Augustine because he'd have hired her through a court reporting service."

Tessa shook her head. "I wasn't paying attention to her name. I was worried about the windows and a possible sniper."

"Mr. Augustine obviously thought there was going to be a sniper," Elizabeth said, "so you probably prevented that from happening too."

"It's my fault," Charles said. "I should have realized something was up when the reporter got into the elevator at the same time. Most court reporters stay to pack up their equipment—they don't leave a deposition as early as that woman did." He shook his head. "I should have been paying attention."

Tessa shrugged. "You're not paid to be paranoid. I am." She turned to Elizabeth. "You know what this means, right? Heath wants you dead."

Elizabeth bit her lip.

"That woman went after you," Tessa continued. "Good thing she underestimated us or it might have been worse."

"Getting hit in the throat wasn't bad enough?" Charles protested.

She finally looked at him, but it was to give him an Are-ya-kiddin'-me? look like Elizabeth had given the officers. "She could have shoved her knife in your throat rather than her fist."

Hmm. Good point.

"But why does he want to kill me?" Elizabeth asked. "I don't pose any kind of threat to him or to his business."

"It could still be all about money," Tessa said. "If you die, he gets it all."

"But if Elizabeth is murdered, her bank accounts would be frozen until they could prove Heath had nothing to do with it," Charles said. "And everything Heath has done would be under a thorough investigation in the meantime. So why would he want to put himself under the microscope like that?"

"But we know Heath has to be involved," Tessa said. "This attack was planned with his lawyer."

"The deposition notice distracted me," Charles confessed. "I should have arranged to hire a P.I. to look into Heath's background, his business, everything. We need to find out why he would prefer Elizabeth dead."

But Tessa shook her head again. "This changes everything. We suspected her life was in danger before, but we know it for certain now. And I'd be stupid if I let them take pot shots at her."

Tessa took hold of Elizabeth's hands and looked her in the eye.

"I'm going to have to make you and Daniel disappear."

••••

They were throwing Elizabeth under the bus. And Charles had this one chance to prevent that.

The hostess looked up as he got off the elevator on the second floor of Lorianne's Café, and he said, "Greer?"

"Right this way—"

"No, I see him." Charles shouldered his way past the reception desk and sat down at a small table across from Manchester Greer.

"You have fifteen minutes before my meeting with the vice chair of the firm," Mr. Greer said, setting down his cup of coffee. "What did you need to speak to me about so urgently?"

"I asked for approval to hire a P.I. for the St. Amant case, but it was denied."

"Yes? So?"

"Why? My justification memo listed the police record of the attack on my client at the Augustine law offices."

"The attack was in the parking garage of a building that holds more than just the Augustine law offices. There's no evidence it was connected to her case at all."

"The attacker posed as the court reporter for the deposition."

"She could have chosen you randomly. All she had to do was walk into a law office, say, 'I'm the court reporter,' and they would have let her in, assuming she was there for whatever deposition they had going on."

"It's possible but a bit … far-fetched." Charles couldn't believe the words were falling from Manchester Greer's mouth.

"Look, Charles, this is a pro bono matter. You were cleared for fifty hours, and your hours are getting too high."

"I'm sorry. I won't write down the rest of my time so it doesn't cost the firm."

"That's not enough. I don't feel this case needs this out-of-pocket expense. Just drop the idea of hiring a P.I."

"Sir, our client is in danger—"

"You haven't definitively proven it."

Only a baby couldn't connect the dots in this case. "You asked me to take care of Elizabeth St. Amant. In order to do that, I need to hire a P.I.—"

"What you need to do is ensure you don't damage your chances of making partner."

The threat was like a slap in the face.

The murmur of other diners in the restaurant faded away, and Charles had a moment of piercing clarity. This had nothing to do with the expense to the firm or proving his client was in danger. He'd been right in thinking it didn't make sense for Heath to arrange the attacks on Elizabeth when it would only cause problems for him.

This wasn't about Heath getting his wife back, or getting revenge, or getting control of Elizabeth's money, or even covering something up. This was about Stillwater Group. Elizabeth somehow did know something about the company or maybe a deal going down. Or at least they thought she knew something.

Mr. Greer hadn't agreed to be lead on this case because of the prestigious St. Amant family. Manchester Greer, senior partner and expert in venture capitalists and private equity firms, knew exactly what was going on with Stillwater Group, and intended to hand Elizabeth St. Amant to them on a silver platter.

And if Charles didn't agree to play by his rules, he could kiss his career goodbye. He wouldn't just not make partner. Mr. Greer could have him blackballed from every law firm in San Francisco. He might even be able to have him disbarred on some trumped-up accusation.

Heath would be implicated in all the attacks on Elizabeth. The angry, abusive husband out to get revenge on the wife who had dared to leave him. No one would even suspect a spoiled Southern belle had been killed because she somehow knew something that would jeopardize a multibillion dollar corporation.

"Your time is up, Charles," Mr. Greer said. "Mark Tyndall will be arriving at any moment."

Charles rose slowly, unable to trust his voice.

"You've done a good job so far," Mr. Greer told him with steely gray eyes that would have pierced him if he hadn't already been numb with shocked realizations. "This little case will have a significant impact on your career at Pleiter & Woodhouse." *Don't forget the carrot I'm dangling in front of you: partnership.*

Charles walked out of the restaurant without speaking to anyone, without making eye contact. At the reception desk, he walked past Mr. Tyndall, the vice chair Mr. Greer was meeting, without even a nod.

He got off the elevator on the first floor and stepped out onto the street and just stood there.

All the thousands of hours he'd put in to making partner at this prestigious law firm, and now it all came down to a choice.

He should do what Mr. Greer said. It would keep his nose clean — or make it brown, depending on how he looked at it.

But it also wouldn't endanger Elizabeth because Tessa was already making arrangements to help them skip town with new identities. Elizabeth would have to find a new bodyguard in her new town because Tessa couldn't violate her parole, but if things ever improved enough where they could return, she had set up a system with him for how to contact them.

Except if Elizabeth really did know something significant,

it would never be safe. They might be on the run for the rest of their lives.

Was his making partner worth the unraveling of Elizabeth's entire life? He was ashamed it was even a struggle with him.

But it was. Because of that dark place inside him, forged with each blow from his daddy's fist. Partnership was the only place where he could finally escape that dark place forever.

But partnership wasn't worth the bruises on Elizabeth's face. And he realized it'd make him just like his daddy.

He shuddered violently.

He started walking back to the law offices. He had some time to think, to weigh his options, to list absolutely everything that was at stake. He couldn't hire a P.I., but he could do his own research on Stillwater Group, about Mr. Greer's possible interests in it, whatever they may be.

They weren't throwing Elizabeth under the bus. They were throwing Heath.

And Elizabeth was collateral damage.

Chapter **19**

Tessa sat outside the principal's office with a stripper sitting beside her, and thought about how much trouble she was in.

Not with the principal, but with her sister. She'd have preferred the principal.

She glanced at the closed door, behind which her niece and Brianna, a student here at Palo Relleno High, were closeted with the principal. The man's booming voice could be heard, although not his exact words, as he delivered a lecture to the two girls that had already lasted fifteen minutes. Brianna's mother, Layla the stripper, also looked at the door.

Tessa and Layla gave identical sighs.

What was more, Layla wasn't just any stripper; she was *the* stripper. The one with whom Paisley's father, Duane, had that first affair. Tessa didn't know how she was going to explain all this to Alicia when she got out of the all-day job interview she was in right now.

Paisley's girlfriend, another eighth grader named Maria, sat on Tessa's other side, swinging her legs since she was too short for the wooden bench. The swinging started getting wider and stronger, so Tessa told her, "Stop that."

"You're not my mom," Maria said with a pout.

"No, but she's coming soon to pick you up, and I can tell her lots of lovely things about your behavior today."

Maria stopped, but she threw her body back against the bench and crossed her arms. "What does it matter? The principal will tell her anyway."

"Except the principal doesn't know the real reason you and Paisley cut school and took light rail to this high school, does he?"

Maria frowned. "Paisley talks too much."

"You shouldn't have roped her into this in the first place." Tessa hadn't met Maria before today, but she could size the girl up pretty easily—a bit of a bully, forcing people to do things for her or with her. Paisley would have been happy to do something for her friend, one of the "cool crowd" at their junior high school.

"She wanted to go with me," Maria insisted. "She wanted to see what Troy looked like since I talked about him so much."

"So was he cheating on you after all?" Tessa asked lightly. She already suspected the answer.

A dark look settled on Maria's features. "Yes."

So much for the secret older boyfriend—now he was the secret older ex.

Maria jumped to her feet.

"Where are you going?" Tessa and Layla demanded at the same time.

Maria rolled her eyes. "In case you missed it the first time, neither of you are my mother."

"If you give me any more lip, honey, I'll give you a spanking to warm you up for your mother," Layla said firmly. "Sit down." For a stripper, Layla sounded remarkably like a soccer mom.

"I need to use the bathroom." Maria pointed to the girls' restroom door, which was in plain sight of the school office doors.

"Fine," Tessa and Layla said, again at the same time.

As Maria disappeared behind the swinging restroom door, Tessa gave Layla a look and found the woman looking at her too.

"I'm sorry Brianna attacked your niece," Layla said. "She said that she got so mad when she saw Paisley on the school grounds—"

"*Skulking* around on the school grounds," Tessa corrected. "She and Maria are not blameless in this."

Layla gave a small smile. "Well, Brianna recognized Paisley because of . . . you know."

"I guess Paisley recognized her too?"

"I'm not sure if Paisley even knew who Bri was. Bri is really upset at Duane, and so she wanted to take it out on Paisley."

"Uh . . . Why is she upset at Duane?" Had Duane promised to marry Layla or something and he broke his promise?

"I don't know if you know this, but Duane lied to me. He told me he wasn't married."

The news shocked her. "He did? I didn't know that." She'd assumed Layla had hooked up with Duane despite knowing about his marriage. She'd been thinking of Layla as the home-wrecker, when all the time it had been Duane just being himself.

"I broke up with Duane right after Paisley's mom found out about us. I was so mad at him and so hurt."

Alicia had mentioned that Duane had broken up with the stripper and was now with the whipped-cream-laden flight attendant. Tessa guessed Alicia hadn't known it was Layla who broke up with Duane, not the other way around.

"Brianna's pretty bitter at Duane because of that."

"I can understand that."

"I've never spoken to Paisley's mom—well, you know why—so I'm glad I got a chance to tell you."

No wonder Brianna had attacked Paisley when she saw her on her high school grounds. "Brianna must have thought Paisley was here to rub it in or something."

Layla shook her head. "I don't know what she was thinking. It's partly my fault. I've been so busy lately with work that I haven't spent as much time with her as I used to."

"Uh ... you work at a club?" Tessa used to know a lot of strippers—had been casual friends with some of them—so she hoped she was being sensitive in asking the question.

"No, I quit the club when I finally got my MBA."

Whoa.

"I used to do a lot of modeling in addition to working at the club, and I just bought co-ownership in a modeling agency."

"How's that going?"

"Better than I expected. We make a lot of money providing hostesses for parties—you know, women to make sure people's drinks are filled, to make small talk, to make sure people are having a good time, that kind of stuff. I used my connections from my years at the club to get some pretty high-end clients. I got some of my girlfriends out of the club to work for me instead. They get paid a lot better."

"I'm really happy for you. I mean it."

Layla gave her a sidelong look and a smile. "Thanks. You're nothing like I expected, you know. I thought you'd be ... tougher. You must be a marshmallow encased in steel."

Tessa laughed. "You're nothing like I expected either. You're so down to earth. How in the world did you fall for Duane?"

Layla groaned. "I have no idea."

Maria finally exited the bathroom at the same moment a flurry of activity sounded from the empty school hallway. Maria turned to look, and her face became white as chalk.

"Looks like Alicia and Maria's mom are here," Tessa said.

Layla's face tightened, but her straight back didn't waver when Alicia appeared in the doorway to the school office. Behind her in the hallway, Maria's mom had grabbed her daughter's arm and was delivering a rapid-fire lecture in Spanish.

Alicia's eyes alighted on both her ex-convict younger sister and the stripper who had caused her husband to ask for a divorce, sitting next to each other on a bench outside a principal's office. Tessa could tell that she was so shocked she wasn't sure who to blow up at first.

Paisley got that honor because at that moment, the door to the principal's office opened and Paisley and Brianna plodded out, both looking mutinous.

"What did you think you were doing?" Alicia and Layla both demanded of their daughters at the same time.

They spared each other a brief look—surprise from Alicia, an inscrutable one from Layla—before both ripping into their progeny.

Ah, motherhood.

••••

"You told me she wouldn't get into fights!" was the first thing Alicia said to Tessa after flaying Paisley's ear off with a tirade that had reduced her to pouty tears as she followed her mother to their car.

Tessa's first instinct was to angrily fire something back, but something made her hesitate. Maybe it was the surprisingly happy hour she'd spent this morning knitting and chatting with Vivian Britton, talking about dogs, since Vivian wanted one; cannoli, since Tessa wanted to learn how to make them; churches, both

Vivian's old one in Louisiana and Tessa's at Wings; and Tessa's efforts to help Elizabeth and Daniel skip town, currently stalled as she waited for paperwork to set up new identities for them. It all culminated with Vivian helping Tessa recover a lost stitch on the scarf she was making.

While salvaging the gigantic hole with some twisty thing she was doing with a crochet hook, Vivian had asked, "Are you going to give this scarf away or keep it?"

"I hadn't thought about it."

"You should give it to your sister."

"Alicia would accuse me of lying when I tell her I knitted it."

Vivian peered at her with blue eyes so much like her son's. "You are too used to the way things were."

"What?"

"With your sister. You keep forgetting you are a new creation in Christ. Your relationship with God changed, but relationships with other people should change too."

"Alicia will never change."

"Maybe not, but the way *you* relate to her should change regardless of what she does."

So now, instead of responding to Alicia's accusation, Tessa shut her mouth.

"And what happens?" Alicia continued. "She gets into a fight."

"It wasn't my fault," Paisley muffled from the back seat.

"You be quiet," Alicia told her as she fumbled in her purse for her car keys, the buckles on the purse clanking loudly. At first Tessa thought the buckles were loose, but then she realized they were clanking because Alicia's hands were shaking.

How strange. Tessa had always assumed Alicia—hard, selfish, and critical—was never distressed. But maybe Paisley getting in trouble and Layla's presence in the principal's office had shaken her up pretty badly. And as upset as she was, Tessa didn't want to imagine her battling rush-hour traffic. She'd probably try to run a Hummer off the road.

"Want me to drive you and Paisley home?" Tessa offered.

Tessa expected control-freak Alicia to say no, but the hand rummaging in her purse stilled. Her bottom lip trembled once—only once—before settling into her usual scowl. "Fine." She shoved her keys into Tessa's outstretched hand.

Tessa climbed into the driver's seat of Alicia's gold-colored SUV. She'd take public transportation to the school tomorrow to pick up Gramps—until then, she didn't think he'd be in any danger in the school parking lot.

They headed out, and Alicia said, "You should have known better than to teach her martial arts."

Again, Tessa had a retort on her lips ... but she let it slide. She'd seen how upset Alicia was. And while her sister was being her usual unreasonable self, she'd also gone through a lot today that wasn't her fault. For this one time, at least, Tessa could give up her right to defend herself, for Alicia's sake. And maybe for the sake of Tessa's sanity too.

Alicia continued, "How could you have thought violence wouldn't cause more violence ..."

Tessa managed to tune her out as she drove. Alicia punctuated her monologue with occasional insults of Tessa, which made her grit her teeth and then purposefully cut in front of some speeding driver.

But then Alicia started to talk about the job interview she'd had that day, which had been the reason the principal had called Tessa after leaving a message on Alicia's turned-off cell phone. And in between ranting about chauvinistic principle investigators and underfunded start-up companies with unreasonable expectations, Tessa heard Alicia's insecurity.

It was a foreign thing to witness. It made the atmosphere in the car seem surreal, like a world outside of the real world. Alicia insecure? But it made sense—after devoting years to helping Duane succeed in his business and raising his daughter, now she had to rebuild her life from nothing and stand on her own.

Alicia began to wind down, and Tessa suddenly wondered if Alicia's constant criticism and complaining was because she didn't know how else to release her anxiety. Maybe her attacks at Tessa weren't solely meant to attack her sister—maybe they were Alicia's first reaction to stress.

Not that Tessa appreciated being a punching bag. But it was something she could relate to, because when she was stressed, she went out for a jog, or she tried to find someone or something to hit.

Alicia hit ... Tessa.

The car became silent for several long minutes. Finally, Alicia said, "I hadn't seen her in a long time."

Layla.

"Did you know Duane told her he wasn't married?" Tessa asked.

Alicia started. "She's lying." But her protest was half-hearted.

"I don't think so. She said that's why she broke up with him."

"No, Duane broke up with her."

"Who'd you hear that from?"

Alicia didn't answer her.

"Brianna was crying," Paisley said softly from the back seat. "She said Daddy hurt her mom a lot."

As Tessa turned down Mom's street, her heartbeat leaped at

the sight of flashing blue and red. *Don't be silly, you're not the only criminal the San Jose Police Department is interested in.*

Except the cop cars were right in front of Mom's house.

Tessa's gut became heavier and queasier as she slowly pulled into Mom's driveway. There were two policemen ringing the doorbell, but of course by this time Mom would be at work as a hostess for Uncle Teruo's restaurant. The two policemen saw the SUV and immediately swarmed the car.

"What's going on?" Paisley asked.

"Turn off the engine and get out of the car," the cop ordered Tessa.

"Not again," Tessa said.

"What do you mean, 'again'?" Alicia demanded.

Tessa complied, but unlike when the police had held her at gunpoint in the parking garage, this time she felt like she was only wearing her Under Armour sports bra and Victoria's Secret boy shorts. And she realized it was because Charles wasn't here.

"What do they want?" Alicia shouted to her as she got out of the car.

"I don't know." But Tessa's words were drowned out by the sound of the men shuffling around her, grabbing her arms and handcuffing her.

"Tessa Lancaster, you're under arrest for the murder of Dan Augustine."

Chapter 20

Charles never thought he'd be doing this, never thought he'd ever agree to do this. Something twisted inside him when he went up to the desk at the San Francisco county jail where Tessa was being held and identified himself, "Charles Britton, here to visit Tessa Lancaster."

The woman whose case he'd researched, the woman whose crimes he knew more intimately than anyone else other than the federal prosecutors. The woman connected with a Japanese crime family.

Mama and Elizabeth had insisted. Naturally. They couldn't see how Tessa could have done what they said she did.

But had she really changed? Or had Charles only lulled himself into thinking that she had?

He entered the jail's visiting area and immediately saw her sitting at a table. Her eyes looked sunken into her face, but her back was straight and her expression stoic. She looked like a samurai warrior about to commit suicide by her sword.

Her eyes brightened when he sat down across from her, and for a moment, he wanted to forget what had happened and crush her in his arms.

But then she registered the expression on his face, and her jaw hardened. "Go ahead," she spat. "Just ask me."

"You know I'm not going to do that," he said, mindful of the people around them.

"You obviously think I killed him."

"The police showed you the crime photos?"

She gave him a dark smile. "Déjà vu, isn't that what you're thinking?"

Just like the murder she'd been arrested for seven years ago, Augustine had been stabbed several times, brutally and viciously. His throat and also his eyes had been slashed in the exact same way that Laura Starling's had.

He tried to erase the image from his mind. "They said they arrested you because your fingerprints were on a carafe in the conference room."

"That and the fact that my uncle is Teruo Ota," she said acidly. "They must have been salivating."

"I explained about the deposition and the glass of water you poured for Elizabeth."

"They said he was killed yesterday. I was home with Elizabeth, Daniel, and your mom." Her hands had been resting on the table, but she suddenly pressed the palms flat. "Does Elizabeth have to come down here to testify that I was with her?"

"No."

"Would they use this arrest to try to get to her?"

He realized he hadn't considered that. "I'll make sure she won't be exposed to any danger."

She gave him a hard look. "Like you protected her by agreeing to that deposition?"

Acid bubbled in his gut. "What do you mean by that?"

"I was against the deposition from the start, but you insisted.

You're the one who put her in danger."

"Excuse me, who has the law degree here? You don't know anything about the legal ramifications." Except she was right. He could have continued to fight the motion to compel. Even if he'd been sanctioned for failing to comply, it would have been just a fine.

But at the time, he had obeyed the lead attorney on this case. He hadn't known that Mr. Greer had probably arranged to hire that assassin and had needed Elizabeth to make the deposition so she could die. Charles had just been a stooge. And that thought made his anger burn against himself.

Tessa's eyes sparked. "Oh, so it's those 'legal ramifications' that made you put on hold the hiring of the private investigator?"

"It's complicated—"

"Everything is complicated with you," she accused him. "What's the problem?"

He tried to rein in his temper and remain calm and detached, but the woman was trying to make everything so simplistic. As if he didn't know what was at stake here. "The firm didn't approve the expense right now, but—"

"Forget the firm. Forget the expense!"

"You can say that because it's not you forking over the cash."

"Can't you just go against your boss or something?"

As if it was just like baking a cake. "Again, you're not the one deliberately disobeying the senior partner who's the lead on this case."

"So what? You'd get reprimanded or something—"

"It's not just a reprimand. It's my entire career. It's throwing away the seven years I've worked to make partner." His voice was rising but he didn't care. Didn't she understand? Was she trying to make him destroy his entire life?

Tessa threw up her hands. "Your career? Why is making partner so important to you?"

"Because my father said I couldn't do it!" he roared.

It had come out of nowhere. He hadn't even been thinking about his daddy, about his childhood, but the words bubbled up with his rage and frustration.

How many times had his daddy beat him and said he would never amount to anything? But every step of his career, from the moment he'd escaped his home, he'd heard his father's voice telling him, "You can't do this," and felt the blows of his fists. And Charles used that pain and those words to spur him to work harder to prove his father wrong.

Was that what making partner was all about for him? Because of Daddy?

Boy, a shrink would have a field day with him.

Tessa had backed down, her eyes large and solemn. As if she understood that dark place inside that he fought to escape from.

Some people on nearby tables glanced their way.

Get yourself together, Charles. He cleared his throat. "Right now, we need to find a way to get you out of this situation. If you didn't kill Mr. Augustine—"

"*If* I didn't kill him? I didn't do it."

This murder, at least.

But in the past few weeks, he'd been starting to doubt whether she'd killed Laura Starling. Or maybe that was what he wanted to believe?

There was a beat of silence. Charles knew he needed to say something, but his mind could only see pictures of Laura Starling and Dan Augustine's bodies.

"Charles." Tessa's voice was low and firm. "I've never killed anyone. Ever."

He had a flash of memory—the parking garage, fighting to get his breath back and struggling through the blinding pain in his throat, stumbling toward the figures of Tessa and the court reporter on the ground. He'd seen Tessa grab the switchblade, swing it wide ... and stop. Stare at the woman's throat. And toss the blade away.

His panicked brain had remarked on it at the time, but he'd forgotten about it in everything that had happened after that. But he remembered it now.

All those years ago, he'd been so sure she'd killed Laura Starling. She'd been arrested right next to the garbage dump where the knife was found, although the knife had been wiped clean, as had her hands. The other evidence had been circumstantial and she'd plea-bargained for manslaughter.

And he'd seen other murders that her cousin Ichiro had been suspected of, but never convicted. He'd researched her reputation on the streets, which had been fearsome—people knew she was violent and ruthless. She accomplished whatever her uncle wanted.

Was it possible she had never killed anyone despite the people who said she could break a man's arm without blinking an eye?

Tessa turned her face away from him. "You don't have to believe me."

But he wanted to. He just ... everything in his head was a muddle right now. Mr. Greer, Elizabeth, Tessa ...

She took a deep breath, then turned back to look at him again. Her face was cool, controlled. "Can you get me out of here? I have to get back to helping Elizabeth and Daniel get out of town."

"I'll make sure the detectives talk to Mama and Elizabeth about your alibi."

She nodded, looked at her hands. Then she said, "I'm sorry I accused you of not protecting Elizabeth. I know you were only doing your job."

He didn't answer her. There was an ugly place in his soul he didn't want to look at right at this moment. He rose to his feet.

"Well, you know where I am," she said.

"I'll get you out of here," he replied before he headed to the door.

But her last look at him clearly said she didn't believe him.

••••

When he came home, he was attacked by a frantic Mama and the smell of cannoli shells frying.

"Is she okay?"

"She's fine, Mama." It wasn't the first time Tessa had been arrested. "Where's Elizabeth?"

"Daniel was distraught that Tessa didn't come home, so she's with him in the room right now." Mama bustled into the kitchen, and Charles followed.

She started filling one of the cooled cannoli shells with sweet cream. "Poor Tessa. People assume she's guilty of all kinds of things when she hasn't done any of it."

Charles sat on a wooden stool at the island in his kitchen. "She has done some of those things, Mama."

"But she doesn't do them anymore." Mama handed Charles a filled cannoli.

He took a bite, but it turned glue-like in his mouth. He set the cannoli down, struggling to swallow. "Mama, she said she never killed anyone, ever."

"She told me that her aunt Kayoko protected her from the

more 'serious' jobs," Mama said. "I thought that might be what she meant by 'serious.'"

"But I was involved in her murder trial."

Mama spread her hands wide. "Charles, I don't know what you want to know. She has never talked about it with me. I don't know if the memory pains her, or if she doesn't want to implicate herself..."

Or maybe she didn't want to implicate someone else. One person the police interviewed had mentioned a rumor that Laura Starling had been girlfriend to Fred Ota, Tessa's cousin. Teruo's son. But there had been nothing more substantial than that third-hand remark.

"Seven years ago, I believed she killed Laura Starling. I believed she killed other people before her arrest. I recommended to the judge ..." He had recommended to the judge that her sentence be extended beyond the maximum in the plea deal. Had Charles been horribly wrong?

But she'd gone into that trial knowing nothing good would come of it, knowing she'd be sent to prison. She hadn't even tried to plead innocent, nor had she ever insisted on her innocence at any point.

"Even if she did kill that woman," Mama said, "she's not the same person today."

"Because she says she's a Christian?"

"She hasn't done anything to prove she isn't."

He knew that, and a part of him wanted to believe wholeheartedly in her, but he just didn't trust himself anymore. Not where she was concerned.

"She's like Paul," Mama said.

"Paul who?"

"Paul the Apostle."

And he suddenly understood where she was going.

"He had been a pretty violent Pharisee himself, and then he found Jesus. Just like Tessa. And people were afraid of him, just like Tessa."

Charles remembered the story from Sunday school. Back then, he'd felt sorry for poor Paul, trying to overcome a dark past.

Since when had he become so self-righteous, so hypocritical?

"Jesus gave Paul a second chance," Mama said. "So I figured I should too."

Did it really matter if Tessa had killed Laura Starling or not? He didn't have the right to stand in judgment over her seven years after the fact. He didn't have the right to determine what God had or hadn't done in Tessa's heart.

Charles was such a Pharisee.

What did God think of *him*?

"Mama, I thought of Daddy today."

She bent her head, staring at her two broken fingers.

"I think … because of him, I've become just like him."

"Oh, Charles, no—"

"I've done everything I can to escape him, to be who he didn't want me to be. But I don't like who I've become."

He'd allowed the deposition that put Elizabeth's life in danger. He'd accepted without a whimper when Mr. Greer refused the application to hire a P.I. He hadn't wanted to jeopardize his career—a house of cards built on a boy's pain, a father's malice.

"Mama, even when I try to escape him, I can't."

"You won't escape him," she whispered. "I can't, even though I finally divorced him." She raised a hand to her lips, closed her eyes for a moment. "But you can rise above him."

"I don't know how to do that."

"When you took on Elizabeth's case. When you offered your home to her and Daniel." She looked at him then, and her blue eyes smiled at him. "You're not just your daddy's son. You're God's son too. And he raised a fine man."

And there was the answer to it all, to the thicket his brain had been since walking away from Mr. Greer at the restaurant. He was his Father's son. Rather than being driven by one father, he had forgotten the One whose approval he should have been seeking.

He knew exactly what he needed to do. He'd hire the P.I. About his career—he didn't want to think about it. He'd just keep walking, with Jesus beside him.

"I'm not just God's son." He walked over to her, wrapped an arm around her, and kissed her on the cheek. "I'm my mama's son. And she raised a fine man."

She colored. "You're just trying to charm me into letting you lick the bowl."

"You mean you weren't going to already?"

"Go eat your cannoli before it gets soggy."

He sat back down on the stool. "Mama, Tessa said she was with you and Elizabeth when Mr. Augustine was murdered?"

Mama shivered at the word, but she nodded. "We were here together all day yesterday."

"I need to establish Tessa's alibi so the police will release her."

"We didn't leave the house. Poor Daniel's getting a little stir crazy, but Tessa didn't want to risk allowing them to go out. She said she almost had everything ready for them to leave." Mama sighed. "I don't want them to go."

"It's not safe for them here."

"I know, it's just ..." She paused in the middle of filling another cannoli. "The UPS man."

"Huh?"

"I ordered a propane torch—"

"*What?*"

"It's a special one for making crème brulee. Anyway, the UPS man delivered it yesterday. Since Tessa answered the door, she signed for it."

UPS had online tracking. "You ordered it online? Do you have the shipping notification email?"

"The what?"

Charles headed to the living room, where the laptop that Mama used was sitting on the desk in the corner. He logged into her mail program—he should get her to change her password, it was too easy to hack—and searched through her email. There, the notice from the online cooking supply website with the UPS tracking number.

Delivered yesterday at 4:47 p.m. Augustine had been seen alive by his secretary at 4:15 p.m., and found dead by the same secretary at 5:45 p.m. Without traffic, from Charles's house it would take a minimum of forty-five minutes to get to Augustine's law office, but 5:00 was peak rush hour. Even if Tessa had hopped into a car and driven to the law office right after signing for the package, she wouldn't have had enough time to kill him before his secretary found him.

Tessa really hadn't done it. Someone was trying to set her up.

And they'd be after Charles next.

Chapter **21**

The look her mom gave her could have spoiled the fish at
the sushi bar.

"So," Mom said as Tessa entered Oyasumi, her uncle's
Japanese restaurant, "you're out of jail."

Tessa approached the reception desk. "They dropped the
charges. I had an alibi."

Charles made sure the police interviewed the UPS driver
who delivered the package to Vivian, and the driver easily identified Tessa as the one who signed for the package. Further proof
was her scrawl on the electronic signature pad.

Praise God for Vivian's love of flammable cooking supplies
that required signature delivery.

Another hostess at the restaurant passed by carrying a tray of
drinks. She paused to titter at Mom in Japanese, "So this is your
younger daughter, Ayumi? How happy you must be that she's
out of jail." She minced off.

Tessa's head flamed as she glared at the woman's back.
"What's that about?"

"Do you know how embarrassing it is for me every time you
get arrested?" Mom scowled.

"It's only happened twice."

"Most mothers would prefer it never happened."

She had a point.

Mom frowned at the seating chart. "Maybe it'll be better after this job is over and you move out."

She hadn't expected it, but a pang twisted in her chest at her mom's words. Tessa originally had been firing her engine in anticipation of getting out of her Close-Encounters-of-the-Mom-Kind living situation, but for the past few months she'd begun to wonder if Mom didn't want her to move after all. And Tessa had begun to think it wasn't so bad to live at home. To maybe show her mom that this "religion thing" had made a difference in her daughter.

She must have misunderstood her mother. Mom's *tatami zori* slippers were itching to give Tessa the boot.

"What do you need?" Mom said. "One of my best customers has a reservation tonight and should be arriving soon." As a hostess at this particular Japanese restaurant, Mom was required to take care of any and all needs for the customers, usually being prompt with drink refills or getting cigarettes or cigars for them. Certain customers preferred her over the other hostesses — Mom could be charming when she wanted — and she always made sure she was available. It kept the customers coming back to Uncle's restaurant.

"I have a problem — "

"I don't want to hear about it." Mom stuck up a hand, her voice strident. "I don't want to know."

"No, not that kind of problem. It doesn't involve anything *illegal.*"

Mom raised an eyebrow. "Considering what you used to do, you can't blame me for assuming."

"It's for Elizabeth."

Her face lit up. "Oh. She is so sweet. Is she doing okay? So what do you need for her?" she asked.

Really? Tessa knew there was a huge difference between jailbird daughter and charming Southern belle, but *really?* "Charles hired a private investigator to poke into Elizabeth's husband's company, to find out what they're up to. He hasn't come up with much yet, but he found out that the company is giving a cocktail party in a few days. It's for investors. I want to try to get hired as one of the wait staff. Do you know how I can do that? How do those kinds of functions hire people?"

Before her eyes, Mom transformed. Suddenly she wasn't the petulant mother Tessa was used to—she was a restaurant professional, talking about her field of expertise. Her shoulders settled back, her chin went up confidently, and she seemed almost pleased to be giving advice. "Most of the time, one-time events like that hire wait staff through a staffing agency, or maybe through an event planning agency, or through the bartending service they hire for serving drinks. The agency decides who's hired for the night—or sometimes they're scrambling to find enough people to staff the event."

"So I need to find out what agency was contracted for the party. How do I do that?"

"You should talk to the Mouse."

"Who?"

Mom gestured toward the back of the restaurant with her head. "You know, Nez."

"The manager? He'd know about the cocktail party?"

"His brother owns a large event planning agency in San Jose, but they have lots of connections with other smaller agencies in

San Francisco. Sometimes he even gets hired for San Francisco events."

"So he might have been hired by Stillwater Group?"

"Maybe, although that's a bit of a long shot. But he would definitely know or be able to find out who was hired."

"Great. Is he back there now?"

Wariness tightened the edges of Mom's eyes. "Yes, but ..." She glanced toward the area near the back of the restaurant that was filled with small rooms, separated by *shoji* sliding doors, which was often used for private parties. There was a raucous one tonight using the largest room. "Your cousin Fred is here."

A greasy fist squeezed Tessa's innards. "In that room?" While it was walled off with *shoji* doors, one door stood wide open so that the customers could flag down waitresses and hostesses. And Tessa would have to pass that door in order to get to the offices in the back.

"I'll run interference for you," said her mother, the 49ers football fan. "Let's go."

They made their way toward the back of the restaurant. Mom went straight to the open *shoji* door, pulling it slightly shut with one hand as she stood in the doorway. "Fred," she shouted above the rowdy laughter, "did you get that order of *gyoza* you ordered?"

While Mom blocked the view from the doorway, Tessa darted past, her head down in case Fred could see above her diminutive mother's head. She didn't breathe again until she was well past the room and heading toward the door marked "Employees only" in the alcove in the far corner.

But then the men's restroom door opened just as she was breezing past it, and Yuuto, one of Fred's friends, caught sight of her.

"Tessa!" he said loudly, possibly to deliberately call Fred's attention to her, but more likely because he was drunker than a skunk. "Long time no see!"

There was a slight lull in the banter in the room, then a hand shoved her mom out of the way and Fred's head appeared. "Tessa!" If possible, he was drunker than Yuuto. "Come here to see your mommy?" His slur against Mom went no further, because his father wouldn't stand for disrespect of his aunt.

Cousins, on the other hand, were fair game. Especially ones he hated because he was indebted to them.

She considered playing the submissive Japanese girl card and trying to slink away when he was done having fun with her, but more likely any un-Tessa-like responses would make him suspicious, and he'd try to figure out what she really needed here so he could do his best to prevent her.

The problem was that her normal response to Fred was to compare him to creatures that had higher IQs than he did, like slugs. Which only made him mad and bullish.

"Come to try to work here now?" he taunted. "No other place will hire you?"

"Of course," Tessa said, chin lowered and eyes blazing. "Why wouldn't they hire me if this is the only restaurant that'll stand the likes of you?"

Fred's face darkened. "You watch it. I own this restaurant."

His friends, sensing the insult to their banana leader, left their places at the table and crowded around Fred in the open doorway. Several climbed out of the room to stand a few feet from Tessa. Some recognized her from seven years ago—some were men she had often worked with when her uncle asked her to do jobs for him—but they didn't hesitate in puffing out their chests and donning fierce expressions.

No one insulted yakuza. Especially not a woman.

Except she wasn't just any woman. "Your daddy owns it, not you."

A triumphant leer slid onto Fred's face. "I own it now. Signed the papers today." Hence the celebration with his friends.

"Oh, did Freddy-weddy finally learn to count to ten?" The insult shot out of her mouth before she could think. While she hadn't wanted to be un-Tessa, she also hadn't intended to insult him so condescendingly in front of his friends, requiring Fred to get ugly or lose face.

And Fred never willingly lost face.

His lips drew back, exposing his teeth. "You apologize or your mom loses her job."

Tessa glanced to her mom's white face, visible a few feet from the crowd of men. "Your father would skin you alive."

"Do you see my father here?" He gestured wildly. Fred couldn't think wisely or long-term if he tried. What mattered to him was the now — Tessa's insult, the chance to show his power by either forcing his cousin to grovel or humiliating Tessa's mom in front of her customers and the rest of the restaurant staff.

This was the enraged pride that had killed Laura Starling.

Seven years ago — no, three years ago, she wouldn't have cared. Would have rather fought them all and broken every rib in her body, along with some of theirs, than be submissive. Would have cared more about her own pride and reputation with the yakuza than the embarrassment and problems caused to her mom.

But she wasn't that Tessa anymore.

With her jaw so tight that it ground a headache behind her eyes, she said, "I'm sorry, Fred."

He gave a toothy smile that Hannibal Lector would have sported with pride. "What? What's that?"

"I'm sorry, Fred."

Fred hooted, as did some of his friends. Some of the men she knew and had worked with stared at her with disgust in their eyes. Behind them all, Mom had her fist to her mouth. Her eyes implored Tessa, and she shook her head. Tessa didn't know what she meant by that head-shake—no, don't apologize, or no, don't make trouble.

"Now, Tessa, I want you to dance like a geisha." Fred struck a girly pose and almost fell over, but recovered his balance by grabbing onto an equally drunk friend.

Every muscle in Tessa's body swelled and tightened, as if they were going to explode off of her bones in her rage. She bit her tongue to prevent the retort that rose to her lips, and she tasted salty blood in her mouth.

"Go on. Dance like a geisha." Fred brayed like a donkey.

Several of the men had evil gleams in their eyes. Tessa, who used to win bar fights, reduced to being Fred's puppet. Tessa, the woman whose fighting abilities were tolerated only because she was the boss's niece, now in the proper role of a subservient Japanese woman.

"Dance, geisha, dance." Fred strode to her and grabbed her arm. "Dance—"

Tessa drew back her fist to punch him in the nose, but a low voice cut through the jeers and laughter.

"Fred, that's enough."

From the front of the restaurant, Kenta approached them, striding through the crowd of men. Some immediately swept back in deference. Others who were dumb like Fred—or simply too sloshed to know better—paused in their catcalling and stared at him with glazed eyes.

"Fred, let go of her."

Fred pouted, but dropped his hand from Tessa's arm. Fred might be his father's son, but Kenta was his father's captain. "It's my restaurant and she dared to insult—"

"Then she can apologize."

There was a pause, then someone said grudgingly, "She did."

"Then she can leave." Kenta looked at her then, with eyes hard and jaw tight.

"I wanted to say hello to Nez," she said.

"Come back another time."

"No, she can't," Fred snapped. "If she does, she'll be thrown out." He leaned close to glare at her. "I'll be happy to do the throwing."

Tessa said softly, so no one else could hear, "Touch me again, and I'll flip you over my hip and dislocate your shoulder."

Fred sneered at her, but he couldn't hide the widening of his eyes and the creases of fear at their corners.

"Tessa." Kenta leveled her a commanding gaze. *Leave, now.*

No, they were not her family. She should never have assumed they were. She was a girl. They were yakuza.

"Ayumi-san, take the rest of the night off," Kenta told her mom.

Mom's eyes were wide and her breathing rapid, but she nodded and followed Tessa.

"Hope you find a job," Fred called after her. "The only job you'll find is as a call girl." He laughed, and a few of his friends laughed with him.

Call girl.

What had Layla said to her? Some businesses used her models as hostesses for high-end parties.

Once outside the restaurant, Mom stood rock still, like a Buddha, but with a turbulent expression rather than one of transcendent peace.

"I'm sorry, Mom," Tessa said.

"Why'd you have to antagonize him?" she said in an anguished voice.

"If I had been submissive from the start, would he have been any less difficult?"

"Maybe. I don't know." Mom turned away from her, her chin trembling, but not crying. She never cried, not even the morning Dad had left. In that way, she resembled her stoic brother.

"Are you okay? Do you want me to drive you home?"

"I can drive," she said snippily. Then in a different voice, "I can try to talk to Nez tomorrow—"

"No, don't get in trouble, Mom."

"I won't." A bullish expression settled over her face. "You know what? I won't stand for that kind of disrespect to my face. I'm not his mother, but Teruo is my brother. If Fred thought his father wouldn't hear about this ..."

"Uncle Teruo would only say I shouldn't have insulted his only son."

"His only son should never have insulted his aunt," she snapped.

Tessa was a bit surprised Mom was angry enough to demand action from Uncle Teruo, but it meant Fred would wish he had the brains of a cricket rather than the considerable amount less that he had. And after Uncle made Fred regret ever mixing thinking with drinking, Fred would take his anger, frustration, and humiliation out on Tessa rather than Mom, so that would be okay.

"I'm sorry I couldn't help you," Mom said.

"Actually, Mom, you did help."

"I did?"

"Or rather … Fred did."

"He did?" Mom shrugged. "At least the pile of rotting fish brains is good for something."

Tessa smiled at her Mom. "Nice."

Mom preened. "I learned from the best."

Chapter **22**

Tessa hadn't thought it was remotely possible for her to achieve cleavage, but Layla had worked a miracle. Of course, it had required an entire roll of duct tape to do it.

She looked at her reflection in the mirror. "You gave me two entire cup sizes."

"Turn around, let me see the backside," Layla said.

The dark blue gown wasn't spandex-tight, but boy did it hug every curve, every roll of fat, every panty line. Somehow, though, seeing sexy-Tessa staring back at herself in the mirror unlocked something inside her. She felt like ... a paper crane being unfolded.

"This is not me."

"Don't hunch your shoulders. Normally you have such good posture—don't let this dress tell you how to walk. Lengthen your neck. Bring your chest up."

"If I do, it'll fall out of this dress."

"It can't," Elizabeth said. "It's duct-taped to the dress."

Vivian bustled into the bedroom. "Here are those shoes ... Oh, my."

"'Oh, my, you look like a million bucks' or 'Oh, my, you're a spaghetti strap short of indecent'?" Tessa asked.

Vivian smiled. "Oh, my, you look like Cinderella at the ball."

Cinderella. No one had ever called her that. More unfolding occurred inside her. "Well, I'll look for my prince among the rich men at that party."

"Actually, as a hostess, you have to make sure all the guests are having a good time, which, at a function like this, means chatting up the wives so the men can do business," Layla said.

"This is such a strange world," Tessa said.

"But you had a lot of money," Elizabeth said.

"I earned it by working for my uncle, but my friends were all the same; they weren't high-class like this. And then when I became a Christian, I gave it all away because I didn't want to live on blood money. So I really don't know how to act around rich women."

"Yes you do," Elizabeth said. "Rich, poor—women are women. Why, some of the women at that shelter were from low-income families, but they were more classy than some of the rich women I met when acting as Heath's hostess for his parties."

Tessa smoothed the blue satin over her hip. "Hopefully I can be classy too."

Vivian appeared behind her in the mirror. "Just tell yourself you're a butterfly. Butterflies are classy just by being themselves."

Tessa didn't want to leave the bedroom, surrounded by these women. They'd seen her at her most vulnerable—as they'd stripped off her clothes in preparation for getting her into the gown, Tessa had had the strange sensation that they were removing old, yucky armor that had served its purpose, but was no longer needed. And she'd emerged with this gorgeous gown on, but somehow she didn't feel as defenseless as she thought she would. Nor did she feel awkward covered in feminine accoutrements.

She was a girly-girl after all. And yet, she was still Tessa.

Take *that*, Alicia.

Actually, Tessa didn't care much for the wig. She scratched at the blonde curls.

Layla slapped at her hand. "Stop that, it'll come off and it took us forever to get it on just right."

"It itches."

"It's supposed to itch. The alternative is being recognized."

Tessa's facial features weren't distinctive or striking, but the assassin in the parking garage had seen her, and Heath's three thugs had seen her. Layla had thought about dying Tessa's hair, but worried they wouldn't be able to make it look natural as opposed to bleached, and she said that a bad dye job was more noticeable than a wig.

They all trooped downstairs, Layla giving Tessa tips on being a good hostess.

"Communication is key," she said. "Be pleasant, ask people what refreshments they want and get it for them, chat with people to make them feel comfortable. If you're smart, you'll hover close to the right people and overhear things."

"I wouldn't know what I'm hearing if I heard anything," Tessa grumbled.

"Well, if you think you might be overhearing something important, turn on the digital tape recorder we taped down your dress. Just don't look like you're groping yourself when you turn it on."

Eddie was in the living room, sprawled out on a chair, one leg swinging over the armrest. "I still don't understand why I can't be the one to come with you," he complained to the ceiling. "Why does Charles get to be all James Bond?"

"Because Charles would understand what people are talking about when they start discussing business," Charles said as he entered the front foyer from the kitchen, "whereas you would..." And then he caught sight of Tessa.

She'd never seen a man's jaw drop like that. His eyes widened and also darkened, making his gaze seem more intense. Her heart beat strongly and rapidly at her throat.

Charles really was James Bond. His black tuxedo made him seem taller, leaner. He'd dyed his golden brown curls into a dark, rich mahogany and he'd cut them shorter than normal, making him look older. She wanted to cup his face with her hands, feel the planes of his cheekbones, the strong cords of his neck, and draw his head down to kiss her.

"Oh my garlic," Eddie exclaimed, only now seeing Tessa at the base of the stairs. He leaped to his feet. "Now I'm really mad I can't go."

"Doesn't she look wonderful?" Vivian gushed. "I wanted to strap a little pistol to her thigh under her dress—I thought that would be so sexy—but Tessa says she can't be in possession of a firearm."

"That's what happens when you get released from prison," Tessa said.

Charles cleared his throat. It sounded like it had closed up a little. "Thanks, Layla, for calling around for us and finding out which agency was hired to send hostesses for this party."

"Oh, it was nothing. Desiree owed me a favor, and it wasn't any skin off her back to send you two as opposed to two of her other employees."

"I hope we do a good job. I don't want it to reflect badly on her," Tessa said.

"I hope we'll be able to overhear something important," Charles said. "We're risking a lot by going tonight."

"I'm more than happy to risk it instead of you," Eddie said quickly.

"Eddie—" Charles started, but Tessa interrupted.

"Eddie, since I have to go with Charles to protect him, I need you to stay to protect Elizabeth. Charles doesn't know mixed martial arts so he'd be hopeless."

Charles looked like he might protest that so Tessa jabbed at his shin with her heel, and he shut his mouth.

Eddie looked thoughtful. "I see your point."

"Be vigilant tonight," Tessa told him. "If Stillwater Group somehow found out we were going to this party and leaving Elizabeth here, they might attack." Okay, well, it was a *remote* possibility, but the anticipation of danger sent Eddie into military alertness.

"I better go find Charles's shotgun, and grab all the knives from the kitchen and stockpile them in the panic room."

"I still need to cook tonight," Vivian protested.

"And batteries for the flashlights in case they cut power. And charge cell phones too ..."

"Gee, thanks a *lot*," Elizabeth groused to Tessa in an aside.

"Would you rather listen to him complain all night about how he ought to have gone?"

Elizabeth sighed. "You're right, you're right."

"We'd better go," Charles said.

On the way, Tessa settled back into the cool leather seats of the Audi and asked, "Are we really going to be able to overhear the conversations we want to overhear while playing host and hostess?"

"I hope so. Most people will be there *for* business, so they'll be *talking* business. My only concern is that sometimes women like to get chatty about other things."

"They might be looking for a little entertainment, sport."

He glowered. "We'll see who's laughing at the end of the night when you're trying to keep some young punk's hands off of you."

"I could say the same of you and some older woman." She laughed.

He'd implied she looked beautiful, desirable. Before, that might have elicited a guffaw of disbelief or the heat of embarrassment, but tonight she actually was beautiful and desirable. She was a paper crane folded right-side-out.

Charles left the car with the hotel valet and the two of them went inside. They found the ballroom where the party was being held and immediately found the event manager.

Tessa and Charles were two of twelve hosts and hostesses hired for the party, and as soon as the event manager saw them, he sized up Charles and said, "You're nice and tall. I'm assigning you to Velma."

"Who?"

"Velma Crackenburg, one of the firm's biggest clients. You'll stick beside her all night and make sure she gets whatever she wants." He turned to include Tessa. "The guests haven't arrived yet, so just hang out here so you can welcome them when they come."

A few minutes later, one of the first guests to arrive was a woman with steel-gray hair pulled into a topknot ponytail, wearing a strapless purple sequined gown. She looked at least seventy-five years old. The events manager stepped up to her, pulling Charles with him. Tessa held back near the ballroom doors but watched them.

"How nice to see you, Ms. Crackenburg," the event manager said to the woman.

She struck a pose worthy of Marilyn Monroe and gave Charles a vertical stare. "And who is this?" Her voice was a low, husky, smoker's voice.

"Charles Carmichael," he said in a tight voice.

"You're one of the hunkiest hosts I've seen in a while." She turned to the event manager. "Good job this time, Danny."

Tessa swallowed a giggle.

"Er, thank you, Ms. Crackenburg." The look the event manager gave to Charles looked part relieved and part pitying. "Charles will take care of anything you need."

"Oh, I'm sure he will," Velma drawled.

Charles offered her his arm and she sashayed next to him into the ballroom.

Tessa looked about for any other guests arriving, and spotted a medium height young man in a tux approaching. He was perhaps in his early twenties, with a square jaw and short brown hair, but the young woman walking next to him wasn't dressed up—instead, she wore jeans and a leather jacket.

And in a second, Tessa recognized Karissa and her housemate, Josh, whom she'd met the time she picked Karissa up to take her to the church at Wings.

"Tessa?" Karissa stopped and stared. "What are you doing here?"

"I was hired as a hostess for this party," she said.

"What happened to Elizabeth?"

"She's okay. I'm still her bodyguard."

Karissa's eyes widened. "Oh my gosh, you're going undercover. How cool! Your life is just so exciting." She turned to whap Josh on the shoulder. "You lucky bum! You get to go all Jason Bourne tonight."

"Hey, watch the tux," Josh said.

"Like you don't have three of them." Karissa told Tessa, "Josh goes to these types of things all the time. He's an old pro."

"This is a party for pretty wealthy investors, but you rent a room in Karissa's house ...?" Tessa asked.

"Oh, Josh is loaded," Karissa said. "He actually owns the house."

"I used to have a condo, but it was kind of boring," Josh said. "The house is more fun. There's four of us, and we sit up late and hang out all the time."

"You have to tell me all about your night when you get back," Karissa said.

"Where are you going?" Tessa asked.

"There's a Chris Tomlin concert tonight at the Filmore— I've never seen him before—and a bunch of friends are going."

Josh sighed. "I'd rather go to the Chris Tomlin concert, but my folks are in Portugal right now and I promised my dad I'd talk to his investor friend at this party tonight."

Tessa smiled. "I'll make sure you have a fun evening, even without Chris Tomlin."

Karissa groaned. "I'm so jealous. I had so much fun driving your car back to Wings. I spotted *all three* tails! It was so neat!"

Tessa winced. She hoped she didn't encourage Le-Femme-Nikita-Karissa to get into too much trouble.

"Whoa, will we get tailed tonight?" Josh asked, his eyes sparkling.

"That would be a no, tiger."

"Aw."

"Gotta run or I'll be late. See ya!" Karissa hurried off.

"Don't worry." Tessa threaded her hand through Josh's tux-edoed arm. "I might need you to help me."

"Do what? Break down a door? Beat up a bodyguard?"

"I might need you to distract a woman named Velma Crack-enburg ..."

Chapter 23

He must have James Bond on the brain tonight, but Velma Crackenburg reminded Charles of a Bond woman who didn't realize she was forty years past her seduction days.

She was also *not* interested in any of the business being discussed at the party.

Plenty of men wanted to talk to her, however.

"Velma." A rotund man who looked like a giant black-and-white blueberry approached them soon after they entered the ballroom. "How lovely to see you here." He leaned in to kiss her on the cheek.

"Hello, Jeffrey," she responded in a bored voice. She scrubbed at her cheek with a hand bejeweled with diamonds. "You really must shave that moustache. It scratches."

Poor Jeffrey's square hand went to his neatly trimmed black moustache. "And here I grew it out just for you."

Velma leaned close to him and leered. "Now if you wanted to get a room, I can show you where I'd like to be scratched—"

"Ahem. Velma, did you get my message about that dotcom investment opportunity?"

"They bombed, Jeffrey, and I won't put a dime into another one."

"No, this one is very promising—"

"Scoot off, Jeffrey." Velma snuggled up to Charles, wrapping him in her Chanel No. 5 scent until he almost gagged. "I'm in more interesting company than yours."

She was approached by a Randolf, a Jeremiah, and a Jackson, all of whom were not-so-subtly propositioned by Velma, and all of whom quickly changed the subject. Velma didn't bother to introduce Charles, and told all of them to "scoot off," some even before they mentioned various lucrative investment opportunities they had for her.

Velma stroked Charles's arm, her diamond bracelets clanking together. "You're so quiet, Charles. Not intimidated by me, are you?"

"No, ma'am."

"Call me Velma."

His throat was tight. "Is there anything I can get for you? More champagne?"

"I love to open men's eyes to new experiences." She parted fire-engine-red lips in a wide smile.

Charles was rescued by a man who strode through the crowd with confidence that was completely real and not faked—it oozed out of him, forming a red carpet on the floor in front of his Italian leather shoes.

Albert Richmond III, one of Heath's business partners in Stillwater Group. Charles wasn't going to let this opportunity go to waste. He whispered to Velma, "I heard they had a problem with a recent special investment."

Velma gave him a long look under smoky eyelashes and murmured, "You have unseen depths, Charles."

"Velma." The man held out a hand, which Velma grasped with less reluctance than she had with the other men. "It was good of you to come."

"Of course, Albert. Lovely party you've put together." She gave Charles a quick glance, then said, "I hear you have a very special investment strategy in the works."

"We always have special strategies. We make our investors money because we keep abreast of innovative developments."

"I also heard you might have had a bit of a sticky problem with your most recent development."

Richmond gave her a tight, condescending smile. "Don't pay attention to rumors, Velma. It's just business as usual."

But she wasn't about to be put off. "Don't give me that, Albert, I know when you're lying. What investment was it that had a problem?"

Richmond didn't quite roll his eyes, but his dark orbs hovered on the ceiling of his eyelids for a moment before he replied, "The problem was resolved."

"Sure it was. You need to work on that poker face, Albert. What investment was it?"

"I'm afraid it was for a fund that has already closed."

"Nothing is closed. Why didn't you tell me about it?"

"The investor came to us and requested an exclusive fund."

"Exclusive?" Her penciled brows reached for her widow's peak, highlighting her swaths of purple eye shadow. "Since when am I excluded from an investment at this firm?"

"You've enjoyed plenty of exclusive investments yourself."

Velma pouted. "But I don't like being left out. Make this one inclusive for me, Albert. I want in."

His eyebrows flattened. "The money has already changed hands, I'm afraid."

Even Velma wasn't willful enough to breach his implacable-ness. "Fine, fine. But at least tell me who the investor is."

"You know I can't do that."

Rather than being rebuked, Velma curled the edges of her mouth upward, and her lashes heavy with mascara became slits. "Fine. Don't tell me. I love a good challenge."

Richmond's lips pressed against each other for a brief moment, then relaxed into an indulgent smile. "I promise you first crack at our next investment opportunity. I'll call on you next week."

"You'd better, Albert." From under all the makeup, the low-cut purple dress, and the girlish hair style, the shrewd business-woman shone out. Velma Crackenburg was a woman who knew her power lay in her money, which she'd multiplied by her own wise choices.

"Go ahead and do your obligatory mingling, Albert," Velma commanded.

Gracious despite her tone, Richmond inclined his head. "Enjoy yourself, Velma."

"Well." Velma pressed against Charles. "You decided to speak like a good puppy."

"I, er, thought you wanted me to ... Velma."

"So I did. And you did me a favor. Now I have a mystery to solve." Her sharp nose swept from side to side, twitching with anticipation. "Who would know about the new investor, hmm? Oh, there's Bernard Hathaway. Let's try him." She sliced through the crowd of people, and Charles followed in her wake.

He couldn't have planned this better if he'd tried. And thank goodness, now Velma had something to occupy her time rather than trying to get Charles to agree to a little extracurricular activity.

"Bernard," Velma barked as she approached the man, who was white and furry like a rabbit. Thick white brows almost touched his curly white hairline as he saw her.

"Uh ... Velma. Hello." He tried to smile, but only his two large front teeth showed, framed by bloodless lips.

"Have you heard anything about Stillwater's problem investment? The one for the exclusive fund that had a spot of trouble?"

"Trouble? I don't like trouble. Especially investments in trouble," he chattered.

"You are as dumb as a dodo. Have you heard anything about it?"

"Uh ... no."

Velma eyed him narrowly. "But you know who has." It wasn't a question.

Bernard tugged at his bow tie. "Al," he gulped.

"Albert? You dimwit, of course he'd know—"

"No, Aloisius."

Velma puckered her red lips. "Oh. You're absolutely right. Thanks, Bernard."

She sailed off again, but after circling the ballroom, slamming down two flutes of champagne, and bumping heedlessly into four of the couples dancing in the center of the room, she hadn't found her prey.

While on their circuit, Charles caught sight of Heath, and his heart sprinted from his chest up to his throat. They were going to pass right next to him ...

But the man's eyes passed over Charles without recognition. *Thank you, God.* While Charles had seen plenty of pictures of Heath, he hadn't spoken to him, just to his now former attorney, and while Heath could have looked up Charles's picture on the firm's website, he obviously hadn't.

But from that moment, he kept a vigilant eye for anyone who might recognize him. He hoped Manchester Greer wasn't here.

Velma stopped a man who'd come in full Scottish regalia. "Chip, have you seen Aloisius?"

"He hasn't arrived yet."

"Darn." She turned to Charles. "Let's dance!"

From the ballroom dancing lessons his mama had made him take, Charles thought that only the woman's hand rested on his shoulder, while he held her other hand and touched the curve of her waist. Velma, however, slathered herself all over him.

But it was while he was dancing that he saw Tessa.

She stood next to a middling-height young man who looked like a kid playing dress-up with his daddy's tuxedo. He shouldn't even be drinking, he was so young. Charles scowled.

"There's Aloisius," Velma said. "Finally. Oh, but he's walking up to Albert. Darn. I'll have to wait until they're done talking."

As the music started drawing to a close, Charles spotted a tall, slender man who looked a bit like a carrot shaking hands in greeting with Albert Richmond. Their expressions were grave, and Charles knew in his gut they were intending to talk about their latest investment and the private investor.

He had to talk to them.

With a few aggressive swirls and by bumping into a few couples, he swept Velma halfway across the ballroom to end the dance close to where Tessa and the Kid were standing. Over Velma's head, he met Tessa's eyes and silently pleaded for help. He had to get Velma off his hands so he could try to overhear that conversation.

"My goodness, Velma Crackenburg? Is that you?" Tessa came forward with hands outstretched. Her dress borrowed from Layla looked as expensive as any other dress here at the party, and there was no way Velma would know she was a hired hostess and not an invited investor. Strangely, the Kid didn't seem to mind her abandoning him to talk to Velma and Charles.

Velma's lips pursed. "Do I know you?" Her tone would have flattened a meringue.

"I'm sorry, we've never formally met, I'm Theresa Blume. I'm, um ..." Tessa's eyes strayed to Charles, standing behind Velma, for some help.

He mouthed, "Albert."

" ... I'm a friend of Albert," Tessa finished.

"Oh?" Velma didn't snub Tessa, but her wary expression didn't drop either.

There was a canny light in Tessa's eyes as they traveled from Velma's topknot to the strapless dress. "The reason I want to talk to you is because ..." She leaned in closer to Velma. "My br— uncle Josh over there really wants to dance with you, but he was too shy to ask himself."

Velma eyed the Kid. "Your uncle?"

"Oh, don't let his looks fool you, he's like, forty. Can I introduce you?"

Velma lifted a hand to smooth her steely topknot ponytail. "Of course."

"Velma Crackenburg, my *uncle* Joshua Cathcart."

Josh's eyes bugged out a little, but he smiled at Velma. "Pleased to meet you."

"Uncle Josh, Velma said she'd be happy to dance with you."

Josh looked like he'd swallowed a spider. "Uh ... great."

Charles touched Velma's elbow and drew her aside slightly to ask, "Would it be all right if I danced with Tes—Theresa while you're dancing with Josh? He'll bring you back to her afterward so I won't lose you."

While he was speaking, Charles heard a protesting whisper, "But she's old enough to be my grandm—aaaaah!" Josh grimaced in pain. Glancing down, Charles noted Tessa's heel squarely stabbing the toe of Josh's dress shoe.

Thankfully, Velma's hearing probably wasn't what it used to be. She smiled at Josh's youthful face. "Certainly."

Josh led Velma out onto the dance floor and Charles drew Tessa into his arms.

He felt as if a circle had been completed.

She looked up at him, her brown eyes glowing with flecks of emerald. He thought she might have stopped breathing—he knew he did. He'd wanted to hold her since the moment he saw her at the foot of his stairs, regal in that blue gown. She hadn't been transformed so much as enhanced—before, her confidence had been in her walk and her athletic grace, but tonight, it shone from every pore, in the tilt of her chin, the sway of her hips, the toss of her head. His hand at her waist tightened.

"The music's started," she murmured, and he realized they'd been standing still at the edge of the dancing area. He swept her into the slow, sensuous tango.

"Needed rescuing, did you?" she asked.

He frowned at her. "You obviously didn't."

"Oh, Josh already knows who we are and what we're doing here."

"You told him?"

She explained about Karissa.

"Do you trust him?"

"Josh assured me that they could torture him like Wesley in *The Princess Bride*, but they'd never get him to tell what he knows about us."

"Oh. That completely reassures me." Then again, she'd gained an ally tonight with the Kid over there, whereas Charles had spent most of his time trying to keep Ms. Crackhead from throwing him over her shoulder and hoofing it out of the ballroom.

"He's been very helpful," Tessa said. "I've been listening to conversations all night, and Josh explained some of the investment stuff I didn't understand, but we haven't heard anything that might explain why they're after Elizabeth."

"We might find out now, if we're lucky." Charles glanced toward the back wall of the ballroom where Aloisius's orange curls could be seen next to Albert Richmond's bald pate in the small alcove formed between two pillars. Charles danced the two of them toward the two men.

The slow music enabled him to move close to the alcove and dance there, but they couldn't get close enough to overhear what the men were saying. Charles kept his back to them in case Richmond recognized him from when he'd spoken to Velma.

"I can't hear anything," Tessa said.

"I don't think I can get us any closer."

"I have an idea." Tessa suddenly stumbled against him, bending down to grab her ankle. "Oh!" she said loudly.

"Are you all right?"

"Help me to the other side of that pillar," she hissed at him.

He walked her there while she pretended to limp, and then the two of them glued themselves to the pillar to try to hear the conversation happening on the other side of it.

"Is she going to cause any problems?" Richmond said.

"No," Aloisius replied. "I'll take care of her."

Were they talking about Elizabeth? Tessa's eyes were only inches from his, and he saw the fear in them.

"She's smarter than she looks."

"She won't fool me." Aloisius laughed, a chuckle worthy of Snidely Whiplash.

"When will you pick her up then?"

"Tomorrow noon sound okay?"

Tessa gasped and grabbed at Charles's wrist. Her fingers burned his skin.

"Her leash will be on the hook by the door," Richmond said.

Leash?

He continued, "Like I said, she's smarter than she looks. She's gotten out of her leash once or twice."

"How long do you walk her?"

"About thirty minutes in the morning, and thirty minutes in the late afternoon. She's pretty good about heeling by your side."

A dog. They were talking about Aloisius taking care of Richmond's dog.

Tessa's eyes crinkled at the corners, and she bit her lip to keep from laughing.

She was still holding his wrist.

He covered her hand with his. Her skin was soft and smooth, and he traced her delicate knuckles, the webbing between her fingers. Her grip on his wrist tightened. Her eyes darkened as they looked up at him.

He was going to kiss her. He shouldn't, for a dozen reasons he couldn't remember right now. But he had to kiss her. He'd die if he didn't.

"So when're they coming?" Richmond asked.

"Any minute now," Aloisius said.

"Keep them out of sight. I already had to field a few questions about them. How do people find out about investors? Who's leaking identities?"

Investors. Was this about their latest investment?

"Remind me again who's who?" Richmond said. "I keep getting them mixed up. Darn Chinese names."

Tessa tensed. She pulled her hand away from Charles and leaned closer to hear.

"Wang is one you've talked to the most. Chang is the accountant. Yang and Ong will be here tonight to represent the Tong family ..."

Her mouth dropped open. She stuffed her fist into it, but her eyes were wide as they looked at Charles.

"We have to get out of here," she whispered.

"Why?"

"Triad members — Chinese mafia — are coming here tonight."

Chapter 24

She wouldn't be in this situation if she hadn't shot Tommy Ong in both kneecaps.

Tessa grabbed Charles's hand and pulled him away from the pillar they'd been hiding behind. They had to get out of the ballroom before the Triad members arrived.

"But you're Japanese," Charles said to her as they dodged waiters with trays of champagne. "They're Chinese."

"I had a skirmish with them years ago." Tessa headed through a door marked "Employees Only" which led to a wide, spare hallway. She guessed it would take them to the kitchens. "Tommy Ong interrupted a —" She'd almost said *drug run.* " — errand I was on with some other yakuza. I was alone, keeping an eye out for ... visitors. He'd just come out of a bar or a party, filled to the brim. He tried to flirt with me, but when I refused him, he tried to rape me."

"What? Wait." Charles grabbed her wrist to stop her. They paused in the middle of the hallway, while a waiter or two passed them carrying trays. "Did he know who you were?"

"Oh, he knew. Which is why I got so mad. I shoved him

off me. When he grabbed me again, I punched him in the nose, pulled my gun, and shot him in the knees."

She said it so calmly. A part of her was sad that back then such violence hadn't been unusual for her, and that even now the memories were muted because, at the time, her conscience had been seared.

"But he was Triad," Charles said.

Tessa nodded.

"What did your uncle do?"

"Tommy Ong is second cousin to a Triad leader, but I'm niece to Teruo Ota. The insult to Uncle Teruo was greater than the insult to Tommy."

"Insult to Tommy? He attacked you."

"It didn't matter—*women* don't matter. But attacking a close blood relation of the yakuza boss—male or female—was unforgivable. Uncle Teruo talked with them and nothing happened, but the Ongs have never forgiven me. Tommy walks with a cane."

She turned away from him so she could grab her cell phone where it had been wedged under her dress bodice. She and Josh had exchanged cell phone numbers earlier—he had insisted they do so in case something happened, although at the time she hadn't really thought anything would. The act of exchanging numbers seemed to make him more excited about helping her, so she'd agreed. Now she was glad of it. She texted him: *Have to leave asap. I'll call u.*

She grabbed Charles's hand. "We can get out of here through the kitchens."

They entered into the kitchen area, suddenly engulfed in the busy sounds of the staff preparing the hors d'oeuvres for the party. They shimmied around kitchen assistants and cooks at the sinks and various worktables. Several gave them annoyed looks, but no one bothered to stop them — no one had the time, it seemed, as the staff rushed to get the food out to the guests. The kitchen was long and narrow, so they had to wend their way down to the far end to reach the doors that would lead out to the back exit of the building.

They were only a few yards from the back door of the kitchen when it swung open and five men in business suits walked in.

Five Chinese men.

She started, which made the blonde curls of her wig dance in front of her eyes. Calm down, she told herself. They won't recognize you.

Why hadn't they come in through the front doors of the ballroom? They weren't Triad leaders — she'd have recognized them on sight — so why this secrecy? She grabbed Charles's hand, lowered her eyes, and started walking.

No shouts. No threatening movements. The men paused when they saw Tessa and Charles, but then kept going, probably assuming the two of them were off for a rendezvous.

The skin all over her arms and legs tingled. She felt the breeze when the first man — a large, hulking figure like a sumo wrestler — strode past. She grasped the fabric of her skirt in her hands, bunching it in her fingers.

Two, three ... they passed each man.

Then the fourth man slowed. Looked at her.

It was Dave Ong. Tommy's cousin.

Pretend you don't know him. She shifted her gaze away and kept moving. Just a few more feet ...

She had almost passed him when he reached out, grabbed her wig, and yanked.

Tessa snatched up a heavy stone mortar someone had left on the table next to her and swung it at Dave before his hand could drop the wig. The edge clocked him above the eye, and he howled and curled away from her.

"Run!" she shouted to Charles. Any kitchen staff nearby either ducked or scattered.

The fifth man, following behind Dave, had frozen in surprise, but he belatedly tried to grab at Charles as he ran past him. Tessa picked up a footed metal strainer and jabbed at his eyes. She delivered a front kick to his stomach that sent him to the ground.

The man in front of Dave reacted quicker. He reached into his jacket and withdrew a gun, but Tessa shot her leg out in a short diagonal kick that knocked it from his hand.

He fumbled for a knife on the table beside him. Tessa grabbed a metal tray of puff pastry tarts and brought the shield up just as he stabbed the knife down at her head. The impact jarred her wrists and elbows, and the knife blade skidded off the surface of the tray to the side, leaving a deep dent in its path.

With his arm now across his body, leaving his head unprotected, she smashed the edge of the tray at his face. He stumbled back, losing his grip on the knife and grabbing his nose.

Tessa ducked and sprinted for the door as a gunshot thundered in the low-ceilinged room. Ahead of her, a few of the tiles on the wall shattered in puffs of powder as bullets hit.

In trying to make the turn to head out the back door, she skidded on the slick floor and fell. But suddenly Charles was there, reaching down for her hand, pulling her to her feet and out the door.

She ran as best she could in heels, but the men behind them were too close for her to pause to pull them off. They burst out the back exit of the building and stumbled down a short flight of stairs into an alley. Would the men use their guns out here?

Charles dragged her to the street and barely hesitated before streaking out into traffic.

A car skidded, and Charles put a hand out, but it stopped inches from them. They kept going. Another car zipped down the lane, and after it had passed they darted out to a cacophony of blaring horns. Another lane, and they were across the street.

Tessa looked back and saw three men on the other side, but they weren't pursuing them. Dave Ong's hateful eyes met hers across the lanes of racing cars.

Tessa knew that this time, the Ongs would make sure she paid.

Then Charles was pulling her, shoving her into a taxi, and they were away.

They sat, side by side, for several long minutes, breaths heaving. Queasiness lay heavy in her stomach.

She'd been afraid in a way she hadn't felt in years. She'd been afraid for Charles, for herself. Before, she'd blithely believed she was invincible. But tonight in that kitchen she'd been abruptly aware that her life was like a breath, that she or Charles could be shot and killed, that she was like a flower of the field, here today and gone tomorrow.

And then, suddenly, she started to cry.

She hadn't cried after a fight since the grade school skirmishes where kids would taunt her because of her family connections to underground crime. Alicia either crumpled into a tearful heap or tried to ignore the abuse, but Tessa fought back—which led to Uncle Teruo enrolling her in martial arts classes. In those classes, she learned how to fight calmly, how to center herself, how to focus herself.

Lot of good that was now.

The tears came in heaving sobs that pulled at her stomach muscles. And then Charles's arms were around her, pressing her face into his tuxedo jacket.

He was warm and solid. His arms gathered her close, made her feel protected.

"It's all right," he said. "It's over. I've got you."

Which only made her cry harder.

She cried until she was used up, and still Charles held her long after the tears had dried on her cheeks, one hand smoothing her back, the other holding her tight to him.

Her arms were around his torso, one cheek pressed to the smooth fabric of his shoulder. His head was bent, his face pressed to her other cheek, making her feel encased and sheltered.

And then she moved her head, and he moved his, and their lips met in between.

His lips tasted like lime. And relief. And tenderness. And just the faintest hint of desire. She never wanted him to stop kissing her. She never wanted him to stop holding her.

And he didn't, for a long time.

A buzz vibrated against her breastbone. At first she thought Charles's fingers were wandering, but then she realized it was her cell phone, still tucked into her bodice. Since it was encased in so much duct tape, it hadn't fallen out.

She pulled away from him. Besides, she needed to blow her nose.

Pulling out the silk handkerchief tucked into Charles's tuxedo pocket, she wiped her face as she dug in her dress for her phone with her other hand. When Charles's eyes flickered to her chest, they immediately shot away, and she could feel the heat radiating from his neck.

She forgot that not everyone grew up as she did, thinking sex was just fun, interpersonal gymnastics. Some people actually grew up with morals.

She snagged her phone on the last ring, recognizing the number. "Josh?"

"Where are you?" he whispered.

"Where are you?"

"Hiding behind the chocolate table. That woman was *all over me.*"

"We ran into trouble."

"*You* ran into trouble? Why couldn't you have rescued me too?"

"Because that might have involved a bullet in your brain."

"Oh. Well, what now?"

Tessa didn't want Velma complaining to Desiree about her escort abandoning her for the evening, so she told Josh, "You need to find Velma—"

"No way!"

"—and tell her that Charles got violently sick."

There was a mutinous silence on the other end of the line.

"I'll tell you where the bullet holes are in the kitchen," Tessa said.

"Really?" he chirped. "Okay. Hang on ..." In the background, she heard Velma's low, hoarse voice getting louder and louder. Then Josh said, "Ms. Crackhea—er, Velma?"

"There you are," Velma said. "You just disappeared. Who are you on the phone with?"

"I just got a call. It's Theresa."

Tessa instructed him, "Tell her that while we were dancing, Charles got really sick."

"She's asking me to tell you that while she was dancing with Charles, he got massively sick. Threw up all over her."

"Oh." There was a rather pleased note in Velma's voice.

Tessa said, "Tell her that Charles had to leave."

"She says that Charles had to leave. He didn't want to throw up on you too."

"And you'll be happy to be her host for the rest of the evening."

Silence.

"Bullet holes, Josh." By the time the party ended, there wouldn't be any danger to him if he wandered into the kitchen.

"I'll be happy to be your host for the rest of tonight, Velma." It sounded like he said it through his teeth.

"So kind of you," Velma tittered. "But what about Theresa?"

"Oh, she can find her own way home."

"Thanks, I owe you big time, Josh," Tessa told him.

He hung up the phone.

Triads. A Triad gang was funding an investment with Stillwater Group.

"Elizabeth said she didn't know anything about Heath's business," Tessa said.

"She must have seen something and didn't realize it," Charles said.

"Triads," Tessa breathed. "No wonder Heath has been so desperate to shut her up."

"Not Heath, his company. And they're setting Heath up to take the fall for her murder."

"Lucky for us, they haven't hired very competent help so far," Tessa said.

"Or Elizabeth just has an exceptional bodyguard."

The compliment warmed her just as if he'd taken hold of

her hand. She realized she was still sitting close to him, almost snuggled against him, although he no longer had his arm around her. She knew she should move away, but she couldn't get her limbs to unglue themselves from the warmth of his body.

She shouldn't have kissed him. She shouldn't have even allowed herself to be attracted to him.

That was like telling a woman with PMS not to eat a Snickers bar.

As the taxi circled back to the hotel so Charles could pick up his car, all she could think about was how much she wanted him to hold her again and make her feel safe.

They arrived at the hotel, and as they waited for the valet to get Charles's car, she said, "I need you to take me to Sea Cliff."

Charles's body became still and tense. Yes, he would know what was in Sea Cliff. After all, he'd been at her trial.

"I should have thought of this sooner, before we sent the taxi away." Except she'd been floating on a cloud, sitting next to Charles. "I'll just flag another taxi down. Or the valet will do it for me."

"Let's talk to Elizabeth first."

"No, I have to talk to him tonight. He needs to know right away."

"Do you ..." His jaw clenched, once. "Do you want me to come with you?"

"I think it's better if you don't."

He looked away from her, maybe to hide his relief. Then he said, "I'll drive you."

"Thanks. I'll find my own way back to your house."

They were silent the entire way as he drove her to the exclusive San Francisco neighborhood of Sea Cliff.

Charles didn't need to ask her what the address was to the seaside home of her Uncle Teruo.

••••

It was a bad sign that even though it was late, Uncle Teruo was still awake. It meant other things weighed on his mind, so he already wasn't in a good mood. And what she had to tell him was not exactly going to make him say, "Let's go to Disneyland!"

Alerted to her visit by the security guard at the front gate, he answered the front door himself, wrapped in a dark blue *hanten*. Underneath the padded cotton housecoat, he wore bright green pajamas printed with turtles—the pajamas Tessa had bought for him a couple months ago for his birthday, because he had a thing for turtles.

The sight of the pajamas would normally make her laugh and tease him. But not tonight.

He gave her a hug, since they were in private, but he didn't smile. He knew that her coming so late wasn't a casual visit to raid his refrigerator for any leftover *onigiri* rice balls and *miso* soup.

He brought her into his den, warmed by a fire in the traditional *irori* open hearth in the center of the room. The ocean wind whistled outside the French doors leading to the terrace, and the occasional roar of ocean waves snuck into the cozy space.

He sat on a cushion beside the square hearth, and she folded herself onto another cushion catty-corner to him. He'd had time to collect the papers he was looking at into a folder that lay next to him on the straw *tatami* hearth mat that protected the wooden floor.

"Uncle, I went to a party tonight and saw Triad gang members there."

His salt-and-pepper eyebrows flattened over his eyes. "Why were you at a party with the Triads?"

"I didn't know they were going to be there. I would never have expected them to even recognize me—I'm not a *kobun*, it's been over seven years since any of them saw me, and I've only been seen in public with you once since I was released from prison. But one of them was Dave Ong."

Her uncle didn't groan, but he exhaled heavily and his heavy eyelids closed briefly. "He recognized you?"

"He attacked me."

His eyes narrowed. "Unprovoked?"

"He, uh ... pulled off my wig—"

"Why were you wearing a wig?" Uncle's voice had risen dangerously.

"I was afraid other men at the party would recognize me."

"That's all he did? Pull off your wig?"

"Well, I didn't think he'd simply drop it and say, 'Oh hi, Tessa, long time no see, let's do lunch.'"

Uncle's mouth tightened.

Watch it, stupid, or he'll slap the sarcasm right out of your mouth.

"Please tell me the Triad members were not there to do business," he growled.

"Uh ..." She bit her lip. "You want me to lie?"

He pressed his lips together and rubbed his forehead with the fingers of one hand. "So you fought Dave Ong."

"And two others."

"Two others?" His eyes bore into hers. "Time and again I have asked you to control your temper, to stay out of trouble.

278

You cannot attack when I haven't given you permission to do so."

She dropped her head. He was right—he had too many other things to juggle, too many intangibles like face and reputation. And yet this time, his phrasing struck a wrong chord in her. "I wasn't attacking. I was defending myself," she said.

"You should have let them give you a few bruises, a few broken bones. They'll heal. You were at a party where a Triad was doing business, which meant you had no right to be there."

She understood this side of his life, she knew what it required, but tonight, his callousness pricked her. "I couldn't just lay down and take it. I wasn't alone."

"Were you with one of us? If Itchy was with you, I'll—"

"No, not Itchy. Just a man."

"Then you should have let them beat him up too."

"They would have killed him," Tessa protested.

"Then you let them kill him."

The dark words echoed off the walls of the room. *Yes, Tessa, you let them kill him. You chose this life years ago. You have to live with the consequences.*

"But I didn't."

His breath exploded out of him in frustration. "Why did you do this? Why did you bring this down on my head? Have you no respect or concern for me, for your family?"

She curled her shoulders against his verbal attack.

"Have you forgotten the Triads outnumber us in the Bay Area? Our relationship with them is guarded at best."

She said nothing, just let his words flay her.

"You haven't told me why you were at that party."

She answered hesitatingly. "It was given by a company I'm investigating for my client. We didn't know a Triad was doing business with them."

"Stay away from that company," Uncle Teruo said. "Do nothing to them."

"But my client—"

"If you stay away from the company, you'll stay away from the Triad's business. This may yet blow over." He exhaled sharply, his mouth pinched. "Leave me now."

She shifted to sit on her knees, bowed with her hands on the floor in front of her. And left the house.

She asked the security guard at the front gate to call her a taxi, and she stood in the shadows of the estate wall and shivered in the sharp sea winds as she waited.

How had it come down to this? She'd thought it was just about Heath and Elizabeth. Not his company, not the Triads. And now she had to choose:

Elizabeth or her uncle.

Chapter 25

"Y'all are throwing me out to drown in a sea of Asian men," Elizabeth complained.

She pointed to Charles's computer screen, where pictures of Triad members were tiled across. "Did you count these? There have to be a hundred faces here."

"Forty," Charles said. "And I'll have you know, it took a lot of digging for the private investigator to get these pictures. Triad don't exactly strike a pose when they see a camera."

"They're more likely to break the cameraman's face," Tessa murmured. She was sitting next to his mama on the couch in the living room, trying to knit a scarf, but she kept tangling the yarn. She'd been quiet since she returned from her uncle's house. Charles hadn't asked her what had happened, and she hadn't said.

He himself was waiting for the hammer to drop. Since the night of the party, he'd gone into work and done his job like normal, but he hadn't heard from Mr. Greer at all. Surely by now Heath's firm would have told Mr. Greer about seeing Tessa there, and it wouldn't be hard to guess the man with her was Charles, sneaking into a party when Charles had been warned off investigating the firm.

He hadn't told anyone, although he noted Tessa's apprehensive eyes on him when he left for work the past few mornings. Mama and Elizabeth may have forgotten about it, but Tessa knew the implications of what they'd done, and how it would affect him soon.

"Mama!" Daniel ran to her side and shook Slasher at her face in a blur of pink flopping limbs. "Slasher! Aarrr! Grrr!"

"Not now, darling. Give me a few minutes. Forty pictures? I know I've lived in California for several years now, but Asian people all look alike to me."

Tessa's mouth quirked. "I could say the same for Caucasians."

"And Heath hosted tons of parties where there were Asians there. How am I supposed to remember them all?"

Even Charles had to admit they might be asking for a tall order. "Just take another look at them—"

"Maybe I can make it easier." Tessa's eyes crossed as she brought a knot of yarn almost to the end of her nose so she could try to untangle it. "Charles, you said the Triad is probably using this investment to launder drug money?"

"Probably a lot of money, hundreds of millions. A private equity investment is perfect for that. There's basically no government regulation and the minimum investment is typically in the tens of millions. It's not unusual for a single investor to put in a billion or more."

"Dollars?" Mama's eyes bugged out. "No wonder they want Elizabeth. What's one woman when there's that much money at stake?"

Elizabeth had paled.

"Thanks, Mama," Charles chided her.

"Oh, I'm so sorry. I was just shocked."

"Mama!" Daniel thrust Slasher at her again. "Aaarrr! Grr!"

"Darling, we'll play dragon later."

Tessa pulled at a string and the knot went tight. "Aargh." She got up from the couch, tossing down the tangled mess of pink and red yarn, and leaned over Elizabeth's shoulder. "Okay, so we know for an investment of this size, the head honchos will be involved. And accountants. Anyone else?"

Charles threw his torso back against the leather recliner he was lounging in. "It could be any number of people who might be involved in getting the money to them ..."

"Well, let's start with just the leaders and the money men." Tessa tapped on the keyboard, and all but fourteen pictures disappeared. "Recognize any of them?"

Elizabeth stared at the pictures for a good five minutes, then slowly shook her head. "I don't know, it's just so hard ..."

"Mama!" Daniel's voice went into a high-pitched scream. "Dragon! You promised!" He threw Slasher on the floor, plopped his bottom down, and began to cry.

Elizabeth reached for him, but Mama got up and picked him up instead. "Don't feel bad," she said. "He refused to nap today so he might be cranky. It's a little early, but I'll see if he'll go to sleep now." She carried him out of the living room.

Elizabeth bent down in her chair to pick Slasher up from the floor, and her hand stilled. "Oh!"

"What is it?" Tessa asked.

Instead of answering her, Elizabeth turned back to the screen, stared intently. "Him," she said, pointing to one of the pictures. "And these three."

Charles shot out of his recliner and looked at who she picked out. Three of the eight main leaders of the Triad, and one accountant. The four men had been mentioned by name at the party — Wang, Chang, Tong, and Yang — although he and

Tessa had deliberately kept that information from Elizabeth.

"How did you—?" Tessa said.

Elizabeth held up Slasher. "I remembered one time Daniel had left a stuffed animal in the living room, and it got shoved under the couch. There was a meeting between Heath, those four Asian men, and a few other Caucasian men. One of the Asian men saw the toy, picked it up, and handed it to me. I was mortified."

"You said other Caucasian men were there?"

"Some men I already knew from the company—Albert Richmond, Chip McFinney, Reginald Duffey. And also some other men, I don't remember their names. But now that I remember that meeting, I might be able to remember their faces."

"I might have their pictures." Charles leaned into Tessa so he could reach the keyboard and mouse. She smelled like rain, and cherry blossoms, and yarn. He wanted to bury his face in her neck and breathe.

But she moved away from him.

He brought up his email program. "The P.I. found out who the principles are in this investment—at least, the legal ones on paper—and he sent me those pictures too." He brought up three photos.

"Him." Elizabeth pointed to Aloisius Rosenstein, his orange curls making his head look like it was on fire on the computer screen.

"Are you sure?"

"Of course I'm sure. Who could forget a man who looks like a carrot?"

Her confirmation should have felt like a victory, but all he could think of was that he'd given her the nails for her own coffin. "According to what the P.I. dug up, the money is supposedly coming from Aloisius. Except for what we overheard Aloisius saying to Richmond at the party, there was no connection between him and the Triad members. None. But your testimony puts him in that meeting with them."

"And that gets Stillwater Group in trouble, right?" Elizabeth said.

"It means Aloisius and Heath and his partners all know the money is coming from the Triad. They've probably erased any other connections that would prove they knew the money was being obtained illegally—except for you. Since you saw them, you can prove the firm knew about the illegality and knew the Triad was behind the transaction. The firm is in deep trouble with the Feds if this comes out."

"Not only that," Tessa said. "If Stillwater Group comes under investigation and the Triad loses its money, they'll kill the people who ripped them off."

Charles told Elizabeth, "When you left Heath, and they realized you might be able to destroy this deal, they panicked. That's why they were hiring men to tail you and try to kill you. They probably didn't want the Triad to know about you."

Elizabeth's lip trembled, and she twisted her hands in her lap. "I can't do it," she whispered. "I can't testify. The Triad will come after me and Daniel too."

"You have to disappear," Tessa said.

Elizabeth shook her head. "How can I know they won't find me? We'll be running forever."

Even if they caused Heath's firm to crumble, it would still set the Triad after Elizabeth and Daniel, and with the amount of money they'd lose, they wouldn't stop until she was dead.

Tessa was staring at the faces on the computer screen. "If we stop this deal," she said slowly, "the Triad will think the yakuza is behind it, because they saw me at the party."

And Charles suddenly saw the larger implications of this. "Would it start a gang war?"

"I don't know." She rubbed her knuckles against her sternum. "I don't know."

"A gang war?" Elizabeth breathed.

"Innocent people would die." Tessa wasn't looking at Elizabeth, at Charles, at anything. It was as if she were talking to herself. "And it would be my fault."

"No, Tessa—" Elizabeth said.

"Tessa—" Charles said at the same time.

But Tessa turned her back on the two of them and walked out of the living room.

The two of them remained silent for a long moment. Elizabeth covered her mouth with her hand while tears spilled over her eyelashes. "There's no way out," she said. "There's no hope. We're going to die."

He should say something, but he couldn't. He didn't know what to say.

And suddenly the doorbell rang.

At ten o'clock at night?

Tessa appeared in the front foyer as if he'd conjured her up. "Get back in the living room," she ordered him quietly.

"I'm not leaving you to face anyone alone," he shot back.

Something shifted in her face, something he couldn't put his finger on, but she didn't protest when he shadowed her to the front door.

But after looking through the peephole, her shoulders became even more tense. He could see the pulse throb at her throat. She opened the door.

Kenta stood there.

Charles's hands curled into fists. The tall Asian man looked first at Tessa, then at him, and their eyes held. Kenta's gaze was black steel. Charles returned it, as hard as stone.

Finally Kenta blinked and said to Tessa, "Your uncle asks you to come."

"Now?"

"He has questions about what you talked about a few nights ago."

"What does he need to know?" Charles demanded.

Kenta spoke to Tessa, not to him. "He needs to know more about the business deal."

"Then I'm coming with you," Charles said.

"That's not a good idea," said Kenta.

"Did your mama drop you on your head too often as a child?" Tessa said to Charles.

Charles gave her a hard look. "Are *you* going to be able to explain to him the intricacies of this deal? Your uncle's a businessman. He does not want the CliffsNotes version."

Tessa and Kenta both hesitated, looked at each other. Charles clenched his teeth at the unspoken communication they had with each other.

Tessa took Charles's arm and pulled him aside. "You don't ask questions unless I say you can."

"So no 'How's the drug running going?' "

"You don't speak unless he asks you a question."

"I'll be quiet as a mouse."

"And you don't repeat anything you hear. Anything."

"My lips are sealed."

She looked like she wanted to seal his lips with her fist. He wondered what would happen if he kissed her in front of Kenta.

She turned toward the doorway. "Let's go."

Kenta gave him a level look. "You're either very brave or very stupid."

"I'm neither."

I think I might be in love.

Chapter **26**

Tessa decided that Charles must have blown a fuse up in the brain box. Otherwise, why would he willingly be here?

The sea air sliced into her lungs when she got out of the car, but she approached the front door slowly. She still felt the weight of Uncle Teruo's disappointment from the last time she'd been here. Coupled with what they'd discovered tonight, she was surprised she could walk upright. If his anger came down on her again, he'd crush her into the ground.

Yet even as she felt the dread of failing her uncle again, she had a slim sliver of hope. Maybe uncle had found a way to solve this situation. Surely he loved her enough to want to do this for her, as well as for himself. Surely there was something she could do to salvage this horrible, horrible situation.

Uncle Teruo met her again in his den, but instead of the intimate gathering around the *irori* open fireplace, he sat behind his massive teakwood desk. Gone were the turtle pajamas and instead he wore his black business suit like *sokutai* imperial court attire.

He didn't look up right away when they entered the room — Kenta leading, Charles and Tessa following. He finished writing on a paper in front of him while they waited patiently, then pushed the pen aside and glanced up. He nodded to Kenta, then looked behind him to see Tessa and Charles.

On the drive here, she had called him, told him she was bringing the man she'd gone to the party with to help explain the business deal to him. He hadn't objected, so she didn't expect him to react with more than a hard look at the stranger.

But Uncle Teruo's shoulders went back and down, his jaw became tight, and he shot to his feet, sending his padded teakwood chair crashing backward. "How dare you come here?" he thundered at Charles.

Tessa took a step backward. She'd seen her uncle angry many times, but this was a fierce anger that roared like a lioness over her cub. It was wild, emotional and protective, not the harsh and judgmental anger he displayed to his *kobuns.*

Uncle's eyes darted to Tessa's face, searching. "He never told you, did he?"

The shaking started deep in her bones, a vibration that made her entire frame hum. Then her muscles twitched, and twitched again, and began trembling with growing force. "Tell me what?"

She looked at Charles frantically, willing him to explain what was going on, but his face was marble as he faced Uncle Teruo's burning eyes.

"He was the law clerk at your trial."

One of her gut muscles relaxed. "He told me that. How did you know?"

"I investigated everyone involved. I could do no less for you. His role was to research the case for the judge."

"Yes, he told me," she said.

Still Charles didn't say anything.

Kenta's face was neutral, but his eyes found Tessa's, crowded with questions she had no answers to.

"He made recommendations," Uncle said in a low, terrible voice. "He wrote the judge a memo."

"How did you get hold of that?" Charles demanded.

"You dare ask me that?" Uncle said. "Here in my own house? She is my niece. That was her trial. She has no father to protect her. I had more right than *you* to know what happened."

Her shaking was making the room swim in front of her eyes. "What happened?" she whispered.

"He recommended the judge go beyond the maximum sentence for you. Because your known associates were suspected in other crimes, which you might have been intimately involved in, he recommended that you not be allowed back into society so soon."

It was harder than she thought it would be to hear her crimes, to hear her case in those specific words, and to think Charles wrote them.

"He is responsible for the seven years instead of five that you served."

Those two years, hateful because at the end of her sixth year ...

After Aunt Kayoko's heart attack, Tessa had applied to be allowed to go see her in the hospital under guard. But she'd been denied because it was an aunt, not a mother or father or child. Her aunt had been alert for a week—Tessa could have seen her one last time. Then her aunt had had another heart attack and died. Tessa hadn't been allowed to go to the funeral either.

The missed opportunity had eaten away at her because Aunt Kayoko had been the brightest light in her world, the sweetest fragrance, the softest touch to a girl who felt unimportant to anyone else.

Tessa turned to Charles in a flurry, slapping him, punching at him with arms weighed down like steel rods. She wanted to hurt him, she knew she could break him if she focused her energy enough, but she found that she was crying too hard, she couldn't draw a breath, and her head swam with the lack of oxygen.

And then she realized that Kenta had stepped behind her and grabbed her arms, trying to pin them to her sides. "Let me go!" She fought him.

"Don't kill him," Kenta said to her in a low voice. "You've never killed a man. Don't do it now."

She'd been to jail. She'd go to prison again. She didn't care. But then her tears started heaving up from her diaphragm, squeezing her lungs, pounding at her heart. She couldn't stop screaming. She dropped to her knees. Through her blurred vision, she saw her tears dripping to stain the wooden floor, the same way they'd stained the inside-out paper crane the day of her aunt's funeral.

The bitterness engulfed her like black flames. "Because of you," she hurled at Charles. "Because of you I never got a chance to say goodbye to her."

That this betrayal should come from Charles stabbed her again and again and again. She hated him. After she wrote that letter to Kenta, she had hardened the protection around her heart because she thought she had lost any chance for a relationship with someone—and then Charles had come along. She had wanted to love him. She had wanted to believe she had a chance for something more.

But he had deceived her.

Her nails dug into the wood of the floor. She willed her tears to stop. Her uncle wouldn't appreciate the hysterical emotion.

She could take care of herself because no one would take care of her. She could find her center and let no one else in.

She willed herself to breathe deeply. Then she rose to her feet, feeling empty and brittle. Kenta helped her with a hand on her elbow, but she gently shrugged him aside.

Her uncle passed her a linen handkerchief, and she realized Charles was gone.

For a moment, she wanted to cry all over again.

You hardly knew him.

True. But something deep inside her had seemed to know him like an old friend.

"Kenta." Uncle Teruo nodded toward the door.

Kenta bowed and left them.

She had a moment of panic. "You let Charles walk out?"

Uncle nodded slowly. "Is that what you wanted?"

Relief rushed in like a chill ocean wave. "Yes."

"But you wanted to kill him."

"For a moment."

"But you are not Fred." He sighed heavily, and went to right his chair and sink into it.

She didn't know what to say to that, so she said nothing at all. She sat in the large teakwood chair opposite him, sliding against the smooth, cool leather.

"I wish you had been a boy," her uncle said. Then in a lower voice, "I wish you had been my son."

She couldn't breathe for a moment. But her lungs burned and she forced them to open again.

He had never before paid her a compliment as deep as that.

And yet, while she was honored by his words, she also realized that while they would have fed her thirsty soul three years ago, they didn't now. She had found another father. She loved her uncle, but there were things he did that she couldn't condone any longer, things she couldn't help him with any more. Their relationship had changed.

She had changed.

Even as she thought it, she cringed. She hadn't changed, not when she had been willing to kill a man only a few minutes before. She hadn't changed at all.

And suddenly, God her Father seemed far away too. She felt alone.

"Tell me about your client and this company," he commanded.

So she did, telling him about Elizabeth, Stillwater Group, the Triad. His brow contracted in confusion over some parts about the business deal, but he didn't ask for clarification — which she wouldn't have been able to give anyway.

When she was done, Uncle Teruo didn't respond for a long time. Then when he did, it was what she expected him to say:

"Come back and work for me."

When she began to shake her head, he said, "You must. I can't save you any other way."

She had never heard that desperate thread in his voice before.

"If you can stop investigating that firm, if you can dissociate yourself from it, then they will kill Elizabeth and the deal will go through."

Everything inside her cringed. No, she couldn't do that.

"The business transaction will not be damaged, and the Triad will not blame us for interfering," he continued. "We can save face and avoid a potential war."

Yes, he had seen that aspect of it, as well.

"She's an innocent woman," Tessa said weakly. "She has a three-year-old boy."

"Innocent people will be hurt or killed if the Triad is angered," he replied. "What is one life compared to many? Even your religion teaches that."

"It would be *murder*."

"Wouldn't a war be many murders?"

Was this how Eve felt in the Garden? So reasonable, so wrong, so tempting. All her problems solved.

"You've had many shocks today." He rose, walked around his desk, and touched her cheek with his large, square hand. His skin was papery and leathery at the same time. His touch was gentle. "Go to your mother's house and rest. And think."

Rest was at Charles's house, with Elizabeth and Vivian.

She nodded and rose to her feet. And then he embraced her, filling her senses with that distinctive cigar brand, brushed with a touch of seaweed from the outside air.

She put her arms around him and knew he loved her.

As she opened the door to his office, he said, "I know you will make the right choice. You will not choose strangers over your family." There was a hint of steel in his voice as he said it, the *oyabun* giving a command.

She let herself out, feeling like she was walking into a dark, yawning pit.

••••

Tessa froze as a figure moved in the darkened living room.

She had just let herself in and disabled and re-enabled the alarm for Charles's house. She hadn't even checked to see that the quiet home she was entering was safe.

She peered through the gloom, her heart pulsing strong in her ears, her skin tingling. Could they see her in the shadowed foyer? What she wouldn't give for a gun, or a knife to throw. She snatched up the umbrella resting against the wall by the door, tested the heft of the wooden knob at the end, the flexible strength of the metal skeleton.

"Tessa?"

Vivian.

For a second, her blood pounded hard in relief, then she set down the umbrella, took a deep breath, and she was calm again.

Vivian flipped on a lamp. She was lying on the sofa, a blanket over her. She yawned. "I hoped I'd wake up when you came home." She paused. "I wasn't sure if you'd come back."

"Elizabeth's my client, no matter what Charles has done." But she didn't feel any anger in her words. She would have expected more bitterness, more sorrow, more pain.

And really, was Elizabeth her client if she chose as her uncle wanted her to? She felt like a hypocrite as she spoke the words to Vivian.

"He feels guilty," Vivian said.

"I don't care."

But Vivian wasn't offended by the harsh reply. She looked at Tessa with her lovely blue eyes, and then she opened her arms to her.

Tessa walked to the sofa and fell into her embrace.

It was a mother's embrace, cuddling her close, nonjudgmental, with only the desire to comfort and love. Tessa had no more tears, but she filled her heart with that embrace, and she filled her lungs with the scent of freshly baked bread, a hint of chocolate, and a bite of chili pepper.

"You made bread, cannoli, and something Thai," Tessa guessed.

She laughed, and Tessa heard it deep in her chest as her head rested on Vivian's shoulder. "Thai red curry. It didn't go that well with the pepper parmesan bread."

"Try rice next time."

"Rice is boring. And I'm never boring."

"No, you aren't." Tessa sat up, and Vivian also sat up on the sofa, tucking her legs under her so Tessa would have room to sit.

Vivian's hand reached out to touch Tessa's cheek. She'd been touched there twice tonight.

"Your eyes are full of pain," she said to Tessa.

Tessa didn't respond.

"But there's also pain at yourself." Vivian's gaze penetrated deeper than the surface.

Tessa closed her eyes and savored the feel of Vivian's fingers, the slight tremble from the two broken ones. "He's ruthless," she said into Vivian's hand.

"Your uncle? You knew that."

"But I'm ruthless too."

"No—"

"You can't tell me I'm not. I almost killed your son tonight."

She said it to make Vivian drop her hand from her face, but she didn't. Instead, the fingers cupped her chin, forcing her to open her eyes and look at her. "But you didn't."

"I wanted to. I was tempted to, like I've been tempted before. I have a very bad temper."

Vivian's eyes widened in mock disbelief. "No, say it isn't so."

"Nothing has changed, Vivian."

"What do you mean?"

"I chose a new life but the old one won't let me go."

Vivian's hand dropped then, and she looked down at the knitted blanket, picking at yarns, staring at her broken fingers. "The old life never lets you go, darling."

And suddenly Tessa wondered how those fingers were broken.

"I left the yakuza. I turned my back on my uncle. But now I have to choose again, and the decision is a hundred times worse."

"You may have a difficult choice, but you're different."

"What's the point of choosing God if I don't get a second chance and a new start? Why can't I leave that old life behind?"

"Sometimes, he doesn't want you to."

Tessa looked away.

"And sometimes, he wants it to shape you more."

"I can't let Elizabeth die. But I can't allow a gang war to start either. I feel completely alone. Where is God, Vivian?"

She expected a pat answer, but Vivian's eyes filled with tears and she said, "I don't know."

The pressure on her was heavy and dark, and she was afraid and she felt stranded. "I'm helpless. There's nothing I can do to make this better."

"Then *ask for help.*"

Tessa had always had to be strong. Strong against her sister's antagonism, strong against her mother's petulance, strong against the men she had to prove herself to and the people she had hurt. "I don't know how to ask for help."

"Then maybe ... maybe that's why God has put you in this place and left you alone."

"Why would he leave me when he said he wouldn't?"

"Would you ask for help if he was with you?"

Was that the point? It seemed like a really stupid point.

"I think you need to make a decision to trust God," Vivian said.

Trust him with a gang war? With Elizabeth's life? What was the point of Tessa trying to protect her all these weeks? "If I trust him, then ..." It meant she would choose what didn't make sense, and trust God. Trust him for what?

Just ... trust him.

"I know it doesn't make sense right now," Vivian said. "But sometimes you have to trust that eventually it will."

They sat there in silence. Tessa didn't exactly feel peace, but she felt resolution. She knew she couldn't murder Elizabeth or abandon her and Daniel. That was all she knew—she had to hope that was enough. She had to *trust* that was enough. The possible outcomes—the consequences—were dark, terrible places she couldn't look into.

Vivian stifled a yawn. "Sorry."

"You should go to bed."

"You should too."

Tessa helped her off the sofa, wrapping the blanket around her shoulders. They walked up the stairs, and at the landing, Tessa said in a small voice, "I wish ... I could hear him."

"Maybe you do."

And Vivian turned to go to her bedroom, leaving Tessa with silence for company.

Chapter **27**

Tomorrow was the day Elizabeth and Daniel would disappear. Tessa had set up everything they'd need, and she had spent all day today doing last minute coaching.

"I wish you could come with us," Elizabeth said as they sat at the kitchen table. "I'm scared to leave without you."

"We'll trust God to take care of you." The words stuck in her throat and came out hoarsely, but they came out.

"I hope your uncle won't be too mad when you tell him tomorrow after we're gone."

Mad? He would be livid, and Tessa would have irrevocably burned a bridge as well as brought a firestorm down on him. But she didn't want to think about that right now. "I admit, I wouldn't have told you about that this morning if Vivian hadn't urged me to." And after what she had discovered about Charles last night at her uncle's home, Tessa realized she didn't want to lie by omission. Elizabeth had taken the information well.

"No, I'm glad you did. If you hadn't explained the situation you're in with your uncle, I wouldn't be spurred to leave as soon as you finished arranging everything. I might have been tempted to wait a few days."

Vivian, making shrimp creole at Elizabeth's request for her "last meal," replaced the cover on the pot and joined them at the kitchen table. "Charles called earlier. He said he's working late and won't be home for supper."

Tessa couldn't prevent a quiet sigh of relief. She hadn't seen him this morning—she hadn't thought she could, after what had happened last night. As for tomorrow, or the next day, or the day after that … she could only take things one day at a time. She knew Charles would too. Unless he could somehow prove Mr. Greer was in collusion with Heath's firm, there was a good chance he'd be fired.

They both had a great deal to lose. But she still didn't want to see him.

"Mama." Daniel wandered into the kitchen. "Computer beeping."

"Is your computer game done?" Elizabeth took his hand and went into the living room with him to restart his game. But then she called, "Tessa, it's Paisley."

Tessa had been instant messaging with Paisley yesterday while working online, preparing for Elizabeth and Daniel's relocation, and she hadn't turned the program off before putting the computer to sleep. When Daniel woke up the computer to play his game this evening, the instant messaging program had fired up, and now a message box from Paisley had appeared in the bottom corner.

Poozy: Aunt Tessa, r u there?

Tessa typed in a message:

TSLan: Hi, P.

Poozy: Grandma found old children's clothes that aren't pink,
purple, or flowered, and asks if Elizabeth wants them for
Daniel.

Tessa laughed. Elizabeth, reading over her shoulder, said, "Sure." Then she tilted her head. "Do you think we can go over to your mom's house to say goodbye tonight?"

It was ten kinds of dangerous, especially when they were so close to being safe—well, safer, anyway. "I don't know ..."

"We've been really good," Elizabeth said. "Daniel and I have been going stir-crazy in this house, but we haven't gone out or let anyone know we're here."

"It'll only be for a couple hours," Vivian said, walking into the living room.

"Plus it's still light outside," Elizabeth said, sensing Tessa giving way.

"Plus we have Charles's car," Vivian added in triumph.

"We do?"

"He took the train to work this morning because I told him I needed the car to go grocery shopping."

"The store is just around the corner. I don't think he would want us driving all the way down to Mom's house in San Jose."

"If he didn't want me driving it, then he shouldn't have let me borrow it," was Vivian's logic.

Tessa's logic was saying, *"Nonononono."* But some weird feeling made her want to take them. And not just Elizabeth and Daniel, but Vivian too. "Vivian, want to come?"

"Oh, I'd love to meet your family. And I haven't added the shrimp yet to the creole, so it can wait."

"Okay, let's go." Tessa sent an IM to Paisley before she changed her mind.

They had a momentary problem when they didn't know how to get Daniel's car seat into the Audi, but Vivian figured it out and they were on their way.

She may think Charles was a piece of flotsam on an ocean of snot, but his car was a pure dream to drive. Tessa still paid attention to the traffic to see if they were being followed—it had become second nature to her whenever she drove anywhere, with or without Elizabeth—but she didn't see any cars. She *almost* wished they had a tail so she could pit the Audi against them.

They were nearly there when Vivian said, "Oh, I forgot. Eddie was going to come over tonight for supper. I'll call him to tell him it'll be late. We'll be back in a couple hours?"

The way the Audi drove, Tessa might be able to make it to Mom's house and back in less. "Sure."

Vivian dialed her son on her cell phone. "Hello, Eddie? Yes, supper's . . . You're already pulling up to the house? Oh, I'm sorry about that, we're in San Jose . . . Yes, yes, if you're hungry, throw the shrimp in, let it simmer until they turn pink, and then go ahead and eat. Just save some for us. We'll be back in a couple hours." She hung up.

Soon Tessa was introducing Vivian to her mom, sister, and niece. Mom made green tea for all of them and pulled out some Japanese cookies for Daniel.

"I'm so sorry you're leaving," Mom said as they sat in the living room. "We so enjoyed having you here."

Tessa sipped her tea. Maybe she just wasn't someone her mom would ever relate to. It was probably for the best that she find a job soon—one that paid real money—and move out.

Paisley, who'd been texting with Maria, suddenly frowned at her phone and knocked it against the coffee table a few times.

"Hey, hey," Alicia protested. "We don't have the money to buy you a new one."

"It's broken. It just suddenly said, 'No Service.'"

A chill raced through Tessa. No, it was probably nothing to worry about. But better to be safe than sorry. She immediately picked up the landline phone, which was sitting on the end table near her.

No dial tone.

Her vision suddenly expanded, and her skin became sensitive and tingly. Had that been a shadow at the window? She shot to her feet. "Everybody, my bedroom, now!"

"Tessa, really—" Mom started to say, but Tessa hissed, "Move, Mom!"

Paisley was the first to move. She sprinted down the hallway just as Elizabeth rose to her feet and Daniel, sensing the changed atmosphere in the room, began to cry.

"Follow Paisley," Tessa told her. She grabbed her mother and propelled her toward the back of the house, and Mom didn't even protest the tight grip on her arm. Alicia and Vivian hastened after her.

Paisley held the door open. "Hurry." As soon as everyone was inside, she slammed the door shut.

Years ago, when she'd had her private collection in this room, Tessa had installed multiple locks, although she'd never had to engage any of them before. She and Paisley scrambled to close all the locks. Next to the door was a metal security door bar that she grabbed and jammed under the knob.

Tessa had stored boards, nails, and a couple hammers in the room to board up the large picture window, if ever needed. "Paisley." She handed her niece a hammer and pulled out some boards. Now she wished she'd been smarter and had reinforced the window with security film and steel rods and security bars.

"Really, Tessa," Mom said, now that her initial alarm was fading. "This is overreacting."

Tessa nailed a board across the window, Paisley working directly below her. "If I am, then we'll just unlock the door in a few minutes and get a good laugh out of it."

She'd been a fanciful teenager, which had fed her tendency toward paranoia and conspiracy theories. Plus, once she had acquired that AR−15, she'd wanted to protect her weapons stash. She had never thought she'd actually use these fortification measures.

She knew she wasn't being paranoid now.

Because of Paisley's help, they finished quickly. If they were under attack, the intruders would know by now that they were in here because of the sound of pounding nails. Well, it couldn't be helped.

Then the creak of a floor board reached them through the thick walls.

Mom turned white. Alicia put an arm around her and held her close, her own expression tense and terrified. Elizabeth wrapped her arms around Daniel and crushed him to her, while Vivian huddled close to her.

Another creak.

Then someone tried the doorknob.

"Paisley," Tessa whispered. She crouched down on one side of her bed. "Help me move this night stand. Quietly."

Alicia moved to clear the stand of the lamp and clock radio. Then Tessa and Paisley grasped each end of the large stand and lifted, carrying it a few feet to the side.

A dark, spiderweb-filled hole gaped at them from the floor.

Mom's mouth fell open. "When did you do this?" she demanded in a whisper.

Paisley's shoulders had risen to touch her ears. "Aunt Tessa," she said, her voice shaking.

"I'm sorry for the spiders, but it's the only way. I made this hole when I was a teenager, and I don't fit in it anymore. It comes out under Grandma's azalea bush."

"No wonder that bush never grew well," Mom groused.

"You need to get out—but carefully, don't let them see you—and go to Mrs. Fleming's house next door and call the police." Tessa glanced at Elizabeth, who was holding a softly whimpering Daniel. "Should we try to send Daniel with Paisley?"

"I want to, but I don't think he'd go down there," Elizabeth said. "And he might cry and get Paisley discovered."

Paisley had screwed up her face as she crouched in front of the hole. Then Alicia came to her with a bandana and wrapped it around her head. "This'll help."

The knob was rattled again, louder and harder.

"Hurry," Tessa said. "Be brave."

"Be smart," Alicia added. "Don't get caught."

With a disgusted squeal, Paisley dove into the hole. Alicia grabbed the covers off the bed and piled them up over the hole to hide it.

"Now what?" she whispered.

The attackers started banging on the door. It wasn't going to hold forever.

"Get under the bed," she ordered them.

"We won't all fit," Elizabeth said.

"Just try."

Vivian, Elizabeth, Daniel, and Mom squashed under the

bed, but Alicia stood next to her. "Please tell me you left a few weapons in here."

Tessa shook her head.

More banging. Then a man's voice spoke in Chinese to someone.

Triad.

A pair of fists twisted and wrung out her stomach. This was not good.

No, no time for self-pity or worrying. She had to think! No weapons? No problem. They'd just improvise.

Bam! Bam! came the pounding on the door.

She scanned the room, depressingly empty. She had taken most of her belongings with her when she first moved out, and since getting out of jail, she hadn't accumulated much.

She pulled out a drawer from the nightstand, dumping out its contents. Nothing useful unless she wanted to squirt Neosporin in the attacker's eye. But the drawer was small enough, not too bulky.

Handing the drawer to Alicia, she said, "Swing it at anything that moves. Try to hit with a corner, not the flat panel."

Alicia nodded.

Bam! Bam!

Tessa grabbed another drawer. How long had it been since Paisley left? Did she escape? How long before the police would arrive?

The wood in the center of the door started to buckle from the repeated pounding. They couldn't break the locks on the edge, but she had never thought to reinforce the center panel.

"Stay back." She sent Alicia to the far corner and she stood a few feet away, waiting for the attacker to get through.

Suddenly a *crash* from the window, and the boards splintered.

Alicia screamed, but gamely swung at the foot kicking in the wood. There was a sound of cursing that Tessa couldn't understand.

Then a figure appeared, only just visible in the closing darkness, and a hand reached in through the window and grabbed Alicia.

Leaving the door, Tessa surged forward.

Alicia struggled, swinging the drawer, but he held on.

Dropping the drawer she held, Tessa got between the man and her sister, then spun so her back was to the window. She grabbed his wrist, tucked her other forearm under his elbow and yanked her forearm up. The arm-bar move dislocated his elbow with a pop. He screamed in pain and snatched his arm back.

The other man kicked in the center panel of the bedroom door in an explosion of splintered wood. Tessa could see him through the narrow vertical hole in the door, saw him raise his hand, saw the barrel of the gun.

She shoved Alicia out of the way as he fired.

One, two, three shots. The first two zinged past her, burning the air in their wake.

It almost seemed like she felt the pain from the third bullet before she heard the shot being fired.

It was a red hot poker stabbing into her liver. She couldn't breathe, couldn't cry out, couldn't move. Fire engulfed her, radiating from that spot low on her abdomen.

Someone shouted, "Tessa!"

The slap of the floor against her back. The water-stained ceiling above her.

They were unprotected, now.

She had failed them.

Chapter 28

C harles had come home early ... he didn't know why. Pain and torture? Stupidity?

But all he found was an empty house and a still-warm pot of creole, sans shrimp, on the stove, which was thankfully turned off. Where was everyone?

He reached for his phone to call Mama when he heard Eddie's key unlocking the front door.

"Mama and company are on their way to Tessa's mom's house in San Jose," Eddie said by way of a greeting as soon as Charles opened the door. He waggled his cell phone. "I just got off the phone with her. But Mama says I can eat—"

It was a bare blur of movement behind Eddie, but it caught Charles's eye. He glanced over his brother's shoulder.

A hulking Asian man ran up and slammed a meaty forearm into the back of Eddie's head. He stumbled forward into Charles, and the two of them staggered into the house.

The Chinese Hulk strode into the foyer, followed by a slender Asian man who looked like a whip of licorice—dressed all in black, narrow body, narrow face, long arms and legs. Licorice Whip immediately grabbed Charles by his shirt front and dragged him into the kitchen, where he threw him against the corner of the cooking island in the center of the room.

The edge of the counter hit him above his ear. Pain arced across his vision. He fell to his knees at the base of the cooking island. His palm flattened against the cold tile, and then he saw drops of blood falling down.

He registered movement to his left. The Chinese Hulk had thrown Eddie to the floor next to Charles. There was a darkening bruise over his right eye.

He let them lie there, towering over them. Charles dimly heard Licorice Whip heading up the stairs.

They were looking for Elizabeth.

But they weren't here.

What had made Tessa take Elizabeth and Daniel and Mama with her to San Jose? Thank God. Thank God. Or else they would have been here.

What was the use of having a security alarm when these two men had been able to muscle their way in through the front door with nothing more than a heavy hand and good timing?

Licorice Whip ran down the stairs and entered the kitchen. He immediately reached down and grabbed Charles's right hand.

Charles fought him, but the pain of the gash in his head made him dizzy. Licorice Whip put a hand to Charles's right shoulder and twisted his arm sharply so that Charles's hand lay palm side up on top of the cooking island's countertop. He tried to rise, but Licorice Whip's hand leveraged on his shoulder kept him completely immobile, at his feet.

"Elizabeth St. Amant." Licorice Whip had only a trace of an accent. "Where is she?"

"Shopping," Charles ground out.

Licorice Whip grabbed Charles's pinky and broke it.

Charles shouted out. It felt like an awl pounded into his hand, even though he knew it was only his pinky bone.

Only.

"Where is she?"

Charles hesitated this time rather than simply snapping out where Licorice Whip could stick it. The pain radiated down his arm from his hand like his blood had turned to battery acid.

Licorice Whip wrapped his fingers around Charles's right ring finger. "Where is she?"

"Federal prosecutors," he gasped. "Putting you away for life."

He broke his ring finger.

Charles hadn't thought it could hurt more, but this felt like a sledgehammer turning his finger into powder with one blow. He screamed.

Licorice Whip started speaking to the Hulk in rapid Chinese. The Hulk pulled out his cell phone and dialed even as Licorice Whip continued talking. Charles heard the words "San Jose."

Oh no. They'd figured out where they were. Or were they simply going to pick up Tessa's family so they would have leverage and make her turn Elizabeth over to them?

The Hulk got off the phone, then gave Charles a nasty smile. "They're already—"

But suddenly Eddie swept a leg out, making the Hulk's legs fly out from under him, toppling him to the ground. In a second Eddie was on top of him, looking like an ant trying to crawl up a molehill. The man twisted and grabbed at his brother, and the two rolled across the kitchen floor.

But ... no. Eddie had managed to trap the man's mutton-sized arm and watermelon-shaped head between his legs. One of Eddie's feet hooked under his other knee, and the Hulk's shoulder pressed against his jaw with the pressure. The Hulk flailed his arms, kicked with his legs, but couldn't escape Eddie's hold on him.

Licorice Whip's hold on Charles loosened.

Charles jerked himself upright and swung a left hook into the skinny jaw.

His knuckles crunched like he'd hit a concrete wall, and for a moment he wondered if they were broken too. Spit flew from Licorice Whip's slack mouth as the blow sent his head flying sideways. Even as he fell to the ground, his eyes rolled back, showing the whites.

Charles curled his body inward, cupping both hands close to him, but unable to ease the throbbing pain. Yeah, his right hand definitely hurt more than his knuckles.

Eddie unlocked his legs, and the Chinese Hulk fell back onto the tile floor, unconscious. "Whoa. That really worked."

"What was that?" The question came out a little louder than a moan.

"Triangle choke."

Maybe that mixed martial arts stuff was useful after all. Then again, he doubted most MMA fighters ever had to contend with a home invasion.

"Quick, get the large zip ties from the garage and tie these guys up. I'd do it, but ..." He held up his swollen right hand.

In minutes, Eddie had tied their wrists together behind them, and then used rope to tie their ankles to their wrists in a hog tie.

"You have to call the police. Not just to come here, but tell them to send cars to Tessa's mom's house."

"You think they sent more guys there?" Eddie stumbled to the phone on the kitchen wall.

"I heard him say 'San Jose.'" His stomach heaved, and he wondered if he was going to cast up his accounts.

"Well, they're definitely not going to a Sharks game."

While Eddie called the police, Charles twisted his less-injured left hand around and dug his cell phone out of his pants pocket. His fingers shook as he brought up Tessa's mom's house address. He shoved the phone toward Eddie as he told the officers about being invaded by two men, and how they'd tied them up.

"The men mentioned this address." Eddie rattled off the Lancaster address as he read it from Charles's phone. "They're friends of ours. You've got to send police cars there right away."

Charles grabbed his phone and dialed Mama's number. He'd barely put it against his ear when it went straight to voice mail.

His stomach became a wadded up piece of paper, pressed tighter and tighter into a hard ball. He tried again, but the same thing happened.

He called Tessa, but it also went to voice mail. He searched his address book and found Tessa's mom's home phone number, but the operator's voice immediately came on: "The number you have dialed is unavailable. Please check the number and dial again."

What? Unavailable?

Was that what happened when a telephone line was cut?

The police arrived within five minutes, and as soon as they saw the two men on the floor of the kitchen, the officers seemed to recognize them.

"Did you send officers to that address?" Charles demanded, even before they tried to call a paramedic. "They mentioned this address." He showed them his cell phone. "We tried calling, but the line is suddenly disconnected."

One of the officers immediately took Charles's cell phone showing the Lancasters' home address and went to make sure a car had been dispatched there.

The next few minutes were tense. Eddie and Charles answered

questions, trying to be calm, but all the while they exchanged flickering glances, taut and razor sharp. Mama. What had happened to Mama?

One of the officers came up to them with a cell phone. "We called the San Jose PD, but apparently your friends had already called 9-1-1. They're okay now. She wants to speak to you." He handed Charles the phone.

"Hello?"

"Oh thank goodness you're safe," Mama said. Her voice had never sounded sweeter to his ear.

He released a breath in a huge whoosh, unaware he'd been holding it. "Mama, you're all right?"

"We're fine."

They were okay. Tessa had kept them safe.

"Well, except for Tessa."

It was almost as painful as getting his finger broken. "Tessa? Is she all right?"

"She was trying to protect us." Mama's voice wobbled. "There was so much blood. Thank goodness the police brought an ambulance with them."

"Mama, *what happened?*"

"She was shot, Charles. The ambulance just took her away. We don't know what's going to happen to her."

••••

Everything was annoyingly white.

What about ecru instead? Or a nice, cheerful lime green? No, that might be pukey. Okay, how about robin's egg blue?

All this white was burning holes in her eyes. And they weren't even open.

"Tessa."

She shook her head slowly. No Tessa here. She went to Disneyland. No, not Disneyland. How about the Bahamas?

"Tessa."

The voice was deep, caressing. It made her insides mushy. Or, her insides would be mushy if they didn't feel like she was birthing a dump truck.

The voice made her crack open an eyelid.

Charles.

The mahogany color hadn't come out of his curls entirely, so they were oak brown rather than golden brown. His blue-green eyes swam above her. Now blue-green would be a nice color instead of all this white.

His hand cupped her face. That felt nice. Maybe he'd kiss her.

The white was too bright. It caused pain to lance through her head, down her limbs, settling into a raging fire in her abdomen.

And in a flash, it all came back to her.

She looked into his beautiful eyes, reminded herself that they were deceitful.

And she turned her head away from him.

She felt his hand fall away from her face. Her cheek became colder than liquid nitrogen.

The white was finally starting to dim, and the pain was starting to dull. Darker, darker.

Darkest.

••••

She awoke to more darn white.

Oh, and pain. In. Every. Single. Cell. In. Her. Body.

"Just shoot me now," she groaned.

"You already were," a deep voice rumbled.

"Oh, you're awake," Mom said, and she appeared beside Tessa's bed, face concerned and relieved at the same time. And next to her ...

"Uncle."

It hurt to talk. It hurt to breathe. It hurt to *think*. She even felt little pulses of pain through her veins that coincided with the *beep ... beep* of the heart rate monitor.

"Am I going to die?" she asked.

"No." And then Mom did something really freaky-weird—she smiled at Tessa. "The doctor said you did perfectly in surgery."

"I don't feel like it."

"That's what happens when you try to converse with a bullet," Uncle Teruo said.

"Ha, ha, very funny. Oh, hey, now I have a bullet wound just like yours."

"Not just like mine." His lip twitched. "I have a cooler scar."

"But I fought off two guys and I didn't have a gun."

"If you want to count stupidity the same as bravery ..."

"I was brave. I took a bullet for someone." She had to pause while the pain roared for a second. "I don't think I want to do that again anytime soon."

"Yes, you took a bullet for your family." He took her hand, squeezing it lightly. "And I ... I can do no less."

What did that mean? But when she tried to understand it, there was that pain again, blanketing her entire head as if her skull was on fire. Maybe it was on fire. She could smell something burning.

"I will see you later," he said. And then he was gone.

Mom did another psycho-bat thing and took Tessa's hand in a gentle caress. She stroked the back of her hand over and over again.

"What happened when I got shot?" Tessa asked.

"Alicia cried."

"She *did*?"

"Well, she also said, 'You moron, I can't protect us!'"

"Ah, okay. That sounds more like Alicia."

"And then we heard sirens."

"Good Paisley."

"She has threatened to spend the next twelve years in therapy after being forced down that spider hole."

"It built up her character."

"She was irate because she got three spider bites in places she wouldn't show me."

It hurt to wince.

"And then it took *six minutes* for the ambulance to come." Mom's voice had gone back to its normal complaining-cadence. Except ... she was complaining *for* Tessa, not *about* Tessa.

"You were shot through and through. And the stupid doctors didn't take you into surgery right away. You were lying on that rolling bed-thingy for almost thirteen minutes."

She had a vague memory of blue-green. "Did anybody ...?"

"I had to shoo that Charles person away — what about 'family only' is hard to understand?"

It was just as well. She remembered turning away from him. Strange, the memory hurt too, like a candle flame under her breastbone.

She could swear she smelled something burning.

"You were in surgery for — "

"I don't know if I want to know, Mom."

And then Mom did a third crazy-bizarro thing — her face crumpled, and tears formed on her lashes. "I thought I lost you." She squeezed Tessa's hand tight.

She had known—or at least had wanted to believe—that she meant something to her mom, but this was the first time she could remember feeling it. It was so foreign, and so nice at the same time.

"You mean so much to me," Mom said.

"I'd do it again, Mom."

"Well, I don't want you to," she said irritably. "Don't do that again, ever."

"Hopefully I won't ever have to."

Tessa realized she hadn't really prayed to improve her relationship with her mom. She'd prayed more along the lines of, *Please help me not to kill my mother.* But God had answered her prayers for a home, it seemed. Maybe it would be good for her to stay with Mom for a while, try to improve this new facet to their complex relationship.

And who knows? Alicia might actually say something nice to her one day. Of course, then she'd know Christ was coming again, so it would be a short-lived nice, but still. She couldn't prevent a snort of laughter. Oh, that hurt like hot coals all along her stomach muscles.

On the side table, Mom had dropped her cardigan, and a sleeve had flopped over a reading lamp—which was turned on. Tessa saw a curl of smoke rising.

"Mom … do you smell something burning?"

Chapter **29**

The man appeared like a ghost.

Charles had just come home from work—still no move by Mr. Greer—to the smell of cannoli and the sight of the San Francisco yakuza boss sitting at his kitchen table.

"Whoa." He jumped back a step.

"Oh, hello Charles." His mama smiled at him but didn't leave her frying oil. "Mr. Ota came by to see you."

Charles approached him cautiously. "Sir."

"Your mother is making me cannoli." He said it solemnly. "She tells me they will cause me to die and then they will stick to my thighs."

"But they are *so* worth it," Mama said.

"They're my favorite," Charles said, more because he wasn't sure exactly what to say. He still wasn't convinced this wasn't a dream—rather, nightmare—or maybe a hallucination induced by the laughing gas at his dentist's office. Except he usually hallucinated about Britney Spears.

Teruo gestured to a seat at the kitchen table. "Sit."

It was his house, but Charles still sat like an obedient golden retriever.

"Your mother has been telling me about you."

Oh, no.

"She says you will be fired soon."

He hadn't thought Mama even realized that. "It has to do with the private equity firm Tessa told you about."

"I know." He slid a folder across the table to him. "I did my research."

The man would have put a law student to shame. "What exactly did you find out?"

"That Manchester Greer and Aloisius Rosenstein supplied money obtained illegally from heroin imported from China for an investment strategy with Heath Turnbull's private equity firm."

"What?" Charles opened the file.

It was all there, documented. Authenticated records, admissible in court.

"Elizabeth St. Amant is now safe," Teruo said. "The Triad will only want to dissociate itself from the situation and Stillwater Group will not say exactly where the illegal funds came from if they value their lives."

"What about … your people?"

"The Triad will be upset about their lost funds, since the money will be seized once the firm is under investigation, but because the blame lies with Greer and Rosenstein, we are not implicated in the fallout."

"What about the attack?"

Teruo gave him a dry look. "I will respond with righteous anger to the Triad's unprovoked attack upon my nieces and sister at her home, as well as the unprovoked attack on Tessa at the party."

"And then what?"

"What will probably happen is that relations with the Triad will remain tense, but will cool down somewhat. Most importantly, there will be no war, which none of us want."

Charles laid his hand flat on the folder. "How much is real and how much has been doctored?"

Teruo Ota gave him a neutral look. "Do you really want to know?"

"No, not really."

"What is significant is that the Triads are not implicated in these documents, but this will destroy Stillwater Group and also Manchester Greer, which I think is what you'd want."

"I didn't want to destroy him, just ... kick him around a little."

Teruo reached out and tapped the folder. "For this, you will not do the kicking. The managing partner in your law firm has been alerted to inconsistencies in Greer's behavior and has been given a copy of these documents."

This was serious. Once the managing partner discovered Mr. Greer had violated firm policy—simply being affiliated with Stillwater Group and yet volunteering himself as lead partner on the case was enough—he would be expelled from the partnership, reported to the bar, and reported to the police.

"You will find your job safe," Teruo said. "I would even guess you will find yourself the object of embarrassed apologies."

"Thank you," Charles said. "Not just for my job, but for saving Elizabeth."

"I did not do this for you, or for her. I did this to save my niece."

"I'm still grateful." He paused, then added, "I'm sorry about what I did seven years ago. I didn't know her then."

Teruo's face remained grave. "But even knowing her past,

you did not tell the Triad members where she was." His eyes fell on Charles's broken fingers.

Charles studied his fingers, also, secured in a cast. They mirrored Mama's broken fingers. He felt rather proud about that.

"Most men do not respond to pain well," Teruo said. "But you are a man who is loyal."

He hoped so. He also hoped he was a man who had changed for the better.

"I give you these documents, but I also ask a favor."

Charles wasn't surprised, but he warily regarded the older man. "What sort of favor?"

"I want Tessa to hire you as a retainer for her bodyguard business."

Charles blinked for a moment, unsure he'd heard him correctly. "My firm ..."

"I will pay her bills."

Of course. "Why me? You have your own lawyers."

"She won't use them."

Ah. No, she wouldn't.

"But I want her to have someone loyal, and you have proven to be honorable."

He'd proven it with two broken fingers. Made perfect sense. Charles supposed that to a man like Teruo Ota, honor *was* proven with broken fingers.

"She will need legal counsel if she continues to take cases of people like Elizabeth St. Amant—people who need Tessa, not just people who need a bodyguard."

"I think I understand what you mean," Charles said. Tessa would take clients she could believe in, not just clients who would pay her.

"You've proven you will do your best to protect your clients,"

Teruo said. "So I want you to protect my niece. Show her this same loyalty in the courtroom."

"She won't want to hire me," Charles said. "She hates me."

"She'll hire you because I'll tell her to." Teruo's jaw was stern. "But do not tell her I am the one paying her bills. It would upset her."

Now that was an understatement.

Charles didn't feel like he could say no to this man, but he also didn't want to. He didn't want Tessa to disappear from his life. "I'll do what you ask."

Teruo nodded regally. "I do not need to tell you what will happen to you if you harm Tessa in any way."

"I would not harm her ... or you." Hoo-boy, would he get in trouble for a statement like that?

"Here you are," Mama said, laying two cannoli in front of them. "Eat up before they get soggy."

Teruo watched Charles intently as he picked up a cannoli and took a huge bite, the shell crispy and flaky, the cream decadent with chocolate chips and chocolate sauce. Teruo followed suit, lifting the cannoli rather gingerly, then taking a bite.

He chewed thoughtfully, swallowed, and then turned to Vivian.

"This will not cause me to die, but yes, it will stick to my thighs."

••••

Man, take a bullet, and everyone forgets about you.

Tessa stared at her bedroom ceiling, counting the water stains. She considered getting up, but she'd rather be bored than in pain.

Mom was getting ready to go to work, Paisley was doing homework, and Alicia was probably scrubbing a toilet.

How pathetic that scrubbing a toilet sounded mildly interesting to her right now.

She'd left her knitting at Charles's house, but since her stomach muscles were still in horrible shape, she couldn't sit up for very long anyway, and knitting on her back would be like washing dishes while standing upside-down.

"Helloooo." She heard a knock at her door.

"Elizabeth! Come save me." Tessa slowly, delicately raised herself to a sitting position.

Elizabeth helped by arranging her pillows for her. "Still in pain?"

"Who knew you needed your stomach muscles for the dumbest things? Like brushing your teeth."

"I come bearing gifts." Elizabeth set Tessa's jumble of knitting on the bed in front of her. "That'll take you at least three years to untangle."

"The prospect is so exciting I can't stand it."

"And Aunt Vivian worried that they'll be soggy, but I said you wouldn't care." With a flourish, Elizabeth uncovered a plate of cannoli.

Tessa took a moment to stare in awe and wonder at the lovely cream-filled cylinders of yumminess. "You are truly superior among women."

"That's what I told my daddy, but he still wouldn't buy me the Corvette."

Tessa took a luscious bite. "Want one?"

"I already had one."

"And the problem is . . . ?"

"Well, if you insist." Her hand snatched up one of the cannoli faster than a magician.

"So how are things at the hotel?"

"You know, I loved your mama's house, and I loved Charles's house, but there is something about room service that cannot be adequately praised."

"So Charles got all your money back for you?" Saying his name was awkward.

"And then some. Apparently Heath had shunted some secret funds into an account in my name alone."

"Sweet."

"Divorce proceedings are going smoothly and my daddy called me last week."

Tessa paused in the middle of a bite. "Your daddy? The one who wouldn't speak to you before, that daddy? Or do you have a different one stashed away somewhere?"

"He was very apologetic." Elizabeth didn't look impressed. "Although my increased bank account might account for some of that."

"Hmm. That's an interesting dilemma. Would I really want a fake apology as opposed to none at all?"

"I'm for the none at all," Elizabeth said. "I'm still feeling rather hurt by the fact that when I was homeless and unemployed with a three-year-old son, they happily kicked me out of their home and hearth."

"Yeah, that would put a damper on Thanksgiving and Christmas."

"But I miss Louisiana. I'm going to move back there. I even found a few old friends on Facebook."

"Good for you. A fresh start."

Elizabeth reached out, took Tessa's hand. "I want you to come with me."

Tessa had been in the act of licking the cream off her fingers. "To Louisiana? But you don't need a bodyguard anymore."

"But I could use a friend. You could either work for me as my full-time companion, or you could find bodyguard positions in Louisiana."

Tessa paused to wipe her fingers and mouth, and then she answered, "I really am tempted. But I've decided to stay at home with my mom and my sister."

Elizabeth's eyebrows arched. "I thought Alicia still wasn't talking to you because you brought danger to the family home."

"Oh, she isn't. But I don't mind so much because she complains a lot less to me, since she has to remember she's not talking to me. But the relationship between me and Mom has started to improve a little for the first time in years ... if ever."

Elizabeth squeezed her hand. "I can see how that would cause you to want to stay and try to make it stronger."

She had to try. Her relationship with Alicia probably wouldn't change much, but she understood Alicia a bit better now, and maybe that would help things improve just on its own. "Also, I really like using my skills to help people. I hope I can get more bodyguard jobs once I heal."

"I'll be happy to write you a glowing recommendation. People will think you can save the whales and end world hunger while you're at it."

"So how is Daniel? And Vivian?"

And they chatted about everything except the one person she really wanted to hear about.

"I need to leave, I have a meeting with Charles at four o'clock."

Elizabeth rose from her seat on Tessa's bed. "Oh, I forgot to tell you. Charles made partner."

His dream. It had seemed to her like he viewed it as his freedom from his father. "I'm happy for him." She even meant it.

"Oh, and his firm, Pleiter & Woodhouse, were *so* apologetic to me. Poor Mr. Woodhouse looked like he was going to cry. And they were practically kissing Charles's feet. Charles said I could sue them for what Mr. Greer did to me, but why would I want to do that? I've got everything I wanted."

She did. And through it all, she'd kept her sunny personality and fierce loyalty to her son.

She had managed to outrun her past — or at least, Heath. It gave Tessa hope that she'd be able to do that too. One day.

"I'll come visit in a few days," Elizabeth said. "And I'll definitely come say goodbye before I go." Elizabeth kissed her on the cheek. "And if you're really nice to me, I might send Charles to come visit so you can get all that information about him direct from the source rather than pumping me."

Tessa's entire chest, neck, shoulders, and ears lit on fire.

"Bye!" Elizabeth disappeared in a cannoli-scented whirl.

Tessa didn't care about Charles. She would feel awkward if he came to visit. She wasn't sure if she had forgiven him yet. She wasn't sure if she knew how.

"Tessa," Mom called. "Your Uncle Teruo is here to see you."

••••

When Tessa heard the doorbell ring, she knew she had exactly thirty seconds to figure out how to forgive Charles.

Instead, she smoothed her hand over her hair and tried to

not look so tired sitting up against her pillows. She wanted to see him, and she didn't want to see him. But she also had no choice but to see him.

He entered her bedroom cautiously. Probably wondering if she would greet him with a lamp chucked at his head. "Hi." His serious blue-green eyes seemed to glow as they studied her face.

She was caught for a long moment, then she looked away. "Hi." An awkward pause. "Thanks for coming."

He nodded, coming a few steps into the room. He dug his left hand into his pants pocket, while the right dangled at his side, immobilized by a cast that left his uninjured fingers free.

"Can you, uh, drive?" What an inane question.

"Yeah. I shift with my three good fingers."

"Oh." She swallowed. *Just get on with it.* "Sit down?" She gestured to a chair set close to the bed. It was both too close to her and yet not close enough.

"Uncle Teruo called on me today." She focused on his knees. Rather nice knees, encased in dark olive slacks. "He wants me to ..." She swallowed. "He wants me to hire you to be on retainer for my protection agency."

There was a moment his expression didn't shift. Then his eyebrows rose. "Uh ... Why me?"

"Because you protected Elizabeth. He wants someone who will be loyal to his client. And Uncle Teruo knows I'd never agree to a yakuza lawyer."

Charles rested his arms on his knees and stared at his hands. "Is this what you really want to do?"

"No." She studied the coverlet on her bed. "But Uncle Teruo has been after me to work for him again, and doesn't understand why I won't. He said that if I hire you, he'll stop bugging me about returning to my old position with him."

He had also said, "You can protect yourself on the streets, but you cannot protect yourself in the courtroom, or with the press. If you insist on doing this bodyguard business, it would make me feel better to know you have help."

But why did that help have to come in the form of this handsome man?

"Tessa, I'm sorry for what I did."

"I don't want to—"

"Seven years ago, I thought those extra years on your sentence would bring justice for Laura Starling's grieving family."

She didn't often think about them, even though they believed she had killed their daughter. Charles had believed she'd killed Laura. Tessa herself had made sure people believed she'd killed Laura.

So why did his betrayal hurt her so much? Her eye fell on her Bible sitting on her nightstand, and the paper crane tucked inside. *Oh, Aunty. I miss you.*

But Vivian Britton had taken Aunt Kayoko's place in the past few weeks, had made Tessa feel loved and cherished. Shouldn't she be able to forgive her son?

And despite her hurt, she was drawn to him. His humor, the way he treated her, the way he trusted her. She looked up and discovered him staring at her.

She breathed, and it was like breathing in his essence as she breathed in the hint of his cologne, his musk, that whiff of sage. Who was she kidding? She wanted him with her, in her life. Him and his wonderful mother and his adventurous brother.

She rested back against the pillows, her injury throbbing with pain. And yet it somehow seemed to hurt her a bit less than before. "Will you draw up a contract for me? And how should I pay you?"

"When you use my services, I'll send a bill."

"And is your firm going to be okay with this?"

He shrugged. "You're a paying client. Also, right now, they're not likely to object to any clients I take on."

"Right." Not after the embarrassment of Manchester Greer and Stillwater. "So I'm your client now?" She held out a hand.

"You're my client now." He shook it.

She had intended it to be professional, impersonal. But his touch made the room spin round and round, with the focal point their two clasped hands. His thumb caressed her knuckles, and her skin tingled, shivered.

Sure. She was his client, nothing more.

She was such a liar.

Her breath came in soft gasps, but he noticed and immediately let go of her hand. "Are you okay? Do you need your mom?"

"I'm fine," she said breathlessly.

He frowned. "I'd better let you get your rest."

"Sure." Maybe it had been a good thing she'd been shot. Maybe it had been a bad thing she'd been shot. She hadn't quite decided yet.

As he headed toward the door, she said, "I'll, uh ... I guess I'll call you if I need you." She had to think of a reason to call him.

Charles, my dog is in need of legal advice. Except she didn't have a dog.

Charles, I have another client whose husband wants to kill her. Cliché?

Charles, I really only just want to breathe your air. Creepy?

He gave her one burning look. "Yeah. If you need me."

She needed him to come back here and kiss her senseless, is what she needed. She bit her lip to keep from saying it out loud.

"Bye." And then he was gone.

But, she knew, not for good.

Read an excerpt from book 2 in the
Protection for Hire series. Coming soon!

Tessa reached to her nightstand and got her laptop, a gift from Elizabeth St. Amant to her *favorite* bodyguard. She'd been using Mom's computer, and Charles's computer when she had been at his house, and it was nice having her own now. She fired up her email program—not that she really had that much email. Most days she opened all the spam just to feel like somebody wanted to chat with her.

Oh, there was a new spam email. Subject line: From dad. Haha, good one. She had to open it just to see. It was probably selling pharmaceuticals to enhance the production of belly button lint.

Dear Tamazon ...

The room suddenly shrank. And yet it also expanded. She had that weird out-of-body experience that she usually only felt if she'd been up for too long playing Bejeweled Blitz and her brain was fritzing.

The only one who had ever called her Tamazon was her father. When they played together, she always pretended to be one of the mythical Amazons, and "Tess the Amazon" had been slurred into Tamazon by her childish tongue.

> I know you're probably surprised to hear from me after all these years. I've wanted to reach out to you, but it's been out of my power. I've watched you grow into a beautiful, confident woman.

Sure — if he really had been watching her, he'd know she just got out of prison. Yup, beautiful and confident ex-convict.

> I'm proud of you for the sacrifices you've made for the family — for Alicia, for your mom, for your uncle. No one else would go to jail for Fred, but you did.

Something inside her grew colder than sub-zero. No one except Fred, Ichiro, and Uncle Teruo knew about that. She'd been alone when she cleaned the knife and planted it in the dumpster. She'd been alone when she was arrested.

How would he know this?

> I have things I need to tell you that are vital for you to hear. I don't know if you'll understand why, but my time is short and I can't risk not telling you. I've come to realize that you are the one thing in my life I don't want to miss.

What in the world did that mean? What was up with all this *Fringe/X-Files* vague, mysterious junk that never failed to drive her nuts?

Below is a postal mailbox I'm using. I will only have it for a week, so please write to me right away. This email address will be deleted as soon as I send this letter.

I love you, little girl,
Dad

Her emotions were like *shabu-shabu*—a mix of a dozen different meats and vegetables combining to create a unique broth. And her feelings were unique, all right. She couldn't decide if her anger was frustrated-anger or disgusted-anger or contemptuous-anger or hysterical-anger.

But definitely anger. That he would dare to write to her now. That he would dare to try to show his affection in words and phrases. That he would dare hint at something more important that had kept him away for so long.

He was twenty years too late.

Dear Tamazon . . .

The girl who played with that man was dead. She died the day he left without a word or note.

But more than likely, this wasn't her father, and she didn't want to get sucked into it anyway.

She clicked "Delete."

If her father did have a good reason for walking out on them, then he could make the effort to find a way to talk to her, face to face, not with a postal mailbox and an email address that self-destructs in fifteen seconds. She didn't intend to go out of her way to make it easy for him.

But this email was just a hoax . . . right?

Share Your Thoughts

With the Author: Your comments will be forwarded to the author when you send them to *zauthor@zondervan.com.*

With Zondervan: Submit your review of this book by writing to *zreview@zondervan.com.*

Free Online Resources at
www.zondervan.com

Zondervan AuthorTracker: Be notified whenever your favorite authors publish new books, go on tour, or post an update about what's happening in their lives at www.zondervan.com/authortracker.

Daily Bible Verses and Devotions: Enrich your life with daily Bible verses or devotions that help you start every morning focused on God. Visit www.zondervan.com/newsletters.

Free Email Publications: Sign up for newsletters on Christian living, academic resources, church ministry, fiction, children's resources, and more. Visit www.zondervan.com/newsletters.

Zondervan Bible Search: Find and compare Bible passages in a variety of translations at www.zondervanbiblesearch.com.

Other Benefits: Register to receive online benefits like coupons and special offers, or to participate in research.

ZONDERVAN®

ZONDERVAN.com/
AUTHORTRACKER
follow your favorite authors